MW01405084

syllables of the briny world

"Georgina Key guides us through the sweeping sensorial landscape of Bolivar Peninsula on the Texas Gulf Coast during one of the deadliest weather events in living memory. Diving deep into the hearts and minds of her characters, we celebrate their private triumphs while mourning the profound losses that come with them. Lush and lyrical, *Syllables of the Briny World* is a gorgeous rendering of life, love, and loss."

—E. Piotrowicz, author
The Currach and the Corncrake
and *Mother of Wild Beasts*

"Beautifully immersive characterization and storytelling that swept me from page to page as the floodwaters rose."

—Hannah Faoilean, author
"A Schoolgirl's Swansong," *Writing Magazine*
Shortlisted for Chimera Fantasy Novel Award

"Georgina Key is a master of the deeply felt novel that can crack open your heart and move you to tears. Houses, humans, and animals are lost, but the wild wind and flooding waters eventually teach these wonderful characters what's really important—the brave connections we build with each other despite the possible heartache living in all moments of deep love."

—Cynthia Williams, author
"An Angel Serves a Small Breakfast," *Tampa Review*

"Part mystery, part love story, part survival saga—with prose that sparkles like the Gulf itself, Georgina Key immerses us in a magical geography which exists between reality and fantasy, in the uncertain realm where ocean meets a sliver of land."

—Catherine Vance, author
The Mountains Under Her Feet

"*Syllables of the Briny World* brings beautiful depth to the sense of place. From the majesty and terror of the ocean to the ethereal dimensions that overlay our very own, Georgina Key's words guide us to the ultimate being: our hearts. You come away knowing that our energies leave a most beautiful imprint behind, an imprint that forever connects us to one another."

—Dawn Adams Cole, author
It's Not the Same for Us* and *Drops of Cerulean

"The pages are filled with tender and often spiritual questions about life and death and the way memory shapes our present and our future. Read to the end and be devastated by the sort of profound joy and solace that literature offers to our most pressing question of how we can learn to love each other despite our broken souls. Heartbreaking and heart-healing, this book is a tender reminder that deep love in all its crazy manifestations is all that matters."

—Robin Reagler, award-winning poet
Night Is This Anyway* and *Into The The

syllables of the briny world

other books by

georgina key

Shiny Bits in Between

syllables of the briny world

georgina key

BALANCE OF SEVEN
Newport, VT

Syllables of the Briny World

For information, contact:
Balance of Seven
www.balanceofseven.com
info@balanceofseven.com

Cover Art by Maryellen Quarles

Cover Design by Fictional Services
www.functionallyfictional.com

Developmental Editing by Amber Meade
ambergmeade@gmail.com

Copyediting by Roberta Templeman

Formatting and Proofreading by TNT Editing
www.theodorentinker.com/TNTEditing

Publisher's Cataloging-in-Publication Data

Names: Key, Georgina, 1964 - .
Title: Syllables of the briny world / Georgina Key.
Description: Newport, VT : Balance of Seven, 2024. | Summary: As Hurricane Ike threatens the Texas Gulf Coast, the residents of a remote community struggle over whether to stay or flee. Warned of the storm's ferocity, a young boy must bridge the chasm between his spirit realm and the living world to save his grieving mother.
Identifiers: LCCN 2024933421 | ISBN 9781947012646 (pbk.) | ISBN 9781947012653 (ebook) | ISBN 9781947012660 (Itchio)
Subjects: LCSH: Hurricanes – Fiction. | Crises – Fiction. | Grief – Fiction. | Mother and child – Fiction. | Ghost stories. | BISAC: FICTION / Literary. | FICTION / Magical Realism. | FICTION / Disaster.
Classification: LCC PS3611.E9 S95 2024 (print) | PS3611.E9 (ebook) | DDC 813 K49--dc23
LC record available at https://lccn.loc.gov/2024933421

28 27 26 25 24 1 2 3 4 5

To our precious briny world,
with much love and respect.

contents

september 10, 2008

3 days before the storm

the lost boys

Finn stood in the foyer of the Sea View Hotel, which was empty except for the furnishings that faded in and out, apparitions hovering between worlds. Its inhabitants were unsettled, restless; something was amiss. Beyond the hotel, sunshine warmed a slim stretch of land off the Texas Gulf Coast, a place where people lived ordinary lives. But within the confines of the hotel, the walls and floors hummed with a powerful charge that couldn't be ignored. And as always, there was a sound of distant whispers, which Finn knew was not the wind.

He needed his tower now.

Once the pride of the peninsula, the Sea View Hotel had glowed white against the blue-green water, a beacon of hope and healing. The newly constructed railroad had brought visitors, who flocked to the Gulf for the mineral cures it offered.

Those lives had left their mark on the place, as had time and tide. Sometimes, Finn would see people gliding through the salon wearing long dresses and hats, dinner jackets and spats, but then the light would change and they'd be gone. Other times, thick vines reached through broken windows and encircled brass curtain rods, only to disappear moments later.

A grand staircase rose before Finn, and he reached for the curved oak banister, his hand brushing its smooth surface as he climbed the stairs. His tower, where he went to be alone and draw, was at the very top of the hotel. Finn preferred that forgotten space, where ghosts of the past tended not to tread.

Pushing the door open, he entered the brightness. The very peak of the tower rose just above the membrane that contained the hotel and up into the world beyond. Sitting at a rickety wooden table, Finn picked up his pencil and rested its point on heavy paper.

The tower overlooked the flint-flaked sea, and he bid his hand draw what his eyes saw—seaskein grays and greens, twisting and curling beneath a calico sky. He added crosshatches of graphite over pale wisps of cloud, the motion of his hand taking on a life of its own. The lead point pressed hard, trenching, tearing, and ripping the paper like the waves gouging the sand below.

Deep in the dark damp, the carcasses of sea creatures lay buried, brittle shell and fossilized bone. Where did their breath—their thoughts—go after they died?

Finn watched his hand scrape and shade the page; it looked like an ordinary boy's hand. When he was alive, he had imagined spirits as vaporous shadows, but his hand looked solid. Perhaps those still in the world of the living would see him the way he saw those who wandered through the Sea View Hotel—drifting in and out of sight.

His eyes darted from the landscape outside the tower to the page before him. Back and forth. Back and forth.

Until they focused on the hem of the horizon, which began to shimmer and unstitch.

It cracked into a thousand pieces, shards like glass piercing the ocean below, each a stabbing pain where his heart once beat. He closed his eyes, trying to block out the truth of what was to come. The sea turned viscous, reaching curled fingers toward the tower. As they wrapped around him, he again felt the intensity of Sea-Mother's love.

Shhhh,

my child,

hushhhh now.

Her voice was the waves themselves.

Do you miss your Sea-Mother?

It circled him,

pulling at his vanishing heart.

Come back to me

so I may love you again . . .

Finn slumped to the floor, giving in to the lull of her words, the immensity of her desire for him. All around was chaos, the wind above roiling her depths so Finn twisted in the undertow, losing all sense of bearing.

Hush my love. She drew him deeper, each crosscurrent pulling him further down, where it was quiet. He rocked in her liquid embrace. *You are safe here with me. Hush now.*

His tower teetered and fell.

Finn's sight slowly cleared. Sea-Mother had shown him a vision—a storm of such magnitude, it would devour everything in its path.

Though Finn knew Sea-Mother to be a capricious, territorial entity, he trusted the vision she offered him. Was she punishing him for abandoning her?

Maybe, but this felt far bigger—a revenge against the vanity of Man. Maybe if he could capture the ocean on the page before him, he could show Sea-Mother she was loved, quell her anger.

Painting is how I love the world.

Finn had heard that once. He picked up the pencil; he would try again.

But time was running out.

clementine

Clementine was vaguely aware of Lou leaning over the bed, his bulk a tether pulling her from her dreams.

"Love you, darlin'," he whispered in her ear. "I'll see you tonight."

He kissed her goodbye, his minty breath cool against her lips. Clem fought the urge to pull him to her, inhale him, and kiss his earlobe until he fell into bed and made love to her in the milky morning light. She wanted to retain the feeling of half-wakefulness, her senses free to roam as if in a dream while her attention distilled into sensations surging through her body.

Clem opened her eyes just enough to watch him—so tall and strong but graceful. She could never get enough of watching Lou move. Chinks of early-morning sun divided the bedroom into segments of light and shadow, and as Lou left, she gave in to sleep once more.

She woke a few hours later to a blaze of sunlight streaming through the thin curtains. The window unit wheezed in an attempt to cool the room.

Realizing the time, Clem threw off the covers and scrambled out of bed. Her friend Dorie was expecting her and did not appreciate tardiness. She wouldn't say anything about it, but her face spoke volumes, each frown line a stronger rebuke than any spoken word.

Clem hastily brushed her teeth, spitting into the discolored porcelain of the bathroom sink. Running a hand through her tangled curls, she headed to the closet crammed with clothes. A loose-fitting dress she had worn a couple of days earlier hung on the back of the door. Throwing it on, she grabbed Dorie's gift from the coffee table and headed out.

Dorie's house in Gilchrist wasn't too far from Clem and Lou's rental on the bayside, but Clem walked briskly to make up for lost time. With every step, sand gave way beneath her feet, and the wind whipped her long hair about so she peered at the world through dark, wavy strands. The Gulf was a muddy green, hiding what lay beneath. Empty stretches of sand were dotted with the occasional beachcomber, who now and then bent to retrieve a shell, examine it, and then either toss it or slip it into their pocket.

Tucking the flat package securely under her arm, Clementine lowered her head and avoided the water, instead swerving between sand dunes and driftwood gifted by the tide.

There had been a time when she loved the ocean, the crimp of waves against her bare feet. But now, when she wasn't blaming herself for her son's death, she blamed the sea. The water had stolen her child and then taunted her, carrying his voice upon the waves, pushing her toward madness. She had wandered the shore night after night, listening for him. And when the moon was full, she had entered the scorched water to search for him. Clementine recalled feeling like a creature of the sea, transformed into something less than human, something primordial.

She had often thought of leaving Bolivar altogether, moving as far away from the water as possible. Perhaps back to Houston or even her hometown in Mexico. But the latter held its own ghosts, live ones she preferred not to revisit—like her father, who haunted her childhood memories still.

Some ghosts, though, she longed for. Back when she still heard Finn calling from the water, she couldn't bear to leave the peninsula. It was all she had left of him—that mournful voice urging her to find him and bring him home. Later, as she came to understand that she could never be with her boy again, his voice quieted. With the help of Dorie, now her best friend, and Lou, the man she loved, Clem emerged from her fog of grief and clawed her way back to the world of the living.

Dorie's house stood above the dunes on tall wooden pilings, its yellow siding reflecting the sun. It looked so cheerful now, unlike when Clementine had lived there.

There had, of course, been happy times. When she and Lou had first moved in ten years ago, they had spent days unpacking boxes of his kitchen supplies and her paints and canvases, claiming their own spaces within the tiny house. Their first night there, Lou had bought fresh crab, and they had laughed as they struggled to break through the shells. Once they had reached the tender meat, they had fed each other crab dripping with butter. And when they made love that night, the scent of garlic rose from every pore.

But that had been a different time, the house's former incarnation.

Clementine climbed the steps to the deck and knocked quietly before opening the front door. Dorie was in the kitchen, filling a carafe of coffee with boiling water. She placed the empty kettle on a metal countertop that had been salvaged from a ship's galley. Along with the thick linen window shades that resembled boat sails and the burnished pine walls, it gave the house a nautical air.

Dorie's graying hair hung loose around her shoulders, unlike the short cut she'd had when Clem first met her three years earlier. Back then, everything about Dorie had been squeezed into as small a space as possible, as if she hadn't been worth the extra room. The beach and the life she had built here had been good for her.

Looking over, Dorie smiled. "I made us muffins." She motioned Clem over to help arrange them in a wicker basket. "A special treat for a special occasion." As Clem approached, Dorie reached out to give her a hug, only then noticing the package under Clementine's arm. "Might that be for me?"

Clementine handed her the gift, and Dorie hugged it to her chest. "Let's get settled, and I'll open it properly." She placed it gently on the kitchen table.

Setting the muffins next to the package, Clementine sat down facing the huge window that framed the water. She wondered where Dorie would hang the painting. It was smaller than the first one Clementine had given her, which hung center stage on a high wall above the living room windows facing the water—an abstracted image of monarch butterflies, a riot of ochre, saffron, and black brought to life by Clem's brushstrokes.

The walls were filled with photos of Harriet and paintings Dorie loved, including the two others Clem had given her. One was of their children, Finn and Harriet, imagined as friends playing together, their heads bent over a small tide pool in the sand. Two splashes of red drew the eye—a red sun hat on Harriet's head and a red swimsuit on Finn, too big for his skinny frame. The other was of the lighthouse.

Dorie loved the Bolivar lighthouse owned by her friend Lynn. Clementine associated Dorie with it, or she used to. Its austere lines, so straight and proud, its isolation—that had been Dorie. Now, Clementine saw both the lighthouse and Dorie as beacons of safety, permanence, and hope.

"There we go." Dorie set the coffee carafe on the table and sat down across from Clem. She poured them both a cup and helped herself to a muffin, taking a large bite.

Clementine took a sip of coffee.

Dorie wiped crumbs from her lips. "So, are you ready for your big day?"

"I think so."

Dorie folded her hands and waited for her to go on.

"I'm a bit nervous about the ceremony."

"Why's that?"

Clem started scraping at her cuticles. "I don't know. I suppose standing up in front of everyone. I kind of regret agreeing to say our own vows."

"You can still change your mind about doing that, you know. Or just keep it short."

"I'm not happy with what I've written so far. Lou has always been better with words than me."

"You have your own way of expressing yourself that's just as important, just as powerful." Dorie brushed her hand across the package.

"So can I just stand there and hold up a painting instead?"

Dorie smiled. "Sure. You can do whatever you want. It's your wedding."

Clem would get it right. She so wanted everything to

be perfect. They probably should have gotten married years ago. Instead, they'd been carefree and irresponsible, moving in together only months after they'd met. Then she'd gotten pregnant before they even learned how to be a couple. They barely saw each other because of Lou working the rigs or Clem shutting herself up in her studio to paint.

All that had been before they understood the unpredictability of life, the tenuous hold on happiness. For so long after Finn died, Clementine had believed she'd never be happy again. But now, she'd had enough glimpses of it. And time—along with those who loved her, especially Dorie—had healed some of her pain. She'd always be grateful to her dearest friend.

"Oh, I meant to tell you," Dorie said. "I was in Galveston last week and came across Lou's food truck. I had to wait in line for almost thirty minutes, but it was well worth it."

Clem smiled. "That's good. He deserves it."

Dorie nodded. "I know. I wasn't sure he'd pull it off, to be honest." She laughed. "Glad I was proven wrong."

"Me too," said Clem, registering a tinge of guilt at oversleeping that morning while Lou got up early to take Roustabout to Galveston. She should have had more faith in him from the beginning. He was making his dream come true.

He'd saved up for the old food truck and refurbished it himself with some help from Pete. And now he cooked for much of Galveston and Bolivar. Roustabout, named after his previous profession, was getting popular. It wouldn't be too long before he could start thinking about a brick-and-mortar restaurant. In their early days, Lou had told her he'd put her artwork up in it. He'd feed the whole island with the dishes he'd cooked for his siblings while his single mother worked day in and day out.

"I'm heading to the ranch later with Rennie to help get the place ready." Dorie took another bite of her muffin.

These days, Rennie and Dorie were joined at the hip. Clem wondered how long it would be before he popped the question. Not long, she suspected, though she wasn't sure Dorie would accept. Not that Dorie didn't love Rennie, but she seemed jaded about marriage.

"If you can give me a ride, I'll help too."

Shaking her head, Dorie swallowed her mouthful. "No, you won't. All you need to do is rest and indulge yourself. We'll take care of everything."

Dorie's version of indulging herself would have included sitting on the deck, reading a book, and sipping from a glass of wine. Clem's, on the other hand, was painting. She felt more herself in the worlds she created on canvas than she did in this one—inhaling the smell of paint and linseed oil until they became her own breath, the paintbrush an extension of her hand.

When Clem realized Dorie was eyeing the package lying between them, she slid it closer to Dorie. Her friend grasped it with two hands and sucked in a deep breath as if preparing herself. Untying the string with care, she wound it into a tiny skein.

Clementine was suddenly nervous. What if she didn't like it? What if Clem's version of the house was too different from Dorie's?

Dorie gently pulled back the brown paper to reveal the painting. She sat very still for a moment, staring down at it. Clementine had rendered Dorie's beloved yellow house by the sea in broad brushstrokes, giving it a slightly abstract perspective. It leaned, all crooked proportions and refracted light. Dorie brushed her hand across the surface, following the outline with her fingers. She lingered on each brush-stroke, leaning closer to examine the lines.

When she finally looked up, her eyes glistened, and a smile had transformed her practical, unremarkable face into dazzling joy.

"It's perfect. Thank you."

Clem let out a quiet breath of relief.

After a moment, Dorie asked, "Do you ever miss living here?"

A montage of memories flashed through Clementine's mind: Lou in the kitchen, cooking feasts for her and Finn, his tall, lean body moving with confidence in the steamy air; Finn listening intently to Lou's bedtime stories of pirates and mermaids, giggling when he did the voices. Finn had loved the outdoor shower, where he would collect frogs in the rain. And he'd learned to count by climbing the wooden steps to the upper deck.

The images in Clementine's mind began to fracture. Dark corners crept closer as shadow memories nudged nearer the surface. Her shoulders hunched as the familiar weight began to crush the breath out of her.

Reaching for Clementine's hand, Dorie clasped it, and the past receded before her spreading warmth. She always knew when to pull Clem back.

Clementine shook her head. "This house healed you in a way it couldn't heal me. You belong to each other now."

Dorie had been so closed off when Clementine first met her. Of course, Clem had been too, in a different way. She'd barely acknowledged Dorie as a real person when she rescued Clem from the sea three years ago. In fact, Dorie still referred to Clementine as a selkie, the fabled sea creature who swam in the ocean as a seal but transformed into a woman on land and sacrificed her true nature for love.

Dorie looked down at the painting again. "You're right, I think. It makes sense that you'd need to move forward, start over. Just like I did here." Dorie squeezed Clementine's hand. "I know it's difficult sometimes for you to come here for our annual memorials."

"It gets easier every year." This ritual was part of Clem's healing, even though it brought up memories she'd worked so hard to release. Not the memories themselves, exactly; she never wanted to forget any of them. But the pain attached to them came too close to the surface at times.

Suddenly, Rosie jumped onto the table, startling them both.

"Oh no you don't." Dorie aimed a swipe at the cat before she could begin nibbling the muffins.

Clementine picked the cat up and placed her on her lap, where Rosie settled comfortably. "Hello, old friend."

"She still loves her first mama," said Dorie.

Clementine smiled and stroked Rosie, her soft fur and increasingly loud purr having an instant calming effect. She wondered what Rosie thought of them. Did she consider them both her mothers? Clementine didn't even remember the moment she had abandoned Rosie, her house, Lou, her entire life. There was a *before* and an *after*. That space in between was a blur of nothingness, a dull grayness, time standing still.

Dorie had moved into the house soon after Clementine left and began her wanderings. Fractured memories resurfaced: a full moon shining the sea silver, a black sky punctured by stars, endless footprints marking the sand, street corners and alleyways where she had been invisible. Dorie had saved her from the waves, where she had searched for her lost boy. Dorie had brought Clementine home. But Clementine hadn't been able to reclaim her place there.

Clem pushed against the memory now—that awful day when she had almost lost the only real friend she'd ever had. Clem looked around the tidy room where they now sat and an image flashed through her mind. Shreds of Dorie's old life lay scattered across the floor—ripped photos of Harriet, torn drawings of stick figures holding hands in a line—remnants of Dorie's precious memories that Clementine had destroyed trying to . . .

What? What had she been thinking back then? She remembered only her manic longing for Finn, that metallic absence that had manifested that night in jealousy and rage. Why should Dorie have had tangible pieces of Harriet when Clem had had none of Finn?

Dorie's anger and hurt had mirrored her own, so they had fought over Rosie. But they had, of course, been fighting over much more than the cat. Clementine had been fighting for the life she'd once had.

Dorie picked up the painting and stood. "Now, where shall we hang this?"

As Clementine followed Dorie around the sunlit living room, her eyes rested on a photo of Harriet feeding her dog what looked like a cookie. Dorie's ex-husband, Hugh, had replaced many of the photos Clem had destroyed that night. Clem had never met him, but she knew he and Dorie had managed to stay friends.

Dorie stood beside her. "I love that photo."

According to Dorie, Harriet's death had been so slow and painful, the cancer making her disappear bit by bit, that when she finally passed, there was some strange semblance of peace to be had for all of them. But letting go was something Clementine had struggled with for so long—even now, four years later. When Dorie had taken her in during the worst period of her loss, Clem had found a soulmate, a friend who understood her as no one else could. Clem would be forever grateful to Dorie for everything she had done for her.

"I think we can squeeze it in here." Dorie leaned the painting against a wall covered in a collage of photos whose arrangement left just enough space for the small artwork. Going to the hall closet, Dorie came back with a hammer and nail. Then she held the painting up. "How's that?"

"Move it up a bit on the left side. Yep, that's it."

Holding her finger in the center of the hanger, Dorie handed the painting to Clem. Once she'd hammered in the nail, she placed the painting on the wall and stepped back.

"Perfect."

Standing for a moment without speaking, they stared at the painting and considered all it held on the small canvas.

"You about ready?" Dorie asked.

"Yep. Let's go."

The two friends walked out the door and toward the beach just steps away.

"These annual memorials," said Clementine. "We must never stop doing them."

Every September, they gave themselves a day to remember, mourn, and celebrate their children, however they needed to. They gave themselves and each other permission to cry, wail, scream, rage, and laugh.

Dorie nodded. "And I hope I continue to get a new painting every year!"

Clementine smiled. "I think you're going to need a bigger place for that."

"Never! I plan to be here until the day I die!"

They clambered over the ragged dunes to the sand and began their search.

"You think we'll find any butterflies this year?" asked Dorie.

To Clem, it was more about the searching than the finding. Three years ago, the seed of their friendship had been sown when they'd come upon a bush full of monarch butterflies resting before their final stretch to Mexico. The friends had shared stories of their children as a kaleidoscope of butterfly wings fluttered and opened before them—Finn and Harriet, both reborn, visiting their mothers, their wings brushing the women's cheeks. Clem and Dorie had watched them zigzag into the blue, higher and higher, until they were just specks against the sun.

pete

Pete woke up to Luanne bitching, complaining that he just used her, that she had feelings too, and that she was getting too old for this shit.

He lifted the pillow he was buried under and peered up at her. Come to think of it, she had been looking her age lately. She had been a beauty back in high school. Not that there had been anything between them back then. They had hooked up after Luanne's divorce—well, during her divorce. She had been lonely, and he'd been happy to oblige.

Now her skin was loose, and she'd lost all the baby-fat plumpness he had loved to grab hold of so he could pull her hips close. Her long blonde hair had gone wiry and thin. Pete wondered how old she was now.

Younger than me anyways. Seemed everyone was younger than him these days.

"So, am I going to be your date to the wedding or not?"

Pete hated when Luanne called him out like that. He hadn't asked her because he wanted to go alone. Wasn't that clear enough?

"The invite didn't include a date," he fibbed.

Luanne narrowed her eyes at him. "So how come Mike invited me, then?"

Having known Mike was after her, Pete wasn't surprised, just relieved. "I guess you already have a date, then."

"I told him I'd let him know." She sat next to Pete on the bed. "I was waiting for you to ask me."

"Didn't you get an invitation, then?"

"No. I don't really know Lou or Clementine." She twirled a strand of hair around her finger and examined the frayed split ends. "Can you believe they're getting married after all this time?"

Pete shrugged.

"I mean, were they married when their kid was born?"

"Nope." Pete leaned over to the bedside table and pulled a cigarette out of a near-empty pack.

"So why bother now?"

"Hell if I know." Marriage was a joke. Flicking his lighter and inhaling deeply, he tried to figure out the quickest way to leave without looking like a complete asshole.

"I mean, their kid died a while ago. And I know they broke up for a bit." She slipped the cigarette out of Pete's fingers and took a drag.

"You sure seem to know a lot about them for someone who doesn't know them." Pete tried to take the cigarette, but Luanne pulled her hand back.

"Mind you, Lou's a doll." She stared at the ceiling, smoke rising from her mouth. "Good men are getting harder and harder to come by around here." She looked pointedly at Pete through the smoke.

Pete laughed. "He's young enough to be your kid."

"Fuck you." Luanne rose quickly from the bed and stomped toward the dresser. Sitting down, she started putting on pastes, lotions, and powders that had always been a mystery to Pete. He watched her for a minute, wondering why women subjected themselves to all that crap.

Still, he appreciated a woman who made an effort. Maybe he should just put her out of her misery and ask her. But then he'd have to escort her around all afternoon, and he'd been looking forward to hanging out with Lou. He missed the old days, when Lou worked on the shrimp boat with him and they'd throw back a few beers after a long day on the water. Who knew how often he'd get to see Lou once he got hitched? Pete liked Clem well enough. She was a looker, for sure. But Lou had been way more fun back then.

"I gotta get to work." Luanne fluffed her hair, preparing to spray it.

Pete couldn't handle any more of this primping. "I'll leave you to it, then." He pulled on his jeans and tee shirt and grabbed his keys, waving the hairspray fumes away with one hand and carrying his boots in the other.

When he glanced at Luanne on his way out, she held the hairspray can aloft, her lips a thin line, a frown merging with the other wrinkles marking her once-fine face. Shutting the apartment door behind him, he breathed a sigh of relief.

When Pete pulled into his driveway, he was surprised to see the blue Oldsmobile belonging to Carol, his ex. She sat on a stack of used tires, smoking a cigarette as she watched the kids play by the bay where he kept his boat. Her knee bounced rapidly, betraying her annoyance and jogging his memory.

Shit!

Carol stood and dropped her cigarette stub to the sand, crushing it with her foot. "Where the hell have you been?"

"Daddy!" Addie ran to Pete and wrapped her small arms around his legs.

"Hey, pipsqueak." Pete ruffled her blonde curls.

"Hey, Dad." Shawn sauntered over and stood a slight distance away, squinting against the sunlight. Pete had forgotten how tall he was getting, his legs far too long for his body. Surely he couldn't have grown that much since Pete last saw him. Pete searched his mind, trying to work out exactly how long it had been.

"Y'all ready for a ride in my *Angel*?"

"Yay!" Addie ran back toward the boat.

When Pete looked at Carol, she was studying his face, frowning. "Are you drunk? It's only two p.m., for Christ's sake!"

He tried not to wince as his head pounded. "Nope."

Pete hated that Carol always insisted on joining them on their boat outings so she could keep an eye on him. It wasn't as if he'd ever hurt his kids or put them in a risky situation. Not really.

"You forgot, didn't you?"

"Course not. I just had to run an errand real quick." Pete extricated himself from her scrutiny and made his way toward the boat. She needed to loosen up, live a little. "Let's go, kids. Ready to catch some fish?"

The shrimp boat's engine started right up, rumbling like a contented cat. As they pulled out of the bay, a warm breeze brushed Pete's skin. Fumes from the engine mixed with cigarette smoke, remnants of the previous day's catch, and the salt air. He inhaled deeply, appreciating the smells he loved most in the world.

Addie came up and tugged on his shirt. "Daddy, *Angel* is named after me, right? Cuz I'm your angel?"

Pete nodded and smiled. "Sure, angel." A white lie wouldn't hurt. No one believed him, anyway, when he said she was named after his first love. Famous singers didn't tend to cross paths with the likes of him. But he happened to be in the right place at the right time. Unlike his wayward angel, who had been in the *wrong* place at the right time. She'd hated living in these parts. She had been a misfit like him, so once they'd found each other, they'd stuck together all through high school in Port Arthur.

Then she had hit the big time and moved to Austin, where he'd followed her. But her star had shone bright, too bright. She'd been impossible to pin down. No one had been able to keep her grounded, not even her. She'd left Austin without telling him where she was going. He'd waited for her to come back, but after six months, he'd returned to Bolivar alone. He'd kept up with her on the news, and when she died of a drug overdose, he'd given up on love for good.

But he had a part of her no one else did, and all his memories of her were tied up in this boat.

"Daddy, I want to be a pirate like you when I grow up." Addie stood on tiptoe, trying to see out the window. "When can we go on your *actual* pirate ship?"

She had been so disappointed that *Angel* wasn't like the *Elissa* that was docked in Galveston, so he'd told another white lie he'd have to figure a way out of in time. Or else buy an actual pirate ship.

"I told you, baby girl. When you're bigger." He held his hand two feet above her head. "And you have to practice lots before then."

"Practice what?"

"Practice how to be a pirate."

"Like how?"

Pete winked. "Well, this for a start . . ." He broke into one of his infamous seafaring ditties.

Now when I was a little boy,
And so me mother told me,
That if I didn't kiss the girls,
Me lips would all grow moldy.

Addie joined in, trying to copy his pirate's brogue, her laughter mingling with their raucous singing. Ever since Pete discovered he was a descendant of the notorious pirate Jean Lafitte, he had emulated his ancestor—or tried to: long hair in a braid, gold hoop earring, tattoos.

Pearlescent water parted for his *Wayward Angel* in a ruffle-edged ribbon that curled as he turned the boat toward the clear horizon.

Finding a good spot, Pete turned off the engine and collected the fishing gear. Carol sat apart from them, scrolling through her phone. He handed a rod to each of the kids and dipped his hand into the live well to retrieve a pinfish for Addie. She giggled as the live bait flailed in his hand and then inhaled sharply as he stabbed the hook into its flesh.

"It's okay," Pete assured as he handed her the rod. "They don't feel nothin'." When Addie glanced apprehensively at Shawn, who had cast his line far into the water, Pete placed his hand over hers, swinging the rod back and then out. The line glinted silver as it arced, landing gently in the waves. Addie squealed with delight and Pete smiled. "You catch a big one, and we'll have it for supper tonight."

Pete wished he could spend more time with his kids, but Carol could be a pain in the ass about visitation. She didn't trust him, not since he'd messed up a couple of times when he was with them: a few too many beers on one trip, and another where he'd hung out with some guys after a morning on the water, passing around a flask of whiskey, before meeting the kids.

As he watched them mess with their fishing lines and bicker about who would catch the biggest fish, he only half listened as Carol went on and on about her latest boyfriend.

"He's a wonderful father. He took his kids *and* Addie and Shawn to Schlitterbahn. They had a blast. I got the whole day to pamper myself. Me and Jen went to the salon and got our nails done." She held her hand out in front of Pete's face. "Like the color? It's called Pink Passion."

Pete's jaw grew tenser by the minute.

"Anyways, Jen told me Frank lost his job at the lumberyard. Remember Frank? Poor thing had to use some of her savings to even go to the salon with me! I swear, what's wrong with men who can't hold down a job? I mean, Clive's a manager at the plant, and he's had that job for eons, so he'd be a good provider."

Pete's own livelihood was spotty at the best of times. He'd been shrimping since he was a teen working on someone else's boat. Then Charlie had retired and sold it to him cheap. He'd been so proud that day. The first thing he'd done was paint over the boat's original name.

Unfortunately, his shrimp hauls had been shrinking by the year. It was said that renaming a boat was bad luck, but he'd scoffed at his friend's warning to at least do a renaming ceremony. Perhaps he should have listened after all, even if he never had been one for tradition or superstition.

Then there was this storm he'd been hearing about. Each hurricane season he worried. One major storm could finish him. Too bad he couldn't just retire now and spend his days cruising around the bay.

Shawn's shoulders slumped. "Dad, there's no fish here. Can we try another spot?" He had never had any patience for fishing.

"Sure, son." Pete turned away from Carol toward the cabin. At least he could get a break from her constant babbling. "Hey, Shawn. You wanna take a turn at the wheel?"

Shawn rushed into the cabin, with Addie following close behind. "No, me, Daddy. I want a turn steering."

Shawn pushed her away. "You're too little still."

Addie ran at him full on and almost managed to topple him over. That's when they started fighting.

Carol grabbed them both by the backs of their tee shirts as if they were puppies and directed them out of the cabin. "I swear, Pete, you never were much of a disciplinarian, were you? I always have to be the bad guy."

Pete tried to block out her screaming. His headache was getting worse.

"If you two don't settle down and behave, we're going home right this minute! I'll tell your father to turn this boat right back around, and that'll be the end of it."

Pete pulled a silver flask from his hip pocket and took a long swig. *Just to take the edge off.* The familiar burn of whiskey going down calmed him, and his grip on the controls loosened.

"Not to mention the whuppin' you'll both get."

Pete took another furtive nip as he focused on the light slicing the waves ahead, trying to ignore Carol.

"Hey, Pete," yelled Carol. "Pete!"

Pulling himself out of his trance, Pete waved his hand. "Yeah, yeah, woman," he muttered. "I'm here. Where else would I be?"

"Come on out here with the kids for a bit and give me a break. I'll take over."

Pete nodded and made his way outside the cabin. At least he didn't have a hangover anymore—hair o' the dog, his favorite medicine.

Carol blocked his way, her face tight and furious. "You've been drinking," she said through clenched teeth. "You bastard."

"I'm fine."

"You stink of whisky. What the hell?"

Pete smiled his most charming smile. "I just had a quick nip. No big deal."

"It sure as hell *is* a big deal. You promised me you wouldn't drink when the kids were on the boat. I'm not about to risk all our lives on this piece of shit."

"Piece of shit? My *Angel* has—"

"Oh, please. If I have to hear that story one more time . . ." Carol pushed past him and took over the controls.

Pete watched the horizon shift as she turned the boat around and headed back. Shawn glared at him, but Addie just looked sad. No one spoke much after that, and even their goodbyes were stilted.

"That's it," Carol hissed as the kids headed to the car. "Never again. You're a bad influence on them, and I won't have it."

When she turned her back on him and strode off, he couldn't help but wince. He couldn't not see his kids. He'd have to make her trust him again. He'd quit drinking and work harder so he could pay the child support on time. Pete tried to remember the last time he'd paid her.

I'll show her I can do better. She'll forgive me. They always do.

agnes and earle

Opening the front door, Earle removed his boots right away, his left hip twinging as he bent over. Sandy had cleaned the place for the weekend festivities, and Agnes wouldn't tolerate work shoes in the house tracking dirt everywhere.

Sandy had taken over cleaning the house after Clementine left four years ago. Agnes said she did a better job than Clem ever had, but she loved Clem so much, she hadn't really cared that she'd been less than thorough.

The house was quiet compared to the impatient longhorns, who had voiced their dissatisfaction as Earle moved hay from the barn to the field. The summer had been an especially hot one, and while the grass was growing back as they eased into fall, it wasn't plentiful enough to feed forty-plus head of hungry cattle. Seemed summers just kept getting hotter and hotter every year.

Growing up in Texas, Earle had worked all day outside as a boy helping his pa with one thing or another. They had planted vegetables to feed the family and sell locally, and the digging and harvesting had been hard work. Earle didn't remember the heat ever being a problem back then.

When he was done with his chores, he would rush to the nearby creek to meet his friends, and they'd swim until nightfall. He used to love that sense of freedom the water offered. Floating in the cool creek, shaded by huckleberry trees and cattails, duckweed coating his body like amphibian scales, he would forget about his responsibilities for a while. He would daydream about his future: a life where he could be his own boss; build a fine home, nail by nail; find a woman who inspired him to be the best version of himself; and maybe have a few kids they could raise the way he had been raised.

All of it had happened, through hard work and discipline. He was grateful to his hardworking, God-fearing parents, who had been devoted to their family and community. He had only hoped to do the same.

His wife sat by the window, checking her watch, her neck stretched forward to get a better look down the driveway. "What time did they say they were getting here?"

The family was coming for a long weekend. It had been a couple of months since they'd visited, and both he and Agnes missed them.

"It shouldn't be long now," Earle said. "You want to wait outside? We can sit in the shade. I'll bring out some sweet tea."

"Good idea." Agnes maneuvered her wheelchair toward the front door. Pausing, she turned her head toward Earle. "Sandy made the bunk beds up yesterday, right?"

"Sure did."

"And will you make sure the fan is turned on? You know how the kids get."

Earle smiled to himself. Agnes fussed over the kids,

spoiling them whenever they were there. As if their parents didn't spoil them enough already. A few years ago, Earle had finished out the back porch for the kids to sleep in, but they were city kids. They loved it during the cooler months but complained about the heat in the summer. Still, it did them good to spend time here, where they could feel the sun and air on their skin, instead of being cooped up in the air-conditioning all day playing those wretched computer games.

A car horn honked outside, and Earle looked out the window. "That's them now."

Hurrying through the front door, Agnes glided down the ramp from the porch to the yard. Earle had customized the house as much as he could for her: built ramps at all the entrances, made smooth gravel pathways outside, lowered the kitchen counters so she could reach. He had wanted to make her life as comfortable as possible.

Coming to a stop, Agnes held her arms wide. "You come give your mamaw a big ole hug!" Dan Jr. climbed onto her lap, asking for a ride.

"Danny, get off. That is not a toy!" chastised his mom, Sheila.

Laughing, Agnes situated her youngest grandson before pressing the lever on her wheelchair. She zoomed across the shorn grass to squeals of delight from Dan Jr. Agnes loved giving him rides, the breeze sweeping back her stray hairs and cooling her skin. She could almost imagine she was riding Levi again, feeling his muscles move beneath her as she pressed her knees into his flanks, urging him faster. How she missed riding horses. Levi had been her favorite, a gift from Earle when they'd first bought the ranch. Earle always knew exactly what made her happy.

"Faster, Mamaw, faster!" Dan Jr. reached for the controls, and Agnes let him take over for a moment, the rush of excitement coursing through them both.

Earle helped Tom unload the car. "We got plenty of food here, son. No need to have bought all this. People are bringing enough to feed us for a year, I reckon."

Tom shook his head. "I know, Pa. I tried telling Sheila that, but you know how she is."

"Well, better to have too much than too little. You be sure and tell her we appreciate it."

Earle grabbed a couple of grocery bags, and they strode toward the house, chatting about Tom's students at TSU. Earle was proud of Tom and enjoyed listening to his tales of helping students navigate university life, both in and out of the classroom.

Academia, however, was a foreign land to Earle. He only read the newspaper, the almanac, and sometimes the Bible if Agnes insisted. He'd quit school after eighth grade to help financially at home.

When he met Agnes, he had focused all his will on her and their life together. Each day, he would return to their cramped apartment, and Agnes would bury her nose in his shoulder when he hugged her hello, inhaling his pine scent—*the smell of our future together,* he would say. She had always been a slip of a thing, especially back then, her bones long and slender like the blue herons lining the bay. He'd saved every penny from his job at the plant for lumber and the small herd of longhorns he bought a few years later. Their progeny now grazed on the fourteen acres of land he'd bought dirt cheap decades ago as a young man working day in and day out.

Agnes was flushed when she wheeled herself into the kitchen, having sent Dan Jr. off to play on the tire swing.

"Don't you overdo it, Agnes." Earle placed his palm

on her forehead and then poured her a glass of cold water. "We got a big day tomorrow, and you need to rest up."

"Oh, Earle, don't fuss."

"Why don't you go lie down for a bit?"

Sheila pulled a large chicken out of one of the bags. "I'll cook tonight. Don't you worry about a thing."

"Perhaps I'll read for a bit," Agnes said as she left the kitchen.

Earle followed her to the sunroom. Bending down, he lifted her frail form from the chair. He loved it when she put her arms around his neck as he carried her to the chaise, her head nestled into his shoulder so he could smell the sweet scent of her hair. He laid her down gently and covered her with a light blanket. Then he poured her another glass of water from the pitcher on the small table and handed her the Bible she always kept close at hand. She smiled up at him, her eyes already heavy with approaching sleep. Agnes patted his hand and held on to it for a moment.

"I'll check on you in an hour or so." Earle kissed her fingertips before letting go and pulled the door closed as he left the room. He fought the urge to go back in and lay next to her; he had work to do. The family could take care of themselves. They'd spent enough time here over the years that it was like their second home. But Rennie and Dorie would be arriving soon to help with the wedding preparations. And Ennis, Earle's right-hand man, was already busy outside setting up the makeshift stage with the help of some local boys who wanted to make a bit of cash.

Still lots to do before tomorrow.

Earle stepped outside and surveyed the preparations. The property had never looked better. The surrounding land was lush and green; even the cows looked content as they grazed, ignoring the hubbub surrounding them.

A large truck pulled up the long gravel driveway. Rennie stepped out, followed by his niece, Izzie, and Dorie. As they made their way over, Earle couldn't help staring at Izzie. She looked like an alien, so skinny, with her too-pale skin and black makeup. And that spiky hair. What made kids today want to look so strange?

Rennie waved. "Morning, Earle. Where should we start?"

"Tables and chairs are in the barn. Let's get those set up right over here." Earle gestured to a wide-open area beside the house. It was mostly shaded by the huge oak tree where Dan Jr. was playing.

"Papaw, come swing me higher!"

Earle strode over to his grandson. Telling him to hang on tight, he raised the tire swing almost to the lowest branch of the tree. When he let go, Dan Jr. cried out with a mix of triumph and fear. Earle swung him a few more times. Kids needed that thrill of excitement tinged with fear; it made 'em tough.

Dan Jr.'s brother and sister joined them. "Us too, Papaw!"

"Sorry, but I got work to do. You take turns now."

Earle left the kids to play and made his way over to the barn. Rennie was talking to Izzie inside.

"Your mom told me you're grounded after sneaking out the other night."

Izzie half-heartedly picked up a folding chair. "How can she even really ground me? I'm eighteen now."

Earle stopped just outside to give them privacy, but he couldn't help eavesdropping.

"You live in her house. She pays for your keep. You listen to what she says."

"I've been looking for a job, but everything's already closing for the off season, so they're not hiring right now."

"Look, I know it's tough, but it's time to grow up. You can't live with your mom forever, and until you get a real job, you can't live on your own."

"I could live with you."

"We tried that once, remember? Unless you follow the rules, it's not going to work. You know I want what's best for you, but you need to want it too."

Earle wondered why people didn't have the same work ethic his generation did. Seemed all people wanted to do these days was nothin'. Rennie painted houses instead of building them. Izzie's mom was a waitress, and granted, she worked hard, but for what? Her family struggled to get by. No wonder Izzie was the way she was.

"You know your mom tries her best," said Rennie. "It's not easy taking care of a family on her own."

"I know, I know."

"Try to put yourself in her shoes—"

"I will never put myself in her shoes." The anger in Izzie's voice was palpable. "I don't intend to have kids and make minimum wage."

"Then you'd better shape up and figure out how you're going to make sure that doesn't happen," Rennie said, his frustration barely disguised.

Deciding this was a longer conversation than he had time for, Earle made his way to the rear of the house to help Ennis. Besides, he didn't want any part of this family drama. He'd had more than his fill of teenage angst. Rennie loved that girl, but he was too soft with her. She needed some tough love.

Ennis was building a stage for the musicians performing at the wedding. Rennie's son, Carl, and his band had come to town for the big day. Earle wasn't familiar with the kid's music, but Rennie had told him he was doing well.

Greeting Ennis, Earle grabbed a board and his tool belt. He buckled the tool belt around his waist and pulled out his hammer, enjoying the heft of it in his hand. He loved the sound of a hammer, that crack as the dense wood gave way to the sharp point of a nail. He'd built every piece of this house over fifty years ago. It held all his hopes and dreams. As a young man, he had known this was the future, one that made him rise with the sun every morning and followed him to his bed each night. He'd whispered a litany of plans into Agnes's ear so they would share the same dreams as they slept.

Tom appeared from around the corner of the house. "Hey, Pa. Want a hand?" He picked up another board.

"That's okay, son. You've had a long drive. Go be with your family."

Tom shook his head. "The kids are playing cards in the bunk room, and Sheila and Dorie . . . well, I'm not sure what they're doing. I just know I'd rather not be a part of it."

"Come on, then. Hold this steady."

After working for an hour or so, Earle went back inside to check on Agnes. Dorie and Sheila sat at the kitchen table, fiddling with various bric-a-brac.

"Hey, Earle," said Dorie. "You want to lend us a hand?" She smiled at Sheila as Earle stared blankly at the table. Dorie held up a square of white netting, and Earle took in the pile of fabric on the table, along with huge bags of sugared almonds and spools of ribbon.

"What . . . ?"

"Wedding favors."

Like Tom, Earle had no idea what they were doing.

Dorie grabbed a small handful of candy, which she wrapped in the netting.

"I-I need to check on Agnes," Earle stuttered.

"Fine. She can lend us a hand when she gets up. So, lucky for you, you're off the hook."

Dorie got back to tying a ribbon around the bundle she'd made. Her fingers fumbled, and the candies clattered onto the table. "Dammit!"

Earle raised his eyebrows and exited quickly. Fiddling with ribbon and lace was not his strong suit.

Agnes was still sleeping when he entered the sunroom, but she stirred when he came in.

"How long did I sleep? You should have woken me."

"Believe me," Earle said, gesturing toward the hallway, his expression still bewildered. "You don't want to go out there."

izzie

Izzie needed to unwind after helping set up for the wedding at the ranch most of the day. Sitting at the kitchen table, she turned up the volume on her earphones and pretended to study.

Nearby, her two brothers argued. While her music drowned out their voices, watching them mime their petty squabbles was like following a movie to her own soundtrack.

Not that the voices raging through her head at full volume were any easier to deal with.

If she had to stay here any longer, she'd lose herself for good. Or murder her family and spend the rest of her life behind bars.

At least then she'd have time alone without her mother yelling at her or her brothers driving her batshit crazy.

And if she was going to get a life sentence anyway, she might as well annihilate the kids at school who made her life a living hell—Jordan, who had forced her into a kiss once and said she smelled like a dyke; Eric, who had plastered her locker with lesbian porn; and Jason, who spat at her whenever she walked by. Rumors had spread before she had even admitted to herself that she was gay.

Izzie wondered how far school shooters were pushed to justify doing such a thing. She knew she could never go that far, though. Anyway, she'd be leaving all that behind soon enough.

Something prodded Izzie's shoulder sharply, and she jumped. Opening her eyes, she found her mother glaring at her, looking exhausted. Her lips moved, forming words Izzie knew she didn't want to hear, but she reluctantly pulled off her earphones.

". . . and the house is a wreck!" screamed her mother. "How do you expect me to work, shop, cook, *and* take care of y'all? I'm not a goddam superwoman!"

"I was helping at the ranch," Izzie said, a sharp edge to her voice.

Shel stopped yelling but turned away. "I'm going to go take a shower."

"I'll cook." Izzie hated cooking, but there was a chance her mother would be in a better mood if she offered.

Izzie unpacked the groceries, keeping out two boxes of mac 'n' cheese, one of the three meals she could cook. Then she tried to get her brothers to pick up the living room while she loaded the dishwasher. Her mom didn't have a shift that night and would probably go to bed early, so Izzie would be able to sneak out and meet Ali at her cousin Shane's place.

She and Ali hadn't been getting along very well lately, but it was better than staying home. They'd only been seeing each other for a couple of months, but Ali was getting too serious. Izzie really liked her, and they had fun together, but Izzie didn't want to be tied down.

Still, Shane was usually generous with his weed stash, which was the best escape Izzie had come up with so far, if only for a few hours.

Izzie made sure her mom saw her at the kitchen table after dinner, studying for her GED. This last summer had been her worst yet—stuck inside a classroom during summer school while her friends hung out at the beach or made money at summer jobs. She'd failed too many classes to graduate and was supposed to take her high school equivalency test in the fall.

Not that she cared. Her mom, however, had grounded her until she passed, and her uncle Rennie was trying to convince her to attend junior college.

No way. I've had enough school to last a lifetime.

When her mom took a second wine cooler into her bedroom after putting Chase and Johnny to bed, Izzie knew it wouldn't be long before she could sneak out. She flipped through the pages of her study guide for a few more minutes, just in case her mom came back out, but all she could think about was her *real* exit plan. One more day and she'd be out of there for good.

Once the house was quiet, Izzie crept to her mom's door and listened for her light snores.

Shane's apartment was across Highway 87 on the bay side of the peninsula, not too far down from hers. She considered taking her mom's car, but that was too risky. As she walked along the track leading to Shane's place, the stink of fish and mud blended with the unmistakable smell of weed coming from the apartment. Shane was Ali's older cousin and had moved out of his parents' place a couple of years ago. Izzie didn't much like him, but her options were limited when it came to partying.

When Shane opened the door, he was already bleary

eyed and slouched. "Hey, Iz," he drawled. "Mommy let you out for the night?"

Izzie dodged past him, not wanting to give him the chance to grope whatever bit of flesh he could get his hands on, but he caught her arm.

"You ain't even gonna say howdy?" His teeth were stained brown from the dip he always chewed; she could smell the bitter tobacco on his breath as he leaned close.

"Hi, Shane."

She squirmed out of his grip and sat on the peeling faux-leather couch next to Ali, who was sucking on a red bong. She wore a look of concentration, as if getting high were a trick she had to master.

As Ali held her breath before blowing out a cloud of smoke, Izzie reached for the bong. Inhaling deeply, she waited for the world to fuzz.

There were several other guys in the room, but no one Izzie recognized. It seemed Shane didn't have any close friends, just a new round of stoner hangers-on each time she came over.

God, what did that make her?

Shane was still staring at her from the kitchen doorway, his eyes holding hers so she couldn't look away.

Ali put her arm around Izzie's shoulders. "Glad you could make it. I was getting kinda worried being here alone with these assholes."

"Thought you said they were cool?"

"Definitely not cool. Just boring."

Izzie hoped that was the most she had to worry about. Shane's taste in music was unbearable. Izzie prided herself on her musical preferences. She went out of her way to find indie bands no one else knew about—well, no one in this backward-ass place, anyway.

She turned her nose ring, still unused to wearing it. Her mom didn't even know she'd gotten a piercing, so she could only put it in when she knew her mom wouldn't see.

Ali pulled Izzie closer and nuzzled her neck. She was definitely high.

"Fuck me!" One of Shane's friends pointed his cigarette at them, a cauldron of ash falling onto the carpet. "Shane, you didn't tell me your cousin was a homo." He laughed, high and shrill like a hyena in heat, and moved toward them. "Mind if I join in?"

"Fuck off." Ali rose unsteadily, taking hold of Izzie's hand. "Let's get outta here."

"Can we at least watch?" Shane's friend had stopped laughing and stood in front of them, his mouth slack.

Izzie looked down at the grubby carpet, counted the dead roaches scattered among the pile, legs raised toward the ceiling like supplicants. One, two, three . . . . The seconds of silence weighed down the muggy air. Four, five . . .

Suddenly, the clamor of the window unit filled the room, and Izzie looked toward it. Faded plastic streamers danced on the air current.

"Hey, that's my cousin, man." Shane planted himself between his friend and Ali, his chest puffed out, shoulders back. If Izzie hadn't been so scared, she would have laughed at his posturing. Tightening her grip on Izzie's hand, Ali dragged her to the front door, yanked it open, and pounded down the stairs into the night.

They headed for the mudflats, checking behind them as they ran. Izzie tried to block out the threat of the boys chasing them, catching them, forcing them to the ground. She sucked at the liquid air, which stuck in her throat, suffocating her.

By the time they stopped running, all was quiet except

for the crabs clicking over shale, hunting for food. Ali burst out laughing, a giggle that became manic. Izzie bit her thumbnail, waiting for Ali to stop. She wanted to go home.

No, not home. Away. Just away.

Izzie sat on a rock next to the water, and Ali plopped down beside her.

"So yeah, assholes." Ali sipped from a can of Budweiser she must have brought with her when they left Shane's. "Look what else I got." She held out a tightly rolled joint. "They won't miss it."

"I'm good." Izzie's head was already spinning, either from the weed or the run.

"It's not for now. I'm saving it for tomorrow, before the wedding. I know we're gonna need it."

Izzie was dreading the wedding. Her mom had bought her a hideous dress from Walmart, saying she needed to look pretty for such an occasion. Iz was weighing the consequences of not wearing the dress against her complete embarrassment if she did. Her mom just couldn't accept that Izzie wasn't into girly things, only girls.

Izzie giggled to herself as she imagined her mom seeing her now: stoned and hanging out with her girlfriend.

Ali smiled and, holding up the joint, sidled closer to Izzie. "Let's meet early tomorrow to prepare."

"I can't. I promised I'd help out again before it starts." At least she'd be busy and not have to think about stuff or talk to people.

"Okay, fine. I'll find you during the festivities, and we can sneak behind a haystack or something." Ali held the beer out to Izzie, who shook her head. "Come here." Ali put her hands on Izzie's face and turned it toward her. "You okay?" She leaned in and kissed her. "I love you."

Izzie's insides clenched, and she stood up.

Ali's arms dangled aimlessly. "What's wrong?"

"Nothing." Izzie wrapped her arms around her stomach. "I'm just tired. And worried about the stupid wedding."

"So you can't say it back?" She reached for Izzie again, stopping short when Izzie backed up.

"Look, I better go. My mom'll ground me again if she finds out I'm not there."

"Like that's ever stopped you." Ali suddenly looked very sober.

"Yeah. Still." Izzie began walking away. "I'll see you tomorrow." She felt Ali watching her and tried not to feel guilty, which only made her annoyed. She didn't owe Ali anything. And she needed a clean break.

Izzie crept up the wooden steps to her front door, avoiding the ones that creaked. The front door had warped some over the years, but she knew to pull up on the handle as she opened it so it wouldn't make a sound. As she fumbled through the darkened living room, she heard a sharp breath—low and filled with something like pain.

"Where the hell have you been?"

Izzie looked down at the scuffed wooden floor, where shadows hid the ever-present grime.

"You do remember me grounding you, right?" Shel was seething, but she kept her voice low so as not to wake the boys. "You were with Ali, weren't you?"

Izzie remained silent, knowing it was the best way to handle her mother.

"I told you not to hang out with her. She's not right."

Yet how could she stay silent? "You mean, *I'm* not right."

Shel let out a long breath, resignation rimming its boundaries, threatening to spill over. "I didn't say that."

"You didn't have to."

"While you live under my roof, I won't have you—"

"Would you be this upset if I had snuck out to meet a boy?"

Izzie already knew the answer to that. She had heard stories about her mom and how wild she had been. Hell, that's what had gotten her where she was now: a single mom with three kids and a part-time waitressing job, broke and miserable. Meeting a boy would have still been a problem for her mom's false morality, but not as wicked as being with a girl. That was a sin her mom could never forgive.

"You can't stay out all hours of the night, mixing with God knows who. You'll end up in real trouble."

"Like you did, you mean." Izzie had never confronted her mom before. A surge of power raced through her body until every cell pricked and burned.

"At least your father made an honest woman of me."

Izzie barked a stab of laughter. "Yeah, for about a month."

"He did the best he could for us—"

"Well, that doesn't say much about your choice in partners, then, does it? At least Ali loves me."

Now it was Shel's turn to laugh. "Love? That girl doesn't love you. It's unnatural."

Izzie headed toward the hallway, fuming, willing herself to keep quiet before this escalated further. She didn't want to have this conversation with her mother anymore.

But Shel grabbed her arm as she passed. "Do not see her again." Each word punctured the still air. "You hear me?"

Izzie nodded once and pulled her arm away. At least that promise was one she could keep. She wouldn't be seeing any of them again after tomorrow.

september 11, 2008

2 days before the storm

the lost boys

The Lost Boys clustered around Leroy as he read to them in the dusty light. He was the oldest and the only one who could decipher the words on pages of books scattered about the hotel. None of the boys could resist the stories Leroy read to them—*Treasure Island*, *The Hardy Boys*, *Huckleberry Finn.* They had heard them all over and over, but they were always sure to listen between the lines so they could hear his anger when it rose nearer the surface.

Leroy was one of the Candy Man's boys. They were the dangerous ones best avoided. Their unmarked graves meant they belonged nowhere, not even with the other Lost Boys. Over time, the unspeakable horrors they'd suffered consumed them bit by bit, until all that remained were shadows that would fill a person who happened upon them with terror, shame, and despair.

Leroy was one of the few boys who had been identified by the coroner working with the sheriff's department. On that day in the 1970s, High Island had been pockmarked with the dug-up graves of the Candy Man's victims. The police had already found the bodies of other teenage boys beneath the serial killer's house in Houston Heights, but a surviving victim had tipped them off to a spillover location on Bolivar Peninsula.

Leroy's spirit was tethered to that place, and the boys watched him grow dimmer by the day.

The Lost Boys listened closely as the spaces between Leroy's words grew shorter and the words themselves grew louder. Exchanging looks of fear with one another, they watched Leroy's face as he read. When it began to crease and hollow, they got up and moved far away from him to safer parts of the hotel. One touch from him could destroy what remained of their previous selves. They had seen it before—shadows that lingered in corners and under beds.

Finn and Jack were the last to go, leaving Leroy to release his torments alone. They sat outside on the hotel porch, wishing they could still feel the briny wind brush their cheeks. It had been so long since they'd been able to feel anything.

"What's it like having a Mother?" asked Jack.

The story Leroy had been reading was about a boy who found a stray dog but whose mother wouldn't let him keep it. There were no Mothers at the orphanage where Jack had spent his short life.

Finn hesitated. He'd had two Mothers once: his Sea-Mother and the one from the other world that he could no longer inhabit. It had been so long ago, he could trace only the outlines of that memory now.

"It's like there's someone who loves you best."

"What's love feel like?"

Finn paused again. Jack concentrated on his face, trying to read tinges of emotion in his friend's features as he tried to remember.

"It's never wanting to be apart."

Jack wondered if he had loved Sister Theresa. She had been his favorite nun at St. Mary's Orphans Asylum, the youngest there and the kindest as well.

Almost every morning after mass, Jack would slip out of the line of children heading to lessons. He'd nimbly climb the wooden staircase, intent on escaping those dingy, suffocating walls, the Vaseline light, and the smell of loneliness that filled the stale air. His one reprieve had been the dormitory balcony overlooking the gulf, half-sheltered behind a row of sand dunes supported by salt cedar trees.

While hiding there once, he had spied Sister Theresa near the water. She had raised her habit to avoid getting it wet, and he had seen her long, pale calves as she paddled in the shallow waves. He had imagined being one of those waves, tickling her pretty toes until she laughed.

"She doesn't call to me in the water anymore," Finn said, interrupting Jack's memories. There were times Finn hadn't been sure whose voice he heard when he lived with Sea-Mother. Had it been her wavesong, a constant lullaby to accompany his eternal sleep? Or had it been his other Mother, calling to him from the shore?

"It's because I saved you and brought you here." Jack frowned. "You *do* still like it here, don't you?"

Finn heard the plea in Jack's voice. "Yes. But I miss her." Had Jack *saved* him from Sea-Mother? His first Mother had loved him just as fiercely but with a tenderness that Sea-Mother seemed only to emulate, her unpredictable power always simmering just beneath the surface.

"How do you know you miss her?"

Finn remained silent. There was a vacant place inside him where something good used to be. That must be it. He wasn't sure how long it had been since they'd parted, because time had no meaning here. He knew things now that he wouldn't have known in the other world, but he had forgotten what love felt like in this one.

"My Mother always smelled good," Finn remembered.

"Did she smell like hot cocoa?" That was the only good smell Jack could remember. Well, not remember exactly. But he knew it was good because they had all looked forward to drinking it once a year, at Christmas. St. Mary's Orphans Asylum hadn't had many good things, but that had been one of them. That was why he'd traveled across the bay to get to the peninsula, instead of staying in Galveston, where the boys were so lost, they didn't even remember who or what they had once been.

Finn couldn't recall her face, but . . . "She smelled like all the colors of the world." He saw splashes of color that smelled of laughter and love with tinges of sorrow.

Jack had no idea what colors smelled like, but he really wanted to find out.

Distant shouts echoed among the shadow-trees surrounding the hotel. Climbing to his feet, Jack ran toward the woods to find his friends.

Finn didn't follow. He never left the confines of the hotel. Beyond the woods were the sand and the sea. He was supposed to be there among the waves, so he didn't want to risk getting too close again in case she took him back. Sea-Mother had claimed him once and would again.

Once, not so long ago, her embrace had rocked him into blissful oblivion. Then one day, Jack had dragged him out of his stupor, severing the hold his Sea-Mother had over him. Jack had said he collected Lost Boys and that Finn was his favorite.

At first, Finn had felt displaced, addled. But he had let Jack take him because he was lonely and needed a friend. It was better here at the Sea View, among the Lost Boys—boys like him who had no one but each other.

Jack ran through the trees, their lower branches flicking against him—half caress, half slap. Not unlike the twist of pain that had made him shudder when Sister Joan tugged on his ear if he forgot the words to the Lord's Prayer.

Jack crossed the threshold of the wood to the sand. He could see the water now, and as he drew closer, wavesong filled his ears. Where the sand met the ocean, the sound grew louder, pulling him in. Beneath the wavesong were discordant mutterings, echoes of a refrain he knew so well—"Queen of the Waves."

He entered the water, that liminal space between this world and the other—between his present state and the past where he had once lived and died. The water began to churn and turn feral, like the maw of a giant sea creature.

He was back at St. Mary's, where battering rain and wind pounded against the dormitory walls, desperate to tear away the fortress and offer its innards to the devouring sea. Sister Theresa appeared like an apparition, an umbilical cord of rope connecting her to four other children, their faces ashen. Jack struggled as she tied him to her waist, the other children's bitter cries like splinters coursing through his veins. Sister Theresa gathered the children close, the incense on her robes the odor of incarceration and God.

The water rose higher, leaning its weight against the red bricks. Jack tugged to release himself from the cord, the sister's good intentions transubstantiated into a sacrificial offering.

Through him, and with him, and in him,
almighty Father,

in the unity of the Holy Spirit,
all glory and honor is yours,
for ever and ever.
Amen.

Jack used his teeth to chew and chew, until the rope began to fray and his jaw ached. But the water came too fast. Swept up in the floodwaters, they struggled to free themselves, but they were bound together, each dragging the other down, sinking farther and farther.

"Queen of the Waves" filled his ears, a dirge of children's voices distorted by the waters that claimed them:

But fear we not, tho' storm clouds round us gather,
Thou art our Mother and thy little Child
Is the All Merciful, our loving Brother,
God of the sea and of the tempest wild.

Until finally, they stilled in the deep,
and like a lily blooming
in slow motion,
each one a petal,
unfurled.

clementine

The ghost of her mother's kiss lingered on Clementine's cheek, and the scent of flowers caught in the back of her throat. Her mother only visited on very special days now, unlike when Clementine was a child. Although she had never known her in the flesh, Clem had received her mother's kiss goodnight every evening with reverence. Would she have been a different person if her mother had survived childbirth? Would the trajectory of her life have taken a different course?

But then, Clem may never have had Finn.

Or never have lost him.

She opened her eyes to marigolds threaded through her bedframe and placed on the sheets around her. Was she finally dead, her body dressed in a burial shroud? Is that why her mother had come, to take her away from the world of the living to another place? The place where she could be with Finn forever.

No, this day was special for a different reason. She was getting married.

A knock at the bedroom door pulled Clementine back to the issue at hand.

"Are you up yet?" Dorie poked her head around the door. "I brought supplies." She dumped a large bag of beauty products onto the flower-strewn bed. "Do you like the flowers? Lou said they're your favorite. It was his idea to do this earlier, while you were sleeping."

Clem smiled.

"Here." Going to the dresser, Dorie opened a drawer and removed a simple wreath of marigolds. "I made this with the leftover flowers. For your hair." She looked almost bashful as she held it out to Clementine. "You don't have to wear it."

Clem took the wreath and placed it awkwardly on her head. "Thank you."

Dorie wasn't usually one for displays of beauty or tenderness. She made her love known in less obvious ways, like always being there for her friends, through thick and thin. Dorie even blushed whenever Rennie was affectionate with her, making a joke of it, though Clem suspected that behind closed doors, there was another version of her only Rennie was privy to.

Dorie laughed. "Hair and makeup first. Then we'll see how it looks with the dress."

The next hour was spent attempting to apply various potions to Clementine's face and hair. Dorie put on her reading glasses and peered at the back of a bottle.

"This says to apply a dab—what's a dab, anyway? Apply a dab to the palm of your hand and rub together. Then pull evenly through hair, beginning at the ends." She looked up at Clem, befuddled.

Clem shrugged. "No idea."

"Your hair already looks perfect. We don't need this

stuff." Dorie threw the bottle on the bed and picked up a palette of eyeshadow. "Any notion of how to apply this? Last time I wore eyeshadow was at my high-school prom, I think. That was over thirty years ago."

Both women stared at the array of beauty products spread across the sheets.

"You know what? This is all you need." Dorie picked up some blush and brushed a few strokes onto Clem's high cheekbones. Then she handed her a neutral-toned lipstick. "Just a dash of this."

Clem looked in the mirror and applied a quick stroke to her full lips.

"Perfect," said Dorie. "Now hair."

Dorie began pinning up Clem's cascade of chestnut curls, bobby pins sticking out of her mouth like a medieval torture device. Every time she made any progress, several stray ringlets insisted on coming loose. Somehow, though, it worked.

Next, Clem put on her dress of antique white lace. It was silly to wear white, really; she'd lost her innocence long ago. But she'd found the dress at a thrift store in Galveston, and she hadn't been able to resist the hand-stitching that reminded her of the dresses her *niñera* had made for her when she was a girl. Her *niñera* was the closest thing she had to a mother, and she cherished every memory she had of her. Clementine's father had treated her like the employee she was, but Clem had loved her fiercely and missed her still.

Dorie placed the wreath of marigolds on Clem's hair. "Exquisite."

Clem stood before the full-length mirror. It had been a long time since she'd put any real effort into her appearance, and she had to admit that perhaps she did look pretty.

Dorie took Clem's hands in her own. "You ready?"

Clem nodded. "Thank you for all of this."

"You deserve only happiness and joy from now on."

Clem longed for that to be true, that somehow this was the turning point, and she really could move forward into a new life with Lou.

"Come on." Dorie led her by the hand as they left the bedroom and walked downstairs toward Earle, who was waiting for them at the bottom.

Clem looked up at him, this kind man who was like a father to her. He had certainly been a better father than her own had ever been.

When she'd first begun working for Agnes and Earle, she'd treated it like any other cleaning job—get the work done and leave. But they'd let her bring Finn, and he had gotten close to them both. When he died and they took her in for a bit, she began to understand how important they all were to each other. Earle had even given her Agnes's silver chain for Finn's shell.

Clem touched the shell. Its familiar shape felt like a piece of her son lingering with her, somehow binding all four of them together like a real family.

She wrapped her arm through Earle's. He stood tall and straight as he escorted her solemnly through the front door of the white ranch house he'd built for his own bride so many years ago. He'd repainted the shutters bright blue just for the wedding, and they contrasted with the bright-white siding. Agnes had planted marigolds in the window boxes, and an aisle between the chairs outside was lined with more orange blossoms. The large clearing in front of the property was filled with tables covered in white cotton tablecloths and surrounded by guests, a sea of faces looking up as the music started.

Carl played a gentle acoustic version of "First Time Ever I Saw Your Face," a Johnny Cash song Lou had sung to her many times. As the words rushed through Clementine's mind, a lump formed in her throat.

The crowd stood as she and Earle made their way down the aisle. At least half the Bolivar community seemed to be there watching her, but they all dissolved as she focused on Lou, who stood at the end. He waited for her, tall and proud that she had chosen him. His expression was so open and clear of any of the troubles they'd shared that she knew this was right. They had wiped the slate clean and were starting over from a place of love and acceptance.

When she reached Lou, Earle released her arm, holding her hand for a moment. Pulling her eyes away from her handsome Lou, she thanked Earle with a kiss on the cheek. Then she turned to her soon-to-be husband, who took her hand in his. His love washed over her, and for a moment, nothing else mattered. Looking into his eyes, she knew she was supposed to be here, in front of him and their friends and family, pledging their everlasting love to each other.

The music stopped, and the crowd hushed. Clementine held her breath as Lou fumbled to find the words he'd memorized for his vows.

"Clem, I always knew this day would come. The first time I saw you, I just knew, like in the song." Looking over at Carl, he nodded his thanks. "We've had our struggles, for sure, but you were always my light. Even in the dark, I felt you with me, always. I told you once that I'd never give up on you, and here we are, promising to spend the rest of our lives together. We can bear anything now; I know that to be true. You can count on me to always be by your side, to always sing to you at night when the light seems so far away.

To make you menudo just the way your *niñera* used to. To be your best friend and to love you fiercely and forever."

Lou took the ring from his breast pocket and placed it on Clem's left hand. She looked down at the antique silver band topped with a diamond that had belonged to Lou's mother.

Murmurs from the crowd brought Clementine back to the ground she stood on, signaling that it was her turn to speak.

"I've never been loved the way you love me. I suppose I didn't understand love before I met you. You showed me how. You make me stronger, a more whole person. I understand myself better through you. I feel safe and able to face whatever comes our way. And you gave me the greatest gift I could have ever wished for—our Finn."

Clem swallowed as her throat tightened. Maybe their boy was watching them now, pleased that they still loved each other and had mended what had been broken.

"Thank you for never giving up on me. For the first time in a long while, perhaps ever, I look forward to my future—our future. I love you."

Reaching into her pocket, she retrieved a plain silver ring, which she placed on Lou's hand. When she looked up into his eyes, they were filled with tears. Leaning down, he kissed her, and all the worry dissolved.

The music started up again, this time the traditional wedding song. People threw golden petals as she and Lou walked through the crowd, arm in arm and laughing with the joy of the moment. They made their way into the house, where they collapsed on the sofa, still laughing between kisses. Clem tried to catch her breath as she stared at her husband—this man she had loved for so many years. Quieting, they kept staring, clasping hands, knowing this was the beginning of something new but also a story built upon something older.

When they finally headed back outside, a small crowd greeted them with congratulations, hugs, and well-wishes. Earle led the newlyweds to the head table, which was draped in white lace-edged cotton and garlands of flowers. Crystal glasses were filled with champagne, and Agnes's best silver shone in the afternoon sunshine. Dorie and Lou sat on either side of Clementine, and Agnes and Earle sat on the other side of Lou. Lou's sisters sat across from them all.

Clementine had been nervous about seeing Lou's family again. She had only met them once before when she and Lou first got serious. At the time, his sisters had lived in Louisiana, so it had been a weekend trip. They were close, and they all worshipped him. She had felt like a third wheel throughout the entire weekend, though they had been polite and friendly. But she knew they had been sizing her up, deciding if she was worthy.

Dorie leaned closer. "You look radiant."

Clem smiled, grateful again for Dorie's uncanny ability to recognize when she needed to be pulled out of her head and back into the moment. "Thank you. So do you."

Dorie laughed and tucked a gray strand behind her ear. "So how does it feel to officially be Mrs. Walker?"

"I'm still a Castillo. I'm not changing my name for anyone, not even Lou." Although she had rejected her father, his surname has also been her mother's—the only piece she had of her. "Will you change yours when you remarry?"

Dorie's eyes widened. "And what makes you think that's a decision I'll ever have to make?"

Clem searched the crowd for Rennie. Dorie was obviously still reluctant to admit how attached she and Rennie had become since they met four years ago, but Clem had a feeling about them.

Clem saw Lou lean closer to Agnes, whose cracked voice straining against the conversations surrounding them. She loved watching Lou with them; he was so gentle and courteous. Clem was proud to call him her husband when he treated her dear friends with such respect. She knew he loved them, too, and had worked hard to earn their trust. They had been so loyal to Clem after her world fell apart, and they had blamed Lou for much of it. They felt he'd abandoned her, when in fact, it was she who'd rejected him.

Earle stood up and called for everyone's attention. The crowd gradually silenced and waited.

"As y'all know, I'm a man of few words. But today, I'd like to honor Clementine and Lou. They've become a part of this community, and we love Clementine like a daughter." Earle looked lovingly at his wife, who nodded and reached for his hand. "And Lou is growing on me." The crowd snickered, and Lou shook his head, smiling. "Lou, you take good care of our girl, you hear." As Earle looked at Lou, his tone became serious. "She doesn't deserve any more hardship in her life, and I expect you to make sure she has only bright days ahead."

Looking at Clem, Lou whispered, "I'll do my best." Clementine took his hand and squeezed, willing him to succeed.

"We'll always be here for you, Clementine; never forget that." Earle raised his glass. "To Clementine and Lou."

Everyone stood and joined in the toast, and Clementine and Lou clinked glasses. When Lou refilled his glass, Clem experienced a touch of unease. But it was a special occasion; a couple of glasses of champagne wouldn't hurt.

the lost boys

Jack could tell he was in the right place. He had searched and searched the peninsula for all the colors of the world since talking to Finn, and this seemed like a most promising source. Jack floated above a dome of light, and when he looked down, everyone and everything glowed with a pulsating energy. A sound he didn't recognize rose up, filling the sky so the air itself danced. Jack began to sway, undulating like the waves he watched from the tower with Finn. He wanted to be immersed in the sound, so he drew closer.

Suddenly, the energy changed, and his body grew rigid. He wasn't sure how to respond to the jarring clamor. Then he began to pick out a rhythm, like rain during a storm, thundering, drumming on the wooden porch of the hotel, a percussive beat that vibrated the air around and through him. Traversing the long grass, he flowed with the surge, his eyes closed in ecstasy.

When he opened them, he was sure he'd finally made it to heaven. That place the nuns had warned them they'd never go, threatening them instead with eternal damnation if they ran or talked too loudly or didn't empty their plates at mealtimes. Before him was the source of the glowing light—more people than he had ever seen in one place at one time. And everyone looked happy, their smiles so radiant, he almost couldn't bear to look.

He located the source of the sound—a group of men on a stage, like the one where the nuns had sat during assembly. Except this stage expelled an energy and sound that made him weak with their ferocity. A man was singing, but not like the choir at the orphanage. This man growled, moaned, and screamed and then suddenly poured out a mellow syrup of song that slowed everything down.

Jack stood mesmerized by the singer and the three other men, who played instruments he'd never seen in real life, only in pictures in books. He'd heard music before, but never anything quite like this.

A crowd of people in front of the stage were hopping and twisting their bodies. They looked possessed. Yet remembering how his own body had felt when he first heard the music, he understood.

Turning, he looked beyond the churning crowd, where other groups of people sat around huge tables laden with food, the likes of which he'd never seen. Jack wished he could still eat, longing to taste each morsel. It was so unlike what they'd been served at St. Mary's, it was almost unrecognizable as food.

Under an oak tree sat a couple, gray and bent. The woman sat in a wheelchair, and the man kept touching her as if he couldn't be whole without her. Jack wished someone had touched him like that, but no one ever had. He drifted over to them and stood close, his hand hovering above theirs so he could almost feel the love and caring that emanated from them.

Then his eyes locked on the most beautiful person he had ever seen.

Everyone was suddenly clapping. Jack looked around at the spectacle of so many people enjoying themselves. But he singled out the beautiful lady who wore a gown like a princess in the fairytales Leroy read to them. Her hair was piled on top of her head, but long, twirling strands fell around her face, reminding him of a mermaid.

He drew closer, bold in his invisibility. He willed her to look at him, to see him. But she looked only at the man next to her, a large man to whom Jack took an instant dislike.

This must be her. This must be Finn's Mother. And the man next to her was the father? Jack recognized the look in her eyes when she watched him. It was the same look he'd seen in Finn's eyes when he talked about his Mother.

Jack wanted to be close enough to know what love smelled like. He drew nearer her chair, so close, he could reach out and touch her smooth skin. Leaning forward, his nose almost buried in her hair, he inhaled. Closer still—

She turned to him. Her eyes stared straight into his.

Jack fell backward, stumbling to right himself. When he looked back at her, she was leaning against the man, her head on his shoulder and her hand on her chest, clasping a shell that hung from a silver chain.

Jack forced himself away. He had to tell Finn. He ran over dunes and along the water, feeling seen for the first time in such a long while. He'd found Finn's Mother—a Mother for all the Lost Boys.

The Sea View Hotel shimmered in the afternoon light, its decay camouflaged by the milky mist that enveloped it. He scampered up the wooden steps onto the wraparound porch, calling out the same name over and over.

"Finn? Anyone seen Finn?"

Charles and Leo were well into a game of marbles and ignored Jack's call. Jack stood before them, scowling, hands on his hips. When Leo dropped his marble, it rolled between Jack's feet. Jack bent and picked it up, examining the blue-green eye trapped within the glass orb.

"Where's Finn?"

Leo lowered his head. "I think he's up in the lookout tower."

Leo's subservience washed over Jack, making him feel powerful. He liked that feeling. He'd never had power over anyone in his other life.

Jack threw the marble in among the surrounding oaks and ran into the house. The downstairs appeared empty.

"What's all the rush about?" Leroy appeared out of nowhere and peered at Jack with narrowed eyes.

Stopping, Jack stuffed his hands in his pockets to keep them from trembling. "Nothin'. Just playin'."

Leroy remained silent. He hated when they had fun; he didn't want to suffer alone. Jack looked down at his scuffed shoes and pressed his foot into the dust.

Leroy moved closer to Jack. "Can I play?"

"I'm done now. Just heading upstairs."

Following Jack's gaze to the staircase, Leroy immediately knew where he was going. "Why you so attached to that boy? He ain't nothin' but a chump."

Jack had suspected Leroy wanted to be his friend, of sorts. No one hung out with Leroy and for good reason. But Jack had gained some authority over the rest of the boys by at least pretending to be in cahoots with him. And Leroy had no other friends; everyone was too afraid of him.

"Yeah, but he might have something we all need."

Leroy stepped closer still. "Such as?"

"A Mother."

Leroy pulled a slim reed out of his back pocket and stuck the end between his lips. One of his greatest pleasures had been to smoke, and now he couldn't. He often complained about it as he blew out invisible puffs after sucking on the slender stick.

"And where is this Mother? How come I never seen her?"

"She's still on the other side. But I'm pretty sure Finn can make her join us here so she can take care of us."

Leroy held the reed out to Jack. "Here."

The end was slick with saliva, frayed like tufts of damp hair. Jack knew that not accepting his offer could be dangerous. No one said no to Leroy. Taking the stick, Jack hesitated, then put it in his mouth. When he sucked on the end, it tasted loamy, like soil deep down where the dead lay.

"You go on and keep that one. I got more."

A darkness descended on Jack, pressing down and into him, filling him with panic. Leroy watched, waited. Jack's insides felt scooped out and laid bare, the pulp of him exposed carrion. Leroy became a shadow before him, touching Jack's nerves, which spooled tighter and tighter, scoured by the barbed air. Agony and terror careened through his every fiber, the marrow of his being festering, stinking . . .

Until all that was left was a dull dread and emptiness, hollow and cavernous.

When the pain eased, Leroy was leaning over him, holding out his hand. "You're okay. Come on."

Jack hesitated once more. He never ever wanted to feel that way again.

As Leroy reached for his arm and dragged him to his feet, Jack tried to decipher what had just happened. His flesh prickled, and his insides thrummed. He hadn't reacted physically to anything since he'd crossed over—until now.

Leroy gestured toward the stairs. "Go on up, then, and see your friend."

Jack walked past Leroy, making sure not to touch him again. Yet they now seemed connected in some awful way, like Jack belonged to Leroy.

He climbed the stairs slowly at first. When Leroy turned and headed to the parlor, Jack quickened his pace. He wanted to get as far away from him as possible and reach the safety of the tower and his gentle friend.

As Jack raced up the two flights of stairs, his footsteps silent on the wooden boards, he left the darkness below. His body shed it as he got closer to the top. Soaring over the gap where the treads had rotted, he landed close to the door of the tower.

He took a breath to calm himself.

"What are you doing there?" he asked.

Finn looked up with a dazed look. "I like to draw what I see from this place."

"And what do you see today?"

Finn held the drawing out to Jack. It was a pencil sketch of the water and sky that Finn had somehow made real. The waves whispered through the window, and the graphite lines seemed to mimic their voices and ripples, scratches and smudges merging and separating, undulating.

Jack studied Finn as he handed the drawing back, wondering what else he saw in those waves. He was always sad, even in the shelter of this magnificent ruin.

"Finn, there's something I have to tell you."

The other boy was already sketching again, his hair covering his face.

"I found your Mother."

Finn's hand stilled, and he looked up at Jack. Again and again, she used to call to him as she wandered the shore and visited the water in search of him. But he hadn't heard her voice in so long. His memories were like dreams. They dissolved as soon as he touched their frayed edges.

"Take me to her." A new light shone in Finn's eyes. He longed to see her face, to feel her touch; he didn't want only memories anymore.

"You know I can't. But I'll find a way for you to be together. Very soon."

Finn smiled for the first time in a long while. He had waited for so long, and now he could have a Mother again, one of flesh and bone, blood and breath. One who loved him more than anything else in the world.

Jack knew Finn's real Mother would take care of them all. She would protect them from Leroy, from Sea-Mother, from anything that threatened to separate them. When he saved Finn from Sea-Mother, he had known it was the right thing.

Jack himself understood that illusion of comfort Finn had with Sea-Mother, what it felt like to be loved by her. She had once pulled Jack close too, suffocating him. Watery arms pulsed where his own heart had once beat.

It had taken him a century to understand how to free himself from Sea-Mother, to understand that he *needed* to free himself. After countless Moon cycles, he knew there was one moment to escape. When the surface above Sea-Mother's liquid skin grew pitch black, when the Moon turned to blood in the sky—that was the moment.

Only during the lunar eclipse could the Moon force Sea-Mother's hold loose. Sea-Mother hissed her hatred for Sister Moon. She groaned and fought against Moon's pull, which dragged her tide farther onto the sand and scratched her underside so she squirmed and fidgeted. Her moans had echoed Jack's own as they both twisted and squirmed in unison under Moon's bloodlust. And when Jack had sensed Sea-Mother's power weaken, he cried out in rage and ripped himself free, rising to the surface, to the Air above.

After that, Jack collected boys, bringing them to Sea View. He learned much, mastering the Earth and the Air. After countless Moons, though, he found Finn.

Jack had hovered over his form, a shadow in the deep bathed in crimson light. How long had Finn belonged to Sea-Mother? Had it been one hundred years for him too, like Sleeping Beauty, like Jack himself?

Sea-Mother had cradled Finn, who was numb in his endless sleep, oblivious to Sea-Mother's intentions. She pretended to love them, to help them, but Jack knew the truth.

She was selfish, covetous.

So, Jack had waited for Moon's silver to darken from Earth's shadow. He watched the Moon dim, slice by slice. When only the penumbra ringed her face, he plunged into the waves—down, down to the deep where Finn lay. He was Prince Jack saving the sleeping beauty after a long slumber, and they would live happily ever after with all the Lost Boys.

He swooped down, sliced through the water to reach Finn. Cupping him in his arms, he soared, soared like the comet he'd just spied in the sky—up, up to the ether.

When Jack looked into Finn's eyes, he saw fear and confusion. *She already has far too many boys. I save them, bring them back to a better place. You'll see.*

The silver halo faded and disappeared. Earth's shadow revealed a fingernail of the Moon, bleeding into the receding tide. Together, they had aligned—Sun, Moon, and Earth—the trinity that had released Jack and Finn from Sea-Mother's grasp.

Pete

Pete had arrived at Beauchamp Ranch first thing to drop off the morning's catch—several pounds of shrimp and crab, which Earle had ordered for the wedding. A few other early birds were there already, sitting at tables and catching up. He took the coolers into the kitchen.

"Mornin', Pete," said Agnes. "Stick 'em in that corner."

When he'd delivered the last one, Agnes offered him some lemonade. Lugging coolers was hard work, especially in mid-September, when the sun was still strong and the humidity high.

"Sure." Pete sat at the table.

Agnes took a pitcher out of the icebox and poured him a glass. He watched her maneuver the wheelchair, wondering how she managed, being a cripple and all.

He had to admit, it made him kind of uncomfortable. He knew she'd walked once, but he hadn't known her back then. He'd still been in Port Arthur and hadn't gotten to the peninsula except to party now and then.

How does a marriage work if you're a cripple, anyway? Agnes and Earle were older than him, but still. *Do you ever stop wanting a woman?*

Pete downed his glass and stood. "All right. I'll see you later, Agnes."

"You take care, Pete."

Pete left quickly before Agnes could engage him in conversation—*or worse yet, start with her Bible thumpin'.*

As he entered the hallway, Agnes raised her voice from the kitchen. "And no shenanigans today."

Pete didn't much like Agnes's company. She kept her Bible too close and her tongue too sharp. Last Fourth of July, he'd gotten a talking-to from Earle and Rennie. He'd shown up at the ranch on his Harley, on the back of which had flown his flags.

It was Independence Day, for Chrissakes. If a man can't be patriotic on the Fourth of July, then what's the point?

Rennie had approached Pete. "You need to take that down."

"Why?"

"It's making people uncomfortable."

"Well, that's their problem, not mine."

"If you don't take it down, I'll do it for you."

He'd suspected it was the Beauchamps who had put Rennie up to this, takin' down Old Dixie.

"Fine, fine. I don't wanna cause no trouble." So he'd taken her down. But it had pissed him off royally.

Pete looked around the Beauchamp grounds with anticipation. Now that the boring ceremony was over, there was only fun to be had. Rennie and Dorie were headed toward him, so he made for the opposite direction. He'd try to stay out of Rennie's way today. Pete was sure Rennie didn't fly any flags and had never fought a war for his country. He needed to get off his high horse and loosen up.

Pete wondered where Lou was. It had been a while since they'd gotten together. Clem kept him on a tight leash these days. It would probably be even worse now they were hitched. He didn't understand why people bothered. He'd married Carol because she'd gotten pregnant, and besides, she'd been a lot of fun back then. He'd never make that mistake again. Still, he had his kids.

Pete saw Clementine standing under the oak tree by herself, watching the crowd. She was a strange one, for sure. He couldn't deny she was good looking, but she was odd. They'd barely ever spoken; in fact, she didn't talk much to anyone at all. He guessed that's what losing a kid did to a woman.

He'd heard the rumors—her going crazy searching for her dead boy, practically drowning herself in the process. Pete had watched Lou struggle with Finn's death, too, during that time. But Lou hadn't gone off the deep end like Clementine had. He'd handled it like a man.

Pete went to the makeshift bar and ordered a whiskey. He'd brought his flask, but he might as well partake of the free liquor.

Rennie's niece stood nearby with her friend—or girlfriend, if the rumors were true. Now *that* he could never understand; it wasn't natural. But hell, whatever floated their boat.

"Hey, mister?" The friend was standing next to him in line. "How about getting us a drink?"

Pete chuckled. "Sure. What y'all want?"

"Two beers."

"Beer? Beer is for wusses."

Izzie joined them. "Beer is fine, thanks."

Pete ordered three drinks and handed them to the girls. "Here you go. Enjoy."

Grabbing the drinks, the girls headed for the barn. He wouldn't have minded seeing what they got up to there. How old was she now, anyway? Must have been eighteen since he heard she graduated—or at least, she was supposed to have graduated.

The girl was a mess, though. And she looked like a freak. *Scrub off all that crazy makeup, and there might be a looker somewhere under there.*

Still, eighteen was probably pushing it, even for him. Besides, she liked girls. Although if anyone could fix her, he could.

Pete searched the grounds again, keeping an eye out for Luanne. Apparently, she had ended up going as Mike's date, but he could change that easily enough.

That's when he saw Lou.

"Hey, man. What's shakin'?" Pete shook Lou's hand, noticing how clammy it was. He clapped Lou on the back.

Lou looked at the ground with a half smile.

"How does it feel? You good?"

"Yeah. I'm good."

"Clem gonna let you out on the boat with me again, or is that off limits now?"

Lou straightened his shoulders. "Course we can go on the boat."

"Let's plan for next week. Been hearin' 'bout a storm heading our way, but it shouldn't be too bad."

"Sounds good." Lou looked around, probably wondering where his other half was.

"Wait here a second. I'll be right back." A couple of minutes later, Pete returned with two shots and held one out to Lou. "Congratulations!"

"Nah. I'm good."

"It's your wedding day. Can't a man celebrate on his wedding day?"

Lou hesitated.

Pete pushed the shot glass into Lou's hand. "Best of luck. You're a braver man than me. Or else a stupider one." Pete laughed and clinked his own glass against Lou's. Man, he loved that sound. "Cheers!"

rennie

As the sun started to go down in the late afternoon, the band went into full swing, and the September breeze induced folks to dance. Rennie stood dead center in front of the stage, trying to avoid getting jostled by the shimmying couples. Lou was two-stepping with Rennie's sister, Shelley, who laughed aloud when he dipped her to the ground. It was nice to see her letting loose and enjoying herself.

"Found you!"

Dorie looped her arm through Rennie's, and he pulled his eyes off Carl for a moment to glance down at her. He could hardly contain his pride as he watched his son perform one of his latest hits. He and Dorie had clapped and cheered the first time it played on the country radio station.

Carl was on national tour now, performing to a full house wherever he went. He even looked like a star. His blond hair had grown longer, and his confidence and talent made him shine brighter than ever.

Yet he still played his old guitar repaired with duct tape.

And he resembled Rennie more than ever: tall and lean, at ease in his body. Rennie had been told that from behind, they could have been brothers, though Rennie's gray streaks surely hinted at his age.

When the number ended, Carl waited for the cheering to die down a bit before speaking into the mic.

"I want to thank Agnes and Earle for inviting me to this shindig. And a huge congratulations to Clementine and Lou. Cheers!"

He grabbed a beer from the floor of the stage and toasted the married couple, which was followed by more cheers and well-wishes from the guests. Rennie noticed Lou drinking from a cup he had set down on the platform. He seemed to sway a bit, likely from dancing with Shelley.

Carl shouted over the crowd that he'd be back for more tunes soon and jumped off the stage.

"Hey, Pops." He pulled Rennie into a bear hug. "Long time, no see!"

"Sounding great up there!"

"Thanks, Dad. Guess that one's a favorite. I'm just happy I don't have to sing 'Margaritaville' anymore." He turned to Dorie. "You taking good care of my old Pa now?"

"She sure is." Rennie pulled Dorie in close to him.

It wasn't so long ago that he had been the one taking care of her. She had told him once that he'd saved her life in a way—he and Clementine both—that he'd taught her how to feel again.

He'd been surprised the first time she'd shown any interest in him. When they first met, she had acted as though she hated him. That was how he had eventually figured out she cared. She just hadn't known how to show it at the time, which was understandable once he found out what she'd gone through with her daughter and all.

It was when she began talking to him about Harriet that their relationship shifted. Dorie opened up about the struggles she'd been through when her daughter was sick, but also the happy times. It was almost as if he had known Harriet, even though she'd died of cancer long before he shared a life with Dorie. Rennie treasured hearing Dorie tell stories about her daughter and looking at Harriet's photos and artwork displayed around the house. Dorie let Harriet be part of her life now, instead of locked away in a place too painful to visit.

Dorie put her arm loosely around his waist and smiled up at him. Thank God she had come around in the end.

"Have you eaten yet?" he asked Carl. "You must be starving."

Leading them to a long stretch of tables he'd helped set up earlier, Rennie marveled at the feast before them. Several large pots of gumbo bubbled on warmers, steaming the air with delicious aromas. Aluminum trays overflowed with Cajun rice. Various casseroles and salads filled in the gaps between platters heaped with barbecue ribs and brisket. And a plethora of desserts in all colors of the rainbow filled the end table. The pièce de résistance was an entire table covered in brown paper stacked with mountains of crab and shrimp, fresh from Pete's boat. Other tables dotted the open space, flanked by neighbors chatting and laughing.

"Where's Iz?" Carl scanned the crowd. "I want to see my little cousin before I take off again. Planning to head out early tomorrow morning. We've got a long drive ahead of us."

Rennie waved a hand dismissively. "No talking about leaving; you only just got here! Can't I just enjoy this day with my son?"

"Sorry, Dad."

"I'll go find her, and you get us a seat at the table. See you both in a sec."

Rennie strode off, head turning in every direction as he looked for Izzie's signature pitch-black hair. Her mom hadn't been able to stop her dyeing it, but he supposed she had to pick her battles.

Everyone was always surprised that Rennie had a niece who looked the way Izzie did. He was clean-cut and pretty old-school in some ways. Even Carl was old country blues.

Izzie, on the other hand, looked like a goth street urchin. Her mom would rip her nose ring out if she saw it, and she would likely ground her for life if she saw the tattoo Iz had hidden under those layers.

Rennie couldn't help a stab of love for the girl as he remembered the day she'd shown it to him—a swallow in flight. She'd made him swear not to tell Shel, and he hadn't. He didn't want to betray her trust, especially since he and Dorie seemed to be the only people with whom she could share any parts of herself.

Besides, it was only a tattoo. Harmless enough.

Rennie spotted her talking to Ali on the other side of the barn. It looked like they were arguing. Izzie was attempting to hush Ali, who was shouting and waving her skinny arms. As Rennie got closer, he picked up some of the conversation.

"Why now? What did I do?" Ali reached for Izzie, but Iz pulled away.

"I told you, nothing. I just have to get my shit together for once."

"But why does that mean we can't be together?"

"I have to do this on my own. Start over—"

She clammed up as she noticed Rennie approaching.

"What's going on girls?"

Ali looked furious but remained silent.

"Nothing. We're just hanging out." Looking down, Izzie pulled her long sleeves over her hands. She'd agreed to wear the dress to appease her mother, but she'd worn a hoodie over it.

"Well, Carl wants to see you before he leaves tomorrow. We're eating, if you'd like to join us."

Izzie seemed ready to get away from Ali. "Sure. See you later, Al."

Her friend had already turned her back, striding toward the gate.

"Everything okay with you two?"

Izzie shrugged. "We broke up."

Rennie couldn't help but feel slightly relieved. Ali was a bit of a loose cannon, as far as he could tell. But he worried for Izzie. "You okay?"

"I'm fine. Not a big deal."

As taciturn as Izzie tended to be, Rennie had spent a great deal of time building her trust, especially after she'd moved in with him for a while. But since Izzie had gone back home again, he hadn't spent as much time with her.

"Well, I'm here if you need anything." Rennie pulled her to him, and she lingered for just a moment. He relished every tiny bit of tenderness he had with his niece. She didn't get enough of it elsewhere; he was certain of that.

Pulling away, Izzie swiped a hand across her face. Then she started walking toward the food tables, as if hurrying to escape. Rennie followed behind. She was probably more upset about the breakup than she let on.

Must be it.

When Rennie reached the table, he sat down next to Dorie and Carl and made room on the bench for Izzie. But Izzie was gone. The girl was more slippery than an eel.

Probably off to find Ali and make up already.

Rennie tried not to worry about it, instead focusing on the animated conversation that had engulfed the table.

Pete shook his head. "I'm just saying it's out there. I'm not telling you what to do."

He must have been talking about the latest storm, Rennie realized. Pete kept a close eye on the weather, as it affected his shrimp business, and word had gotten around about a tropical storm from Cuba that had recently been reclassified as a hurricane. Supposedly, it had grown even stronger after moving into the southern Gulf of Mexico.

Various other voices at the table chimed in. "Well, I ain't bothered. It probably won't even make it to us."

"I heard it's only a category two."

"Yeah, it's just an itty-bitty thing. Won't affect us."

"I lost two days of work when we evacuated for Gustav. Boarded up the house, and all for nothin'."

"Whatever." Pete shrugged and tipped his flask, taking a long swig. "Y'all do what y'all gotta do."

Glancing at Dorie, Rennie realized she wore that worried look she got sometimes. It was always the newbies who took these things too seriously. The locals had been through so many storms, they were immune by now. He'd watch out for her, though, make sure she was safe.

clementine

Clementine stood apart from the crowd, needing a reprieve from all the noise and excitement. Hopefully no one would miss her for a bit. The sky was turning gold as the sun continued its descent—as if blessing them from above.

Clem watched a family pay their respects to Agnes and Earle, who sat under the enormous oak tree shading that side of the house. The air hung heavy with humidity, yet Agnes sat regally in her wheelchair, her white hair scooped up into a pleated bun. Earle held her slender hand, his knuckles like tree burls. He leaned closer to adjust the thin embroidered shawl she wore, lingering to whisper into her ear.

Clem turned to the sound of chickens squawking as they ran from a group of young children. Finn had so loved the chickens. They had entertained him while she cleaned the ranch house, before Agnes and Earle became her found family.

Reaching for Finn's shell, Clem turned it on the thin

silver chain that Earle had given her. She wondered about the strange sensation she'd experienced at the table, as if some unseen presence had been observing her. Her thumb grazed the shell's surface, and she pressed the tip of her finger into the aperture, feeling the empty, smooth space—as if she could find him hiding there.

Or herself, perhaps. Except she had no smooth interior. Only cracks that went beyond the surface, deep inside every chamber of her being.

But Finn's shell meant she was a mother. Still.

Mabel, Agnes's cat, brushed against Clementine's legs. She was another member of the feline family they all shared. Dorie's cat, Rosie, was Mabel's grandma, and Dorie had given her baby to Clem three years ago. She wondered how many generations they would share among them.

Clem picked Mabel up and nuzzled into her fur. She looked toward Lou, who was in his element at the barbecue grill, replenishing the platters. There was a line forming next to him, and not just for the food. Women couldn't help flirting with him; just a glimpse of those eyes through that thick black hair was enough to draw them in. Lou was so friendly and confident, everyone loved him. He was especially animated now with the excitement of their wedding day.

Dorie was making her way toward Clementine. "We've been looking for you." She gestured toward the main table, which now boasted a towering white wedding cake. Agnes had spent two days making it and decorating the surface with piped buttercream flowers. "It's time to cut the cake." Dorie rubbed Mabel's chin before looking up. "Then you can be alone with Lou for your honeymoon night." She winked, and they both laughed.

Lou was waiting at the table, a wide grin on his face and a knife in hand. "You going to help me with this?"

Smiling, Clem stood by his side. Cameras were already flashing, and boisterous voices cheered them on.

Pete swayed nearby, his eyes unfocused. "Watch what you do with that knife, Lou."

When Lou brandished it about like a sword, Clem backed off a little. Pete laughed, egging his friend on. Lou looked up at the crowd, grinning from ear to ear. Only then did Clem notice his eyes, which were as bleary as Pete's. He made an elaborate bow, as if he'd just performed a fight scene from *Hamlet*.

And then he stumbled, reaching for the table to steady himself.

Time seemed to slow as their beautiful wedding cake wobbled and began to slide off the table. As it fell, the fresh flowers decorating the top of the cake tumbled to the floor, bloom over stem, twirling like ballerinas. Clem held out her arms as if to catch the cake, but they hovered, useless, in midair as buttercream roses splattered the ground, reduced to smudges of pale muck.

Toppling along with the cake, Lou sat among a ruined heap of sponge cake and icing. A hush settled over the scene—except for Pete, who cheered at the spectacle of it all. His laugh boomed amid the low murmurs of the crowd.

Clem looked at Agnes, who had worked so tirelessly on the cake, wanting it to be perfect for their special day. Agnes sat very still in her chair, a look of patient disappointment on her face. Clem looked down at Lou, who scooped up a large hunk of cake and held it out to her.

"Here, babe. It's still good."

That's when she knew. He was drunk.

When Clem didn't take the cake, Lou took a large bite himself. He made appreciative noises as he spoke, crumbs falling from his mouth.

Earle moved toward Lou. "Come on now, Lou. Let's go." He attempted to get him up from the ground.

Lou shook himself free and stood, swatting at Earle. "I'm fine."

Earle straightened his stooped shoulders. He still didn't reach Lou's six-foot-plus height. "You need to come on with me for a bit."

"I said I'm fine." Lou's voice was low, a sound Clem had hoped she would never hear again. He turned toward her. "Time for the bride and groom to dance." He grabbed her upper arm and dragged her toward the stage. "Play somethin' sweet, Carl."

Tripping on the hem of her dress, Clem lost her footing, and she fell to the ground in a heap of white lace. Rennie stepped forward, holding out his hand to help her up.

Lou pushed him away. "You leave her alone." He tried to pull at Clem's arm, but Rennie intervened. Lou stared hard into Rennie's eyes.

"Come on now," Rennie said, his voice firm but calm. "We don't want any trouble."

"If that's true, then you need to move out of the way." Lou's voice grated against the tension in the air. "Right now."

Rennie didn't budge.

That's when Lou tackled him.

"Stop!" cried Clem.

Arms and legs flailed as the two men rolled in the dirt. Grunts and curses filled the sodden air. Clem turned away. She couldn't watch the obscene spectacle. Both men could do serious damage to the other if they wanted. Lou's bulk overwhelmed Rennie's wiry build, but both of them were strong and angry.

A couple of guests stepped forward and tried to secure

Lou. He swore and kicked like an animal wanting loose. Rennie sat on his knees, breathing hard, his head lowered.

Dorie rushed over to Rennie. “Are you hurt?” Helping him stand, she ran her hands over his torso as if to heal him.

Rennie winced. “I’m fine. Go see to Clem.”

Dorie looked over at her friend, who was still on the ground, watching Lou be led away.

“Clem, come with me.” Dorie was by her side, helping her stand. “Why don’t we go and sit down for a bit while they deal with Lou.”

Clem hesitated as she watched the men half carry Lou toward the barn. Then she nodded and followed her friend into the house.

izzie

The Greyhound bus Izzie had been on for over an hour reeked of greasy food, bad breath, and unwashed bodies, hers included. She hadn't even changed out of the stupid dress her mom had made her wear for Clementine's wedding. But it hadn't been worth the risk of getting caught to go back to the house, so she had hidden her backpack behind a hay bale on the ranch and snuck out while everyone was busy stuffing their faces.

Izzie tried to ignore the man sitting next to her. She had hoped to have a seat to herself, so she'd been mortified when the disheveled older man shambled onto the bus and sat down beside her. He had fallen asleep almost immediately and snored in her ear the entire trip.

Izzie nudged him sharply when his head lolled once again onto her shoulder. He snorted awake for a moment and mumbled before dropping off again.

She also tried to ignore the stab of guilt when she recalled Uncle Rennie's hug after her fight with Ali. He was the only person who trusted her—except maybe Dorie.

They had both been so patient over the years, and she had betrayed them. She loved her uncle more than anyone, but she couldn't risk telling him about her plans. He would surely have told her mom or, at the very least, have done everything in his power to stop her from leaving.

She could hear him now: *be sensible, you owe it to your mom, it's rash and irresponsible*, et cetera, et cetera.

She promised herself she would call him once she was settled.

Izzie was more than relieved when the bus finally pulled into the depot in downtown Houston. Hopefully she'd get a chance to change before Frankie showed up.

The first time Izzie met her friend had been in eighth grade, when Frankie's family moved to the peninsula from Houston. Even then, Frankie had had a laid-back, cool vibe that made everyone want to befriend the new city kid.

But she'd chosen Izzie.

About three weeks into the fall semester, Izzie had been sitting in her usual hiding place at recess. No one ever hung out by the math classroom because it was close to the dumpsters, which tended to stink in the lingering summer heat. But it was worth putting up with the stink if she could avoid the other kids, who already bullied her.

Frankie had turned up out of the blue. She'd worn her hair in braids back then, and her preferred style had been black leggings and extra-large flannel shirts, even in the heat.

"This must be where the cool kids hang out."

"Yep. I guess you found me."

Izzie held her gaze, ready for some wisecrack insult to follow. But Frankie sat down on the gravel drive beside her, crossed her legs, and took a large bag of Cheetos out of her backpack. It was already open, and she offered it to Izzie.

Izzie shook her head. "I only like the puffy ones."

Frankie shrugged and stuck a handful in her mouth, crunching with relish. "I'm Frankie," she mumbled. She held out her hand, fingers coated in orange goo.

Izzie refused to shake. Not only was her hand gross, but who shook hands?

Frankie began licking her fingers, one by one. Izzie swallowed hard. Then Frankie wiped her hands on her pants and held her hand out again.

Izzie paused for a second, then took it. "Izzie."

They shook, and Frankie smiled an orange-toothed grin. Izzie wondered if she tasted like Cheetos.

"So, Izzie, what's there to do for fun around here?"

"Nothing much."

"Well, that sucks. I was hoping you knew all the secret places." Frankie looked around, taking in the dumpster and the bland brick walls of the math building. "So far, everyone either wants to play softball or Pokémon." She shook her head. "Not really my scene."

"Yeah. Mine neither."

"So, what do you do for fun, then?"

"Listen to music, mostly."

"Who do you like?" Leaning closer, Frankie picked up Izzie's MP3 player from her lap and scrolled through her song list.

When the bell rang for the end of recess, both girls stood up reluctantly.

"Hey," said Izzie. "Meet me after school. I'll show you something cool. You got a bike?"

"Skateboard," said Frankie.

They walked together, splitting ways once they reached their homerooms.

Izzie had watched the clock for the next three hours

until school let out. She had wondered if Frankie would show up and had been surprised to see her waiting outside Izzie's homeroom, a skateboard tucked under her arm.

"You might not get too far on that," said Izzie.

"I'll manage," replied Frankie. "And if not, I'll jump behind you on the bike."

Izzie showed Frankie the best places to hunt for blackberries. Their hands were soon scratched from the thorns, blood mingling with red juice as they stuffed berries into their mouths. Izzie laughed at Frankie's stained lips.

"You look like a vampire."

Frankie went for Izzie's neck. "I vant to suck your blood."

That was the first time Izzie kissed a girl. Berry juice blended with the faint taste of Cheetos.

She and Frankie had been each other's armor. The kiss hadn't led anywhere except to confirm that they would be best friends. So when Frankie's parents had moved back to Houston the summer before their junior year, Izzie felt unmoored. She had tried to find the same bond again with someone new, but they either thought she was a freak or just wanted a secret friends-with-benefits arrangement.

She had stayed in touch with Frankie, though, and even managed to visit her a couple of times.

Frankie had sounded thrilled when Izzie called two weeks ago while her mom was at work. She had spoken in hushed tones so her brothers wouldn't overhear her escape plan. And now here she was.

Izzie spotted Frankie through the grimy bus window. It took Izzie a second to recognize her friend, who had shaved her head. She'd dyed what little hair was left a bright blue that almost glowed neon under the harsh fluorescent lights of the depot. Frankie glided between people on the sidewalk, her body twisting and bending like the tall reeds that lined Highway 124 when the beach was getting close. She stopped at the bus and popped her skateboard, hugging it under her arm.

As soon as Izzie stepped onto the sidewalk, Frankie pulled her close and put her arm around her shoulders, smiling widely.

"Girl, you made it!"

Izzie was warmed by the familiarity of the gap in Frankie's smile where she had lost one of her teeth in a skateboarding accident in ninth grade.

"This all you have?" Frankie nodded at her backpack.

"Yeah. You know me; I travel light."

Izzie's attempt at nonchalance didn't quite work. As Frankie looked at her closely, Izzie started walking. She'd had to leave most of her stuff behind at her mom's place to cover her tracks. Still, her mom would figure it out soon enough. And then what? Izzie's stomach rolled, and she didn't know if it was from hunger or guilt.

"How far is your place?" Izzie asked.

"Just a couple of blocks. And it's not my place, as such."

"Meaning?"

"We got a few roommates."

Izzie hadn't expected to be sharing with strangers. She was not a big fan of strangers. In her experience, strangers were unpredictable—not that people she knew were much easier.

"You'll love them. There's Jules; she's a DJ." Frankie ticked them off on her fingers. "Then Dez, who's in a band. They're playing at the Continental Club tonight. We'll go so you can check them out. They're pretty good. Although not as good as Dez thinks they are. And then there's Mikey, who . . . you know, I'm not really sure what he does. But he's cool. As long as we pay rent, it's cool."

"Jesus, Frankie. When did you adopt so many roommates?"

"Rent in Houston is high, Iz. You're not living in the boonies anymore."

Izzie wasn't sure she'd call Bolivar Peninsula the boonies exactly. Although, wasn't that why she'd left? "So, is that job still up for grabs?"

"Yeah. I'll take you over there tomorrow. They always need waitresses."

Izzie cringed. "You sure they don't need a bartender?"

"You have any experience?"

Izzie shrugged. *Please don't make me become my mother. I'll never be like her: a small-minded, bigoted hick with a dull-as-shit life.* All her mom did was work, watch dumb TV shows, and bitch about everything all the time. And she was constantly exhausted and broke.

No, Izzie would *not* have a dull-as-shit life.

Izzie's backpack began to feel heavier in the downtown bustle and heat, even at twilight. They passed disheveled men who slept curled up on the sidewalk like bundles of discarded trash. Two guys up ahead started fighting, and the girls swerved around them, the men's words garbled by whatever elixir they were on.

Frankie glanced at Izzie with a side smile. "You're a city girl now, Iz. You'll get used to it."

I've gotten used to worse, Izzie thought, recalling the constant groping and bullying she'd experienced back home. She'd played spin the bottle at a party once. Some classmates had started a bonfire on the beach one night, and she'd gone because someone she'd thought might be her friend had asked her. When Jordan spun the bottle and it pointed at her, she'd stood up to leave. Jordan, however, had grabbed her, pulled a stick from the fire, and held it close to her face.

"Let me get a proper look at the goods before I decide whether to partake."

Everyone had held their breath as he swayed, staring into Izzie's eyes.

"Nah." He had turned to the group sitting around the fire. "Anyone else interested? Maggie? I bet Iz would love that." He had moved closer, until she'd smelled the acrid scent of her singed hair. Izzie had turned and run, her feet sinking into the sand.

No one had followed her.

Turning off the street, Frankie walked up a broken asphalt driveway. "Home, sweet home." She unlocked the door, and they entered a dim hallway. Narrow stairs creaked, their footsteps echoing in the empty space. On the third floor was a beat-up bike leaning against the wall and a dead plant in a plastic bucket.

"Not sure who's home right now." Frankie opened the apartment door to reveal a room with scuffed wood floors and sparse furnishings. A burly guy lounged on a frayed mustard couch, smoking from a bong and reading a music mag. The wall behind him was covered with scraps of paper—random drawings, photos, scribbled handwriting she couldn't decipher—all stuck up with tape. He slowly raised his eyes when they came in.

"Hey, Frankie." Everything about him seemed to work in slow motion, even his voice.

"Mikey, this is Izzie. She's our new roommate."

He nodded. "Hey." He went back to his magazine.

Frankie led Izzie through a hallway with three closed doors. "Mikey's okay, just doesn't say a whole lot." She opened the last door. "You're sharing with me."

Izzie walked across the threshold into a sizable space that shone with glazed light. She looked around her new room, which was surprisingly tidy; she hadn't taken Frankie for a neat freak. Posters were tacked onto most of the walls, mainly skateboarders Iz didn't recognize, but also bands she did: Woozy Helmet, Kimya Dawson, The Gossip, Nina Simone. Unlike Ali's cousin and most everyone living on the peninsula, Frankie had awesome taste in music.

"Sorry you have to share with me," said Izzie. "Won't you miss your privacy?"

"Privacy! There's never any privacy around here. Besides, my old roommate only left a week ago, so it's not like I'm used to having my own space."

"Why did she leave?"

"Oh, I don't know. She said family crap, but I think she lost her job and couldn't pay rent anymore."

Izzie prayed she'd get the job Frankie had mentioned and be able to stay, even if it was waitressing. Hopefully she'd work her way up to bartending. She had some savings with her, but they wouldn't last long. Her mother had tried so hard to force onto her a life resembling her own. The closest to home she'd ever felt was when she'd lived with Uncle Rennie.

Izzie's stomach rolled again as she pictured her uncle when he found out she'd gone. He'd always done right by her. If it weren't for her mom, maybe she'd still be there. But when her mom had made Rennie kick her out for not living up to the deal and failing school, she'd had to go back to her old life, and she just couldn't do that anymore.

"So, how's Ali? Y'all still together?"

Izzie shrugged. "Nah, not really."

"That's too bad. She seemed cool."

Ali was the first girl Iz had ever been with—well, properly been with. A quiver of regret passed through her.

"She is. But I'm *here* now, so—"

"Damn right! And we need to celebrate! We'll head to the Continental Club soon; consider it your baptism by fire! I 'borrowed' a bottle of vodka from the bar, so we're all set!"

A warm breeze came through the open sash window, and Izzie inhaled. Instead of the salty air she was used to, she smelled freedom: a mix of aged wood, dust, and weed. And something she couldn't yet identify, the smell of a city and all its secrets, which she would uncover in this new life she was inventing for herself.

Izzie was ready.

She threw her backpack on the floor and jumped onto the bed, where she started doing snow angels on the sheets.

"Girl, you know I love you, but this one's mine. You're over there." Pulling Izzie's arms, Frankie dragged her off the bed, and they tumbled onto the floor, giggling and wrestling like the children they still were.

rennie

"What the hell are you doing, son?" Rennie sat Lou down against a hay bale in the back of the barn, where he slumped forward, mumbling incoherently.

Earle stood back and wiped his forehead with a handkerchief. "Best to leave him for a bit, I reckon. Doubt he'll be showing himself again anytime soon."

Both men watched Lou for any residual anger, but he was sprawled on the packed-dirt floor, quieting into oblivion. Exchanging a look, they recognized the shared disappointment in this man who had promised Clem he would do right by her.

Sighing, Earle headed out of the barn. Rennie glanced at Lou one more time before following Earle out.

"I certainly had my doubts," said Earle, "and now here we are. I thought Clem might finally get the happiness she deserves, but she chose that knucklehead. I'm not sure he'll ever change."

"Anyone can change if they set their mind to it and the time is right." Rennie thought of Dorie and her transformation from a heartbroken woman who hid herself away to one who was capable of love and joy. It was never too late to change.

However, Earle was protective of Clementine, and he and Agnes didn't have a whole lot of patience for bad behavior. In fact, if Agnes had been present for this conversation, she undoubtedly would have quoted some Bible verse or other.

Earle dropped his head, muttering to himself. Outside, the guests had thinned considerably, having gotten the hint that the party was over. "I'm going to help Ennis clean up." Earle headed for the stage area.

"Right. See you in a bit." Rennie went toward the house to wash up before going upstairs to check on Dorie and Clementine. On the way, he was stopped by Pete.

"Hey, Rennie, how's our boy Lou doin'?" Pete still looked like he found the entire episode highly entertaining.

"You have anything to do with this?"

"Huh?"

"You are aware that Lou is trying to stay sober, right?"

"Could have fooled me." Pete chuckled. "Jeezus, it's his wedding day. Ain't a man allowed to celebrate on his wedding day? We just had a couple tequila shots, is all."

Rennie watched Pete sway before him. "More than a couple, by the looks of it."

"Man, why y'all overreacting? He was just having a bit of fun."

Rennie shook his head. "Best you get on home now, Pete. This party is well and truly over."

Pete shrugged. "Too bad. Things were just getting interestin'." He turned and scanned the few remaining guests before setting his sights on Luanne.

Going to the washroom, Rennie cleaned up, tried to

smooth down his hair, and force himself to calm. He made his way up the stairs, calling Dorie's name. She came out of the bedroom Clementine had stayed in the night before, a look of concern etching her stern face. "You okay?"

"I'm fine. How's Clem?"

"Upset. Angry. How's it looking out there?"

"Okay, I guess. We left Lou in the barn. Earle looked like he wanted to punch him—probably went back in and dunked him in the cow trough by now."

"One can only hope," grumbled Dorie.

"I sent Pete home. I'm pretty sure he had something to do with it."

"That man is a bad influence. Just keep them away from each other."

Rennie knew she was right to be concerned. Back when Lou worked with Pete on his shrimp boat, Rennie always worried they'd have an accident or Lou would end up in jail again after a drinking binge.

"And don't let Lou in here yet. Clem needs some time," said Dorie.

"Oh, you won't be seeing him for a while. He's out cold. But don't you worry. You just focus on Clem."

Dorie gave Rennie a quick peck on the cheek and thanked him, before walking back into Clem's room and shutting the door. It was going to be difficult for Lou to charm his way out of this one.

When Rennie got back outside, most of the guests had left. Earle and Ennis were starting to fold up the tables. Rennie asked if Lou was still in the barn, praying he hadn't left with Pete. He couldn't help imagining Lou hog-tied and hanging from the rafters after Earle had gotten done with him. He gathered a stack of folded chairs and carried them toward the barn.

It seemed a lifetime ago that Lou had suggested they convert it into a painting studio for Clem. They'd all helped clear out the rusty old farm equipment and paint the exterior red. That was back when she had stopped painting.

Dorie had told him Clem associated painting too much with losing Finn. It was when she'd been engrossed in bringing to life a world on canvas that he'd slipped into the water. Back then, she had barely even been there—as if she were willing herself to disappear, to follow Finn to that other place. In fact, she had almost dragged Dorie down with her. Rennie had tried so hard not to let that happen.

Lou had been right about the barn, though; it had brought Clementine back to them. That was when Lou had been on his best behavior and had been trying hard to win her back. Rennie envisioned Lou sprawled in the dirt back there. Now that he'd won her, would he screw up all over again?

Rennie, Earle, and Ennis finished clearing the tables and chairs. The ranch was set right once more. When they entered the house, Dorie and Clementine were in the kitchen washing dishes and cleaning up. Rennie noticed most of the food was gone—either eaten or packed up for people to take home.

"You just relax, Agnes. We've got this," said Dorie.

Ignoring her, Agnes motioned for a towel to dry the clean bowls. "It's Clementine's wedding day. She doesn't need to be doing the cleaning up, and I'm perfectly capable. Now pass me that towel."

"Where's the family?" asked Earle.

Agnes gestured to the back room. "Oh, the kids were hyped up after all the excitement—and not a little scared, I'd say. Sheila and Tom put them to bed a while back. I'm sure they're all asleep right now." She turned to the three men. "There's some plates made up in the ice box, if y'all are hungry."

Must have read my mind, thought Rennie.

They gathered around the table to eat, all of them exhausted after a busy day of preparing for the party and then the drama of the evening. There wasn't much chatter. Rennie figured everyone was avoiding the elephant in the room so as not to further upset Clementine.

Rennie noticed Clem hadn't eaten much. Instead, she kept looking anxiously toward the door. Rennie swallowed one last bite and stood up. "I'm going to check on Lou. Can't very well leave him out there all night."

"It's not any less than he deserves, after making such a mess of things," said Dorie.

Clem bristled. "Dorie, please don't. He overdid the drinking. It's not the first time, and it won't be the last." She nodded at Rennie.

Earle stood and followed Rennie to the barn. It was dark out, and their eyes took a moment to adjust now that the strings of party lights had been taken down. Lou was still passed out. Rennie nudged him in the side with his boot. Lou mumbled and attempted to roll over.

"Lou, wake up." He nudged him again, a little harder. "Time to go."

Hauling Lou into the house, Earle and Rennie dropped him on the couch, where he passed out again. Clementine grabbed a blanket from a nearby chair and laid it over Lou. Then she turned and began climbing the stairs very slowly.

Dorie frowned as she watched Clementine ascend the stairs. "Time for us to go."

Everyone said their goodbyes, and the full moon lit their way as they walked to their cars, a chorus of cicadas serenading them in the silver light.

Rennie opened the passenger door for Dorie. "How about you stay at my place tonight?"

Dorie didn't answer. Stepping into the cab, she collapsed onto the leather seat and rubbed her hands together. Giving her space, Rennie didn't push the invitation. As they pulled out of the ranch, though, he looked at her, unsure which way to turn onto Highway 87.

"Not tonight. I'm exhausted and wound up all at once. I just want my book, my cat, and silence."

Rennie nodded. "You got it." He turned left, heading for Gilchrist.

"He's not good enough for her." Dorie's tone was leaden rather than scolding, as if she had given up all hope for Lou and was simply stating a fact.

Rennie knew it had stung Dorie when Clem reprimanded her about Lou. Dorie was a woman with strong opinions who struggled to keep them to herself, especially when her convictions were tested.

She stared at the road ahead, the truck's headlights mapping their course. "Maybe it's not too late to change her mind. She could get an annulment."

"I wouldn't get your hopes up on that turn of events." Rennie said, wanting to prepare her so she wouldn't be disappointed yet again.

Dorie shot him a dirty look. "One can dream."

Rennie chuckled and took her hand. "Clem is stronger than you may think."

Dorie sighed. "I suppose."

"And you had a part in that, you know."

"I just don't want her to get hurt again."

"I know. But she's ready to move forward with her life now, and she chose Lou to do that with. She knows what she's in for. You need to let her go."

"You make her sound like my daughter, and I'm her overprotective mom."

Rennie smiled. Dorie could read him like one of her books. "You care about her. Not overprotective, just looking out for her best interests. As I am for yours."

Dorie squeezed his hand.

Who's still rooting for Clem and Lou now? Thought Rennie. He wasn't sure how he felt about Lou. He knew Lou loved Clem and would do anything for her, but was he capable of making her truly happy?

Rennie pictured Dorie moments from now, sitting on her deck with a book and watching the ocean, Rosie rubbing against her ankles and settling on her lap. Dorie didn't need Rennie to be happy. It was one of the things he loved about her. She was independent and knew how to be alone.

When they arrived at the little yellow house, Rennie didn't bother turning off the engine. Dorie wouldn't change her mind. She needed her alone time to decompress and understand the bigger picture. That was one of the things he respected about her. She might be impulsive at times, but she always reflected on her actions and how they affected people. That's why she was continuing to grow into this version of herself—a version Rennie liked very much.

Dorie sat for a moment, staring at her hands.

"Just be there for her when she needs you. Like you always are. You're a good friend, Dorie. It's one of the many things I admire about you."

Dorie turned and kissed him. "I'll see you tomorrow, yes?"

Rennie nodded. "Yes."

As he drove away, he wondered if Dorie would be willing to spend the rest of her life with him. He'd been wanting to ask her to marry him for a while now but hadn't quite had the nerve. And Lou screwing up again would have just reinforced her attitude toward marriage.

He'd hold off for a little longer, at least until the Lou-and-Clem drama settled down. Maybe in a month or two, the timing would be better; he'd ask her then.

izzie

Izzie and Frankie sipped vodka as they got ready. Dez's band wasn't due to go on until ten or so, which probably meant eleven, so they had plenty of time.

Frankie handed Iz some fishnet hose, which she put on under cutoff denim shorts. Assessing herself in the mirror, Izzie decided something wasn't quite right yet. After finding some scissors, she cut the bottom off her Sonic Youth tee shirt. It was already two sizes too small and now exposed more of her than her mother would have allowed.

After another shot of vodka, Izzie let Frankie fix her hair. She now wore it slicked into a Mohawk with shaved sides. It changed her face so much, she almost didn't recognize herself.

Her beat-up Converse completed the look and were the only things she wore that really felt like her. But she kind of liked her disguise.

The band snuck them into the Continental Club so they wouldn't need to show their IDs. Izzie had been there a couple of times before when she'd visited Frankie, so she didn't feel too out of place. As she sipped a beer and listened to the band warm up, Izzie started to enjoy this new version of herself. She had left the old Izzie back on the peninsula; now she could be whoever she wanted.

Iz was surprised by how good her roommate's band was. They had an energy and freedom on stage that she had never been able to unleash in herself. She'd always felt enclosed within a fragile shell that could crack if she moved too fast or spoke too loudly. Even now, she realized, she held her beer close, both hands wrapped around the bottle.

Closing her eyes, she synchronized her head-bobbing to the deep sound of the bass as it passed through her. Concentrating on loosening her body, she began to sway to the slow drone of the guitar.

Cheers erupted when the song ended, and Izzie opened her eyes, joining the applause.

"You a fan, then?" A girl stood next to her. Her blonde dreads were piled on top of her head, making her seem taller than she really was.

"Yeah. You?"

"They're all right. I came for the main act. If you like these guys, you'll love them."

"I guess we'll see."

The girl seemed to evaluate Iz, as if she could see through her protective casing and was deciding whether she liked what she saw. "I like your hair."

"I like yours too." Izzie decided she liked more than just her hair.

When the girl headed into the crowd, Izzie was suddenly very alone. Her roommate's band had left the stage, and the lights had dimmed. She wondered if she should go backstage and find the rest of them.

Izzie looked around for Frankie, but there was no sign

of her. Draining her beer, she went to buy another. Dez had gotten her a wristband so they wouldn't card her, but she was still nervous. Luckily, the bartender was swamped and barely acknowledged her as he handed over the beer. Fresh beer in hand, Izzie wandered back toward the stage, hoping Frankie would be there by now.

When the stage lights came back on, a syncopated guitar riff filled the room. The audience quieted. One by one, the band members came out onstage and began playing, until the room was filled with a sound that wasn't quite music. The drone resembled a living creature, hypnotizing the audience into submission.

Abruptly, the energy shifted, and a banshee wail filled the space. The crowd roared, and the volume of the music seemed to double, yet the screaming still rose above it all.

A creature sprang onto the stage, dressed all in black, long blonde dreads whirling through the air as if she were Medusa. Her petite body moved like a disjointed insect—arms and legs flailing as she bounced from one end of the stage to the other.

Izzie was transfixed.

A surge of bodies began pushing Izzie closer to the stage, and she found herself in the middle of a mosh pit. Jumping, pounding bodies flung themselves into her, so all she could do was push back.

The singer spoke a language beyond words, one that Izzie understood well—anger and pain but also a fierce independence and strength that rose from deep within.

Izzie felt invincible and transported, so when the last note played and the stage darkened again, she was dizzy and exhausted but buzzing with a manic energy.

"There you are!" Frankie appeared beside her, panting and grinning.

Izzie laughed. "They were amazing!"

Frankie nodded, her eyes wide with adrenaline. She guided Izzie toward a door that led backstage, into a room filled with cigarette smoke and the smell of beer and sweat. Her roommates were chatting with the band who had just finished, and Izzie's attention landed immediately on the singer.

Frankie rushed up to the singer and slung her arm around her neck. "Awesome as always, Jess." She turned to Izzie. "Meet Jess. Jess, meet my new roommate and old friend, Izzie."

Izzie suddenly felt shy. "You were great."

Jess winked. "Told you."

Frankie looked confused. "Y'all know each other?"

Izzie shook her head, but Jess just stared at her again as if she did know Izzie.

"Jess, you coming back to our place?"

"Sure."

The van was packed with equipment and people, everyone sitting on someone's lap. Jess's drummer drove, and Jess sat up front on Frankie. Izzie wasn't even sure whose lap she was on.

As soon as they arrived at the apartment, the party got going. Frankie and Dez started arguing about the playlist. Mikey and Jess's bandmates fired up the bong, and Jules put beers into a cooler. Izzie watched Jess, who sat at the rickety table, strumming a guitar. She seemed so different offstage, smaller.

Izzie moved closer to hear what she was playing over the blaring music. Glancing up, Jess smiled, so Izzie joined her. The notes she played were soft and melodic.

"That's nice," Izzie said.

"You like it? It's just something I've been working on.

I don't really have a chance to play this stuff; it's not exactly Angel Spit material."

Izzie liked the name of the band. It seemed to personify Jess pretty well, as far as she could tell. "You should do some solo shows."

"Maybe."

Picking up a broken crayon from a pile on the table, Izzie doodled on a piece of scrap paper as she listened to Jess play. She wanted to tell Frankie to turn down the music so she could make out the lyrics Jess whispered under her breath, her neck bent so her thick hair hid her face.

Looking over, Jess paused and picked up the drawing. "That's cool."

Izzie laughed. It was an abstracted image of Jess's hair, her guitar just visible.

"Seriously. I really like this."

"It's just a doodle for the wall." Izzie gestured toward the wall behind the couch that was covered in drawings, quotes, ticket stubs, photos—mementos of their young lives.

"Can I keep it?" Jess asked.

"Sure. If you want."

Folding the drawing, Jess put it in her pocket and continued strumming. "How long have you known Frankie?"

"We met in middle school."

"Oh, you're an ex–beach bum too, then."

Izzie shrugged. "I wouldn't say that, exactly. I never really liked living there."

"So now you're here. What do you think?"

"It's cool."

"Different from your life there I expect."

"Yeah. Thank God."

"Why's that?"

"What?"

"You weren't happy living in paradise?"

"It's hardly that. Besides, my mom made my life hell."

"In what way?"

Izzie wondered why Jess was so interested in her, why she was being so nosy. But somehow, she couldn't not answer her questions, even though it felt like a layer of skin peeling off. "She didn't understand anything."

Jess stopped strumming and stared, waiting for Izzie to go on.

"She doesn't approve of my lifestyle choices."

Jess smiled. "Most parents don't."

Iz shrugged. "I guess. But it's more complicated when your mom thinks being gay is a sin and you're going to hell for it."

She immediately doubted herself for opening up to this stranger. But somehow, Jess didn't feel like a stranger.

Jess nodded. "I hear you. And that sucks. But you're here now in the Queer Capital of Texas, so you're safe to be who you want."

Iz wondered how true that was. Montrose was known for being gay friendly, but she was aware of the ongoing violence toward their community. In the past, she'd gone with Frankie to the Westheimer Street Festival, when the main drag was filled with rainbow flags, cross-dressing, fake eyelashes, big wigs, and stiletto heels—a day of celebration for the gay community. Yet a police presence had hovered on the periphery, their faces grim, their holsters filled with that menace that could both protect and kill.

Jess leaned over and kissed Izzie softly on the mouth. "Is this okay?"

Izzie shivered and nodded.

Standing, Jess held out her hand. "Want to go somewhere more private?"

Taking her hand, Izzie followed her to the bedroom.

september 12, 2008

1 day before the storm

clementine

The bed sank beneath Lou's weight as he lowered himself next to Clementine, his bulk nestled against her back. It was still night and quiet in the house. He nuzzled into her neck, breathing deeply into her hair, dark, wet breath like a wounded animal needing comfort. She reached back and raked her hand through his thick hair.

"I'm sorry." His hoarse whisper conveyed so much more than those two words.

Rolling over, Clem looked into his ravaged face. "Why do you do this to yourself?" Lou's eyes didn't leave hers. She stroked his stubbled cheek, and when she kissed him, he tasted of salt.

Lou's shoulders shook as he buried his face into her neck and wrapped his body around her as if encompassing her entire self so they were one strange creature, not of this world. Clem stroked his hair until she fell asleep.

She opened her eyes to an early light. The sheets were warm from their enfolded bodies, almost stifling. Events from the previous evening weighed on her in a way she couldn't shake off. A night she'd thought would begin a new chapter of her story, one of second chances, would instead be a constant reminder of the disappointment always hovering in the periphery.

Yesterday, when she and Dorie left the party and came upstairs, Dorie had told her how scared she had once been of Lou. Back when Clem was missing and Dorie first moved into the yellow house, Lou had shown up looking for Clem right after he'd gotten out of prison. His confusion and disappointment had manifested into anger, terrifying Dorie. Afterward, he went on a major drinking binge that got him into trouble again.

That had been when he was working for Pete. Neither Clem nor Dorie were fans of Pete—nothing but trouble. Yet as far as Clem knew, Lou hadn't drunk for almost four years—until now. He'd told Clem that prison had forced his sobriety, guilt over almost killing a man had strengthened his resolve, and love had made it stick.

So what happened last night?

Clementine extricated herself from Lou's grasp, and he groaned and rolled over. Stepping across the wooden floor, she crushed the wilted marigold blossoms Lou had scattered there the day before.

Wanting to rid herself of thoughts of Lou for now. She got dressed and crept downstairs.

Everyone still seemed to be sleeping, so Clementine sat on the front porch with her coffee. The morning air held a freshness that promised the arrival of fall.

No one could have guessed there'd been a wedding there the day before. Everything was in its place, both inside and outside the house—all neat and tidy, as if trying to conceal yesterday's ugly scene.

Clem wished she could do the same, but Lou's violence

toward Rennie replayed in her mind. It was something she could not abide. She preferred the wounded animal over the dangerous one, but she wished she could exorcise both.

Clem knew about living with guilt—how it made a person do things they regretted. It was easier to bury fear and grief by any means available, such as booze or disappearing. He had done so much over the last few years to exorcise *her* demons. Surely she could do the same for him.

But she already knew that was impossible. She'd tried and failed countless times. Only he could do it.

Clem knew he loved her. He just didn't love *himself* enough. *That* she could help him with. Good intentions weren't enough, but he'd keep promising her, and she'd keep trying to believe him.

A hum announced Agnes's arrival onto the porch, Earle following close behind.

"Morning." Earle set two coffees and a newspaper on the nearby table. "How you feeling today, Clementine?" He glanced at the ring Clem was twisting on her finger, then opened his newspaper. "Lou doin' okay? Looks like he made his way up last night."

Clem nodded. "Yeah. He's okay."

The newspaper rustled, and Earle looked over at her. "He apologize to you?"

Clem nodded again, wishing he had apologized to his hosts as well. "I'm so sorry about ruining everything. You both worked so hard to—"

"*You* didn't ruin anything. He did that all by his own self." Earle flicked the newspaper so it cracked in the air.

Agnes patted the Bible she held in her lap as she spoke slowly and deliberately. "Forgive, and you will be forgiven."

Earle raised the paper so it covered his face, his grip creasing the pages. A few minutes passed in silence.

"Says here we're under evacuation orders."

Agnes tutted. "They always make a big deal outta nothin'."

"Best to be prepared, just in case," said Earle from behind the newspaper. "I'll check the supply shed."

Clem wondered how bad the storm would be. But if Earle wasn't worried, then she wasn't either.

As the scent of cooking food wafted through the door, Clem realized she was starving; she hadn't eaten much at the wedding. Her spirits lifting a little, she smiled at Agnes. "What's cooking?"

Agnes shrugged. "I haven't started fixin' breakfast yet. Seems like someone beat me to it."

The three of them made their way into the kitchen, where Lou stood in front of the stove. His hair was wet from the shower, and the curls at the end stuck to his neck. Clem longed to reach out and smooth them. His deft hands moved between the various pans and the fridge.

The first time he'd cooked Clem breakfast had been when she'd gone home with him after they'd danced at a club. How her blood had hummed along with his whistling.

She had fallen hard. They both had.

Lou glanced over his shoulder. "There's scrambled eggs, bacon, hash browns. Hope y'all are hungry."

Sitting at the kitchen table, they waited for Lou to finish. When Agnes asked Earle for the crossword, he removed a sheet from the paper, folded it neatly, and handed it over. Clem and Agnes bent over it, working out the clues.

Clem occasionally glanced up at Lou, who moved with grace, even with what must surely have been a pounding hangover. He hummed as he cooked, and the smells made Clem even hungrier.

Setting out four plates, Lou began loading them with

the feast he had prepared. Whatever spices he had added to the simple breakfast heightened it to another level. Even Earle dug in despite his reluctance to forgive Lou, finishing his plate before Clem had hardly made a dent in her own.

Lou stood from the seat he'd claimed at the table. "Earle, you want some more?"

Earle shook his head but held Lou's gaze. They locked eyes for a moment, and Clem watched them, twisting the napkin in her lap. Lou finally looked down and nodded slowly.

Standing, Earle stepped closer to Lou. "You make sure you clean up after yourself. You hear?"

"Yes, sir."

Earle nodded once and left the room. Clem breathed.

Agnes wiped her mouth and placed the napkin on the table. "That was good, Lou. Thank you."

Lou smiled, his face relaxing a little more. "Anytime. And, Agnes, I'm truly sorry about yesterday."

Smiling gently, Agnes wheeled herself toward the living room to find Earle. "Don't you make too much noise, Earle. The kids are still sleeping."

"It's well past daybreak. Time to start the day."

"Oh hush, now. They're here to relax."

"They need to head on back to town sooner rather than later with this storm comin'."

Their voices faded as they went outside.

Lou joined Clem at the table. She took his hand and squeezed it. "Looks like it might be worse than expected. We've been told to evacuate."

Lou's brow creased. "I don't want to risk staying. Let's head to my sister's place in Houston, just to be safe."

"Do we have to? Earle doesn't seem too worried." Lou's sister's wasn't exactly her idea of a honeymoon.

"I'm not risking it, Clem. We'll pack up a few things, just in case."

"Why don't you head back home. I need a walk." She smiled at him to make sure he knew things were all right.

"I may take the truck out for a bit, see if I can make some extra cash for gas."

"Okay. I'll see you soon." She needed to clear her head before returning to their shared space. Besides, she felt the urgent tug of the beach.

As Clem scrambled down the loose sand of the dunes, the air was still and saturated. In the sky, a row of pelicans headed west after a busy day of diving the Gulf waves. There was no telling how long it would be before she could walk the beach again. If they had to evacuate, hopefully the storm would pass through quickly, and they'd be back in a couple of days.

She hated to leave the peninsula; it felt like abandoning Finn. Reaching for Finn's shell, Clem held it against her chest to ease the old, persistent ache.

She tried to imagine the gentle roll of waves just a few hours from now, the transformation the storm would bring. Clem knew only too well the capricious nature of the ocean. Soon, the blue-green translucency would turn a viscous slate, churning with violent retribution. This paradise was an illusion, and the ocean would reveal her true nature.

Clem breathed in the briny air carried on the ocean breeze that whipped her hair about her face. It entered her lungs and diffused, reminding her that she, too, had briefly belonged to the sea.

At the periphery of her vision, a movement caught her eye—a bird, graceful and fluid as it landed. When she turned, a young boy was walking toward her. His pale skin and silver hair reflected the sunlight. Her arms prickled with goose bumps. There was something oddly familiar about him. He looked young, about ten or eleven years old—close to the age Finn would have been now.

Stopping, he looked up at her, his eyes almost as pale as his hair. Clementine scanned the empty beach. Surely he was too young to be walking alone.

"Are you lost?" she asked. The boy nodded but didn't seem distressed. She looked up and down the shoreline again but could see no one. "Your family must be looking for you. We've been told to evacuate."

"Evacuate?" His voice sounded far away.

"There's a big storm coming, and we've been told to leave the peninsula."

The boy's eyes never left her face. "We're not leaving. Everyone's just making a big deal out of nothing."

Clementine pursed her lips against the urge to agree with him.

"Are *you* leaving?" He tilted his head, pale eyes boring into hers.

Clementine hesitated. "Probably."

"So why are you here, just walking?" He looked at her as if assessing her true desire to leave or not, and for a moment, she saw Finn in the strange boy's eyes.

Touching her stomach, she felt a stirring. "Where do you live? I can take you home if you like."

He turned and walked away from her, his back so small and straight. A frayed length of rope swung from his waist, bouncing against the backs of his knees. Clementine wondered what game he had been playing. She took a step toward him, compelled to reach for the rope in case he really was lost and needed her.

Shimmering silver, he disappeared as a shaft of sunlight caught him just right.

rennie

A small group of men gathered around the television, which blared news about the impending hurricane. It was the stuff of myth: Men in suits prophesying. The bizarre practice of naming them—a christening. Alphabetized to evoke some semblance of control: Fay, Gustav, Hanna, Ike. They were being ordered to evacuate the peninsula, but not everyone was convinced.

Rennie was determined not to get sidetracked. He already had a firm plan of action, and besides, he was in Ace Hardware. He probably went far more often than he needed to, according to Dorie anyway. But the smell of freshly cut wood and paint, the reassuring smacks on the back and handshakes, the bragging about who caught the biggest fish—it was like church. This community of men who spoke the same language and understood each other, the camaraderie filling him up.

Today it was packed.

Next to him, Al laughed and shook his head. "What you worried about, Jim? You're just wasting your money on all that plywood—not worth the effort. You're gonna have to take it all off again in a couple days."

Jim told Al he was a fool and went to pay at the register. Other men began arguing about preparing for Ike.

"I bought four cases of water, batteries, and canned food—"

"The wife make that list for ya? Cuz I know you didn't think of all that!"

"Whatcha doin' with your cats, Bob?"

"Ah, they'll be fine. Those beasts can handle anything."

Bob kept a collection of big cats out back of his property. Rennie had taken Shel's kids there more than once to check them out—a tiger and a couple of lions, as he recalled. They seemed harmless enough, probably had all the fight domesticized out of them. Still, Rennie wondered how well they'd fare in a hurricane, though they'd probably experienced one or two over the years; it seemed like Bob had had them forever.

"Scared of a little wind, buddy?"

Margie at the cash register had heard enough of the jeering and carousing. "You boys just take it down a notch. I got a headache from all your fussin'. Just get what ya need and get the hell outta here."

"Aw, Marge. Come on now. We're all in this together."

She rolled her eyes and beckoned the next customer, who yes-ma'amed her until she cracked a sideways smile.

Rennie bought enough plywood to board up both his and Dorie's houses, as well as Shel's cabin. Better safe than sorry. Dorie was getting anxious about that beloved yellow house of hers—though Rennie had to admit he had grown fond of it, too, over the past few years. It had good bones, but when she first moved in, she hadn't been in any state to make it a real home. Sure, it had looked the part, with all her fancy furniture and art and books. But now it was cozy and welcoming. She had infused herself into the walls and floors, imprinting herself on the place.

Rennie hurried to finish his errands so he could get to Dorie as fast as possible. He could never get enough of her and hoped she felt the same way. These days, he often felt more like a teenager than the middle-aged man who had sworn off women after his divorce years ago.

When they first met, she had been impervious to any attempts at friendship, let alone a relationship. He'd shown up every day to paint her house when she first moved in, and all she'd done was act testy as she sat with her back to him, staring down at the newspaper. She still tapped her pencil against her teeth while doing the crossword, but now he found it endearing.

Rennie loaded his pickup with the last of the plywood sheets, his lean, toned body making easy work of it.

When he arrived at Dorie's house, he watched her through the window for a moment. She was bent over her desk, probably editing some pages for work. He liked to savor the calm she possessed now, her movements slow and natural. So different from when he'd met her four years ago. Although there were still remnants of the grief that had shut her off from the world, there were now healing and joy as well.

He recalled an incident when Izzie had been living with him. His niece resembled Dorie in some ways. They both tended to keep their troubles to themselves, putting on a strong exterior to cover the pain. It took a great deal of trust for them to show their vulnerability.

Izzie had been upset about some kid at school who'd been giving her a hard time. Watching Dorie with her, the way she listened intently, the care he saw in her eyes, the pure empathy when she held Izzie close while she cried—that was when he had first known he loved her.

Dorie opened the front door. "Well, were you ever going to knock?"

Smiling, Rennie walked into the little yellow house that Dorie loved so much. "I bought plywood to board up the windows."

"Already? How am I supposed to work here in the dark?" She'd spent way too much time in darkness and wasn't eager to return to it.

Rennie pulled her close. "We could always light some candles, get romantic." He nuzzled her neck, and she pretended to push him away.

"Silliness." She blushed but leaned into him.

They were interrupted by multiple footsteps clamoring up the deck stairs. Shel opened the front door and walked in, dragging her two boys behind her.

"I could kill that girl!"

Dorie quickly pulled away from Rennie and smoothed down her hair.

Rennie sighed. "What did she do this time?"

"She didn't come home last night!"

Rennie kept his voice low and calm. "When did you last see her?"

"Yesterday!"

"When yesterday?"

"I don't remember! I was busy with the boys at the wedding."

Dorie gathered Johnny and Chase. "Why don't we go outside and see if we can find Rosie, shall we?"

"Who's Rosie?" asked Chase.

"My cat, remember? She's usually asleep under the rosemary bush. Let's go see."

As Dorie closed the deck door, Shel's voice rose higher. "At first, I assumed she was with Ali. I mean, it's not the first time she's stayed out all night doing God knows what, is it?"

Rennie remembered Iz and Ali's argument. He forced his voice to remain calm. "Have you called Ali?"

"Ali doesn't know where she is or isn't saying. Apparently, they had a falling out." She muttered something under her breath.

"What was that?"

"I said, it's about time. I told you it was just a phase," she spat, as if the words left a bad taste in her mouth.

Rennie scratched his head in frustration. He hated that Shel was still unconvinced that her daughter was gay. She just refused to accept it, which pushed Izzie further away.

Shel's voice cracked. "I've called everyone I know, and she's not anywhere." Her face hardened. "She'll get in touch with *you*, I imagine, for money or something. She knows damn well I don't have any. And you're always soft with her."

She pointed at Rennie. "You'd better tell me if she calls you! And don't you give her any cash. If she wants to be all independent, she needs to learn how to support herself."

Rennie loved Iz, but she could be a pain in the ass at times. He couldn't deny it. However, he also couldn't help feeling it was partly his fault. When she'd begged to live with him, Shel had only agreed under the condition that she pass school and not get into trouble. Izzie had been doing well for a while. Her grades were decent, especially with Dorie tutoring her. And she hadn't missed school or stayed out too late.

But it hadn't lasted long. He'd had to stick to his word, so he'd sent her back to her mother, as promised. He wasn't surprised by her disappearance, but that didn't make him any less concerned.

A sudden thought hit him. With this storm coming, it would *not* be good to lose track of Izzie. She never kept up with the news and may well be oblivious to the threat.

Shel had become quiet, as if sensing Rennie's thoughts. She sat on the sofa, and Rennie sat beside her, rubbing her back. "Shel, we'll find her."

Rennie now wished he had bought Iz that cell phone she had begged for. At least then he would have been able to call her.

Shel swiped at a tear. "Stupid girl. Stupid, stupid girl."

clementine

Earle and Ennis were busy covering the windows with plywood when Clem and Dorie arrived at the ranch. Having heard that Earle was staying, Dorie had told Clem she felt it was her duty to convince him otherwise. They had been ordered to evacuate the peninsula, even if Hurricane Ike's projected landfall was one hundred miles south of them.

Clementine was supposed to be packing because Lou wanted to go to his sister's place in Houston in case the storm was worse than expected. But she hadn't been able to turn down Dorie's request for reinforcements, and anyway, she wanted to see Agnes and Earle before she left.

Earle pounded another nail into a sheet that Ennis held against the window, blinding the house to the threat of the impending storm. Dorie raised her voice above the hammering. "You are not staying."

"Been here goin' on fifty years, and this house has stood through more storms than I can count." Earle hammered another nail. "Half the peninsula evacuated for Gustav, and that turned out to be a complete waste of time. We ain't goin' nowhere."

Dorie waved a hand at him dismissively and walked toward the house. Clem wished she could stay with them. Holding Finn's shell, she brought it to her nose, but it no longer smelled of the sea. She rubbed her fingers up and down the silver chain, remembering the day Earle had given it to her under the oak tree. They had taken such good care of her after she lost Finn. They were her family now, and she longed to stay with them inside their cozy house, safe and sound, as the storm blew through.

Clem followed Dorie into the front hallway, smaller and dimmer with each new piece of plywood.

"You all right in there, Agnes?" Dorie yelled.

Agnes replied from the front room. "Can't see a dang thing! Earle, you gonna cover all them windows so we gotta run the electric all day and night?" She continued muttering to herself. "Not only am I stuck in this blasted contraption, but now I'm blind as well."

Following the sound of Agnes's wheelchair, they found her wedged between the sofa and a side table that was threatening to topple a lamp.

"Here, let me give you a hand." Clem steadied the table and reached for Agnes.

"I got it, I got it." Agnes put the control in reverse and righted herself as Clem backed off. Knowing Agnes's testiness was due to worry about the storm, Clem ignored her grumbling.

"Agnes, you need to talk some sense into him," Dorie said. "It's not safe. And it'll be too late if you change your minds later."

"He won't change his mind. You know that."

"What about you? Don't you want to leave?"

"I'm not going anywhere without Earle." Agnes looked toward the window where sharp strikes sounded—one, two for each nail—her hand cupping her lined face. "He will protect us."

Clem glanced up at the cross on the wall above the fireplace and wondered who she meant: Earle or God. A large family Bible sat on a wooden pedestal, open to pages marked with their lineage. Early entries were faint, the ink faded to sepia calligraphy. *Agnes Mary and Earle Lee Beauchamp*, followed by their children and grandchildren. The last names were written in a bold black script, declaring their place in history. Clem looked around the cozy living room, hoping it would remain intact and that her beloved friends would stay safe.

"Hold that straight now. Last one." Earle hammered the final nail, wiped sweat from his brow, and surveyed the work they'd done with satisfaction.

Then he remembered what they were preparing for. He looked toward the water and the sky above, so clear and blue. He had made their newlywed dreams real so long ago and had faith that nothing would take them away now. Besides, Ike was only predicted to be a category-two hurricane; they'd been through far worse. Carla back in sixty-one had thrown them all for a loop, but a new roof and some repairs to the lower floors had had everything shipshape soon enough.

Earle nodded at Ennis. "Come on in now. Agnes made some sweet tea earlier; it'll make all this work worth it, guaranteed."

As they entered the house, Agnes gestured toward the table, which was filled with eggs, ham, and a fruit salad. "Y'all ready to eat?"

Earle clicked off the radio before joining them at the

table. "I'm sick to death of hearing all the doom and gloom about this darn storm. Let's just enjoy this food prepared by my lovely wife."

Agnes and Earle bowed their heads to say grace. Dorie and Clem glanced at each other before following suit. They always did so out of respect for their hosts. As soon as the word "Amen" sounded around the table, the two men began eating with far more enthusiasm than they had shown while praying.

Dorie shared the news about Izzie. "Did any of you see her leave yesterday?"

"We were a bit preoccupied, so no." Earle looked pointedly at Clem, who looked down at her plate. She hated it when Earle reprimanded Lou's behavior. Although she understood why he did.

"I'm sure she'll turn up," said Agnes. "You said she's a bit wild, right?"

"Yes, but Rennie's really worried. We need to find her before this storm hits."

Clem spoke up. "Earle doesn't think it'll be too bad."

Earle nodded, and Dorie tsked. "Well, we're leaving, so hopefully she'll show up very soon." Dorie picked half-heartedly at her sandwich. "I'm meeting Rennie at his place, and we'll leave from there this afternoon with Shel and the kids." Dorie looked at Clem. "When are you two leaving?"

Clem hesitated. "I'm not sure. After Lou gets back from work and loads up the truck, I guess."

"He went to work today?" asked Agnes.

"Just for a few hours." They needed the money. Her part-time job at the gallery barely paid anything, and though the food truck was successful, it was early days yet.

Dorie stood and looked at Earle and Agnes. "Well, since I obviously can't convince either of you to leave, I'm heading out. Don't want to keep Rennie waiting. Clem, you ready?"

"Sure." Clementine knew she needed to get home and show she'd made some obvious progress in packing for their trip out.

Agnes and Earle followed them out, and they all hovered by Dorie's car, unsure how to say goodbye.

Earle turned to Clem. "You stay safe now, you hear."

She could sense the worry beneath his words, his eyes betraying all he held back. She fought the urge to throw her arms around his neck and beg them to let her stay close through the storm. Instead, she nodded and swallowed the lump in her throat.

"We'll see you after this mess is over." Earle and Agnes turned and headed back to the boarded-up ranch house.

"Wait." Clem ran after them and clasped their hands in hers. "Be careful. I'll miss you."

Earle nodded and smiled. "Don't you worry about us. We'll be just fine." He patted her hand.

Clem forced herself to turn from them and head back to Dorie's car, knowing her friend would be getting impatient by now.

Clem and Dorie drove in silence, neither able to sort through the mess of emotions enough to articulate what they were feeling.

When Dorie pulled up to Clem and Lou's house, she turned to her friend. "Please take care of yourself. Don't delay. I know how hard it is for you to leave here." She glanced through the car window toward the water. Clem knew Dorie understood. "Stay in touch. I want to know you got out safely." Dorie reached for Clem's hand. "I'll be thinking of you."

"Me too," said Clem. "All this will be over soon."

Even as she said the words, she hoped they were true. Bad things had a way of lingering in her experience.

Dorie squeezed her hand. "See you soon."

Clem leaned over to hug her, and they held on, each the other's anchor in the storm.

izzie

Izzie woke up feeling lighter than she ever had before. Was this what happy felt like? Turning over, she looked at Jess, who breathed quietly next to her. Izzie remembered the feel of her hair in her hands like golden rope, the scent of something bright like a pine forest. She kissed Jess on the shoulder and got up, laying the covers back over her sleeping form. Iz pulled on a tee shirt and jeans and left the bedroom, shutting the door behind her.

People were splayed out on the sofa and floor among a litter of beer cans and ashtrays. Noises came from the kitchen. She hoped someone was making coffee.

When she walked in, Frankie glanced over her shoulder, then returned to banging mugs against the counter and turning the faucet on full blast so that it gushed into the coffeepot.

"Shut the fuck up," grumbled someone on the couch.

"Morning." Frankie ignored Izzie. "You okay?"

Frankie turned. "What the fuck?"

Izzie stood still, confused by Frankie's outburst.

"You hooked up with Jess last night, right here in my apartment."

"Our apartment."

"I had to sleep on the floor."

"I'm sorry. You could have slept in your bed."

"And listen to you two all night!"

Izzie's skin burned. She wasn't sure if she was embarrassed or angry.

"You are aware she and I are together, right?" Frankie demanded.

"No, I wasn't aware." Angry. Definitely angry.

"Well, we are. How could you do that? I thought we were friends."

What kind of crazy shit was this? Was this what city people did, share each other's partners? Izzie didn't know how to feel. "Maybe you need to talk to Jess."

"No shit!" Frankie slammed down the coffeepot and headed toward their bedroom.

Izzie did not want to be part of this showdown. She walked out the front door, shutting it behind her, not sure where she was going.

The street outside was already bustling with people walking dogs, stores opening for the day, and cars honking as people tried not to be late to work. The noises of city life made Izzie's blood pump faster—that and the residual anger she felt toward Frankie and Jess.

Why would Jess sleep with her when she was seeing Frankie? Iz couldn't do that—share her friend and a lover. Maybe her family's uptight morals had embedded themselves into her psyche more deeply than she cared to admit. Maybe she needed to lighten up—though Frankie obviously hadn't been happy about it either. The admiration and desire she had felt for Jess just hours earlier had weakened.

Now all that remained was that persistent dull grayness she knew so well.

"Got any change?" An older man held a handwritten sign that said, *Hungry—anything will help*.

Izzie dug her hand into the pocket of her jeans and pulled out a crumpled dollar bill. He eyed it like a dog eyeing a bone, and his hand shook as he took it from her. Tipping an invisible hat, he smiled a gap-toothed smile that made his eyes crinkle and shine. Then he placed something in her hand and walked away.

When she looked down, she was surprised to see an origami crane folded out of old newspaper. The sepia-stained paper and faded type created the impression of feathers. Izzie held it gently so as not to crush it.

This is definitely going on the wall.

How could a person who was so obviously struggling still find beauty in the world and make something so delicate and perfect? If she were in his shoes, she'd cling to every material possession she owned, let alone made with her own two hands. Yet he had given it to her in exchange for a dollar. It was worth so much more than a dollar. What sort of life must he have? Had his family given up on him?

Her shoulders slumped. Had her family given up on her? No one had tried to contact her since she left. Not that they could, she supposed. Her tight-ass mom wouldn't give her a cell phone, and the apartment didn't have a landline. And to be fair, she hadn't contacted them either.

She wondered what they were thinking right now. Did they even care that she was gone?

Oh, to hell with them. I'll get that job, and I have a roof over my head. I don't need them.

Once Iz had pounded asphalt enough to clear her head and dissipate her anger some, she made her way back to the house. She needed to shower and change before her interview at the restaurant that afternoon.

When she opened the front door, the entire apartment sounded empty. Taking off her shoes, Izzie crept across the wooden floor to her bedroom. She let out a breath when she found no one there. Frankie must have gone to work already.

Grabbing a towel, Izzie headed for the shower. Hot water must have been scarce with four roommates, but the cold rush felt good on her sticky skin. Asphalt-walking brought out a sweat, especially when anger and nerves about her upcoming interview drove up her energy level in the September heat. But she made the shower quick so she wouldn't be late. Wrapping herself in a towel, she opened the bathroom door, leaving wet footprints on the floor.

Izzie was surprised to see one of the bedroom doors open. Her roommates seemed to guard their private spaces, so after making sure no one else was home, she took the opportunity to peek inside.

Computer monitors filled three folding worktables, which spanned almost the entire length of the bedroom. She counted five of them arranged at different levels, wires clustered and tangled in knots on the floor below. She'd never seen anything like it.

Who the hell's room was this?

She crept inside to take a closer look. Boxers and large stained tee shirts were discarded on the floor. Trails of Cheerios led from open cereal boxes to takeaway boxes spilling leftover food, their smell mixing with . . . weed.

Mikey's room.

But all this computer equipment? Izzie leaned in to read what was on the screen closest to her, but it was just a bunch of indecipherable code, glowing green on a black background like an alien language. What did Mikey do? Frankie had never said. Izzie didn't think he'd left the house since she'd been there—until now—and was usually holed up in his room. Izzie had assumed he was just getting high all the time or sleeping.

Guess not.

Suddenly remembering she was running late, Izzie headed for her bedroom. She pulled on the only clean clothes she had left: jeans and a slightly wrinkled tee shirt. Whatever. It was just a waitressing job, not Wall Street.

As she made her way to the restaurant, she recited to herself: *I will not become my mother. I will not become my mother.*

When she arrived, she was told by an older woman that the manager wasn't available. They were closing early because of the storm.

"Well, is there anyone else who could interview me?"

"Man, you're enthusiastic. Don't get your hopes up; this job sucks." The woman exchanged her wisecracking tone with a more patient one. "Look, we need people, and you seem as good as any. Come back when all this is over. Now go home. It's gonna be a doozy."

On the walk back, Izzie wondered just how bad this storm might be. She hadn't kept up with the news and assumed it would be just like most other Texas storms—a pain in the ass but nothing major. She couldn't quite dispel the thought of her family back home and what they were doing to prepare. Maybe she'd call Rennie from a phone booth just to check.

But first, food. She was starving and not quite ready to face Frankie again after her outburst that morning. Izzie wondered what Jess was doing and how she'd reacted to Frankie's wrath.

Izzie cringed. What had she gotten herself into already?

clementine

Lou still wasn't home when Dorie dropped Clem off, which was a relief. Clem went into her art room and looked around at the beautiful clutter of it all. Lou had suggested she pack her paintings and art supplies to put up in the attic in case water got into the house. But where to start?

She began placing her paintbrushes into a bag one by one. Specks of color flecked their wooden handles, hinting at the countless lives she had brought to life on canvas. She smelled the bristles, which tickled her nose, the scent of paint and linseed oil her healing tonic.

She wasn't sure how much time had passed when the front door opened.

"Hey, beautiful," Lou cried out. "Where're you at?"

His boots clomped on the hardwood floor, and he poked his head around the door. A thatch of hair hung over his eyes, and he pushed it back, a habit that always made her pulse quicken. She smiled up at him and rested the tip of a paintbrush on her lower lip.

Lou went to her and reached for a lock of her hair, twisting a curl around his finger and bringing it to his nose. "Why do you always smell of the sea?"

Clem looked into his eyes. "Perhaps I really am a selkie like Dorie said and I belong in the waves." She smiled at him, but Lou looked serious.

"No. You belong here with me."

She kissed him then, long and slow, and inhaled his earthy smell of barbecue smoke and sweat. Her stomach rumbled.

"Did you forget to eat again? I swear, if I didn't feed you, you'd disappear."

She knew that was true. She'd disappeared once and could certainly do it again.

Lou must have read her face because he kissed her cheek and pulled out a large packet of barbecue from his bag, a smile on his face. "Why don't you set the table while I wash up."

The barbecue was good, but she picked at it and didn't end up eating much. Lou talked about the few customers he had sold to, all grateful he was out and about so they could stock up for a trip out of town or a long night waiting out the storm. Clem half listened but was distracted.

"What's the matter, darlin'?"

"I met the strangest boy on the beach earlier."

"Strange? Strange how?" Lou stuffed another handful of fried okra into his mouth.

"I'm not sure. He just seemed so lost and alone."

Lou stopped eating and looked at her. She knew what he was thinking. She forced a laugh and got up from the table. "He was just a bit odd, that's all. You know how kids can be."

She took her dishes to the sink and began washing them, relieved her back was to Lou. She hated when he worried about her. She was doing just fine now.

His chair scraped, and Clem felt his hand on her shoulder. He turned her to him and looked into her eyes.

Clem smiled and rolled her eyes. "I'm fine. Promise." Then she kissed him on the forehead before walking toward her art room. "Got to keep packing."

A stack of canvases leaned against a wall, and Clem began going through them one by one, a litmus test of her mental well-being. By the time she reached the last paintings, she recognized the threat of a covetous sea.

Reaching for one painting, Clem felt a chill shiver through her being. An image of the full moon shone back at her. She had painted Finn onto canvases that had begun dark when he was lost in the shadows. Instead of painting to love the world, she had done it to purge the horror of losing Finn.

Clem picked at her cuticles to reveal the lunula underneath, then tore the skin off with her teeth and tasted the paint crusted at the edges. She still felt the moon's pull sometimes and had to convince herself that everyone was right: she'd had a nervous breakdown after Finn drowned, and needed to focus on getting well. No more searching the waves for her lost boy. No more listening for his cries.

And she *was* feeling better. Her part-time job at the gallery in Galveston helped distract her, and Lou was bringing in money with his food truck. Sure, he'd slipped up at the wedding, but it had been a stressful day for them both, and he had been nervous.

Clem thought of the painting she'd done of the monarch butterflies four years ago. That had broken through the weight of her suffering, and now her paintings were ablaze with color. They shone and glimmered, and over and over, she painted the light.

Clem picked up armfuls of paint and dropped the tubes into a box, filling it quickly before moving on to another. She and Lou would be back soon enough, and life would continue as it was.

"Clem, what are you doing?" Lou stood at the door.

"I'm packing."

He looked around the room as if assessing her progress. "Remember, we need to be ready to get out of here soon." He glanced at the box in her hands. "Don't bother with the paint and brushes. Just help me move your paintings."

Clem hesitated. "Are you sure we need to leave? Agnes and Earle are staying, and they've been here forever, so they should know."

Lou huffed in exasperation. "We're not staying, Clem. I told you, it's not worth the risk." Entering the room, he picked up a stack of canvases. "Come on. Let's just get this done so we can head out."

Clem knew Lou meant well, and she had learned it was easier not to argue with him. But it had been a big decision for her to move out of Agnes and Earle's place and into a tiny house on the bayside with him. She missed them. Not to mention, she had rushed into her relationship with Lou the first time, and look where that had gotten them. The thread that bound them had been broken and mended, but she still felt those frayed edges.

rennie

The wind had picked up, and a dusting of sand spooled between Rennie and Dorie. Slate clouds shadowed the sun, but patches of blue remained. Rennie could almost convince himself that things might not get so bad.

Shel's truck bed was filled with towering shapes covered in tarp and roped down, a monolith of memories. Dorie stood beside Rennie as he ushered Chase and Johnny into the back seat of the cab. Shel held out the keys for her brother.

"You go on ahead," Rennie said. "I'm staying."

Shel hesitated and then nodded once. Squeezing his hand, she got behind the wheel of the truck.

Rennie turned to Dorie and took her hands. "You need to go with Shel and the boys."

Dorie shook her head.

"I'm not leaving without Izzie," Rennie insisted. "As soon as I find her, we'll head out, and I'll meet you at my brother's place."

Dorie pulled her hands away and stuffed them in her

pockets. "And what if she's not here?" she snapped. But Rennie knew her well enough by now to understand it was fear of losing him that made her push him away.

He looked at the ground and kicked the parched sand so it dusted his boot. "Until I know for sure, I'm not leaving. I won't have her come home and find no one here."

Dorie planted her feet more firmly on the ground. "Then I'm staying too."

Rennie shook his head and took her elbow. She could be stubborn, but he would not let her win this argument. "Shel needs you, and the boys." He directed her to the truck, meeting with resistance, and opened the door, which screeched on its hinges. Dorie looked at Shel and the two boys, who had begun to feel like family. "Y'all need to stick together." Shel waited for her at the wheel, her face tense and focused on leaving. "Go. I'll see you soon."

Dorie grabbed him and held on tight, as if she'd never let go. The frantic energy that had possessed him only moments before stilled. Rennie sank into her, this woman he had come to love, slowly but ever so surely.

Then he brought himself back to the task at hand. Time was of the essence.

"Dorie, look at me." They both stepped back, and he stared into the face he wanted to see for the rest of his days. "I'll be okay. And it'll help me get through this knowing you and the rest of my family are safe. Please do that for me."

Dorie stared fiercely into his eyes, and all the joy, sorrow, strength, and resilience he loved so much about her seared against him, until he felt he could do anything. He recognized that look, had seen it before whenever Dorie had to face a trial she couldn't escape.

"You come back to me." She looked into his rugged face, holding it in her hands. "Promise."

"I will." He kissed her. "I love you."

"I love you too." Dorie turned and reached into the passenger seat to pick up Rosie's cat carrier. Slumping into the truck, she placed it on her lap. Then she stared straight ahead at the dirt road leading to Highway 87.

Rennie watched them back out over the dirt track and then pick up speed as they reached the asphalt, willing Dorie to turn around, even as he knew she wouldn't. She didn't do goodbyes.

Getting in his truck, Rennie headed back to his place. If Iz were to come home, there was a good chance it would be to his house and not her mother's. Surely she'd heard about the storm by now and would realize they needed to leave.

Rennie glanced at the row of cars heading in the opposite direction. Some faces were familiar, and he raised his hand to wave as they headed toward Highway 124. He nodded to himself, glad that people had the sense to follow the evacuation orders. Hopefully he'd find Izzie before it was too late.

The house was silent and dim due to the boarded-up windows. Rennie opened the front door and called out her name, but he sensed she wasn't there. He tore off a corner from a house sketch he'd been working on and scribbled a note. Then he stuck it on a nail on the outside of the front door.

Izzie

Looking for you. Stay here and wait for me.

Uncle Rennie

The beaches were completely deserted, as they should be. Waves crested high, as if warming up for the big event, their song wild and discordant. Pelicans flew in Vs, somehow sensing the impending chaos to come. Where would they go to sit out the storm? Gulls shrieked as they swooped and dove, riding air currents that tossed them gracelessly, so they swerved and looped off course. Rennie drove up and down the shoreline, the wet-packed sand hard beneath his wheels. It would soon become saturated and swarm with movement as the waters churned up its treasures.

He remembered taking Izzie beachcombing when she was younger; they had always been more successful after a storm. She had had a gift for finding shark's teeth—or *sparrow-beaks*, as she called them. She had always been a fanciful little girl, but she'd changed. Perhaps she found it difficult to fit into the world now because so much of the world rejected her. But the world was at fault, not her.

Craning his neck to see behind the dunes and between the houses, he pressed on the brake at every sign of movement: a shrub shivering in the wind, a tern taking flight. The tide was already high now, so he had to exit and find another way onto the wider stretches of beach. Geotubes, like giant black worms, lined the dunes, and in parts of the beach, the water already lapped more than halfway up the barriers. Rennie knew they wouldn't hold the surge, that it wouldn't be long before the water reached the houses and possibly beyond. He estimated that he only had an hour or two left to evacuate.

He decided to check Ali's house, just in case. Maybe the girls were hiding out there, despite Shelly's insistence that the family had evacuated. He parked the truck on the shoulder of the road, just to be safe. Rennie knocked, but of course, no one answered. He peered through the cracks between the plywood on the windows, but it was impossible to see anything.

He pounded against a board. "Anyone home? Izzie, answer the door. Ali, let me in." Rennie waited, hoping against hope. "Girls!" He raised his voice, his desperation mimicking anger. "Open up right now! This is serious."

He was talking to an empty house. Where the hell was that girl?

An hour or so later, Rennie returned to his house, praying his niece was inside. His heart dropped. The note was still on the door, fluttering in the wind that had started to pick up. He'd just have to wait for her inside and hope she showed up in time. He gathered some candles for when the power went out and filled the bathtub with water. Then he found whatever receptacles he could and filled those as well.

There wasn't much food in the house, as he'd expected to be gone by now. The pantry was stocked with canned beans, soup, bread, and peanut butter. The refrigerated food wouldn't last too long, but there was some cheese and bologna; bologna was nonperishable, right? He'd always told the kids it had so many preservatives in it, it would outlast them all. If they had to wait out the storm, there should be enough for a couple of days. It would pass over, and they could probably leave for Houston sometime tomorrow.

He turned on the weather channel. Ike was predicted to hit in the early hours of the morning. He looked around his house. It was solid. He had designed it to withstand hurricane-strength winds; it would hold.

Rennie busied himself doodling house plans. He'd told his friend, Ken, that he'd given up design work for good after leaving New Orleans. But he secretly scribbled drawings on pages that he later threw away. He had to purge his mind, which was constantly brimming with ideas. As long as he didn't execute any of them, he could convince himself he wasn't an architect anymore. Rennie associated his past occupation with his ex, Claire, and their crazy life filled with angst. He had known she could only be married to an ambitious, successful man, so he had made sure he became that. And when she found someone else, Rennie became another sort of man with a different kind of life.

Rennie scribbled harder, adding structural beams to the house he was drawing, making it able to withstand the strongest of storms.

He wasn't sure how long he'd been sketching when he became aware of a loud rushing noise outside. He went out to the deck.

Rennie had expected a six- to eight-foot surge with a category-two hurricane. But the water was already high. Walking down the deck stairs, he was surprised to find waves lapping under the house and the wheels of his truck partly covered.

There was no getting out now, and there was little chance of Izzie showing up at this point. He sat outside and watched the water recede, then surge again—nothing too bad. Surprisingly, it wasn't raining or windy yet. That would come later.

clementine

Clementine finished packing while Lou loaded the food truck. The rheumy air felt different and pressed upon her as she added to the stack of boxes outside. As she sat down on a shorter one, she saw him—a shimmer of light in the darkening sky. He walked behind the house, and she got up to follow the silver boy.

"What are you doing here?" Clem asked him.

"Looking for you. I want to show you something." His voice was sweet like a promise.

"What?"

"Come with me."

"I can't. We're about to leave. The storm is close now."

"I know, but this is important." He held out his hand, and Clem hesitated.

She ached to go with the strange boy.

By the time she reached for him, he had turned and was walking away from her. She followed behind, concentrating when she lost sight of him as he slipped between fingers of light. But soon he became clearer, and the tug of an invisible tether pulled at her, as if he had attached the rope flicking at his rear.

She walked as if in a dream. They traveled over grass and sand, always close to the water. The sky hung heavy, bloated with millions of droplets waiting to fall. Clem didn't take her eyes off the boy, his young body so agile and light, he almost floated.

In a matter of moments, or perhaps hours, they arrived at the woods on the far-east end of the peninsula. The sun was weakening, and shadows mimicked morphing forms, so Clementine was unsure what she was seeing.

"I live here." The boy gestured to a vacant area among the trees.

Clementine's skin prickled. She didn't remember seeing trees this close to the water on High Island before. She blinked to adjust her eyes. Rain fell lightly, and the wind had picked up some.

She followed the silver boy toward a door that emerged from the veil of rain. They crossed over a threshold into a large room lit by candles. Figures appeared and disappeared, so Clementine was unsure for a moment who stood among the flickering shadows, watching her.

"Mama?"

Clementine wondered if she had again slipped into that in-between space after all these years of healing. Looking in the direction of the voice, she saw a small figure flicker in the candle flames.

It was him. She had no doubt.

Clementine walked toward Finn, afraid he'd disappear with each step she took. His pale skin was translucent, and he receded into the half-empty space and emerged again as she drew nearer. Her throat constricted, choking her with too much love and hope to bear.

When she looked into his eyes, she almost doubted for a moment that it was him. They held far too much for his years, the innocence displaced by a strange knowing. What had he been doing this whole time? How was he here?

She knew it was not up to her to reach for her lost boy, as much as she longed to pull him close and never let go again. So she forced herself still.

As she stared into Finn's eyes, filaments of memory drew him closer to her. "How are you here?" His voice was faint, a hushed whisper, like a language born of the sea.

Clementine tasted salt water as tears slipped into the corners of her mouth, a communion of sorts between mother and son. Looking around, she pointed at the silver boy. "He brought me here."

Finn nodded. "Jack's good at that. He found me too." He paused before asking, "How come *you* couldn't find me, Mama?"

Her heart broke for the thousandth time. "I tried so hard for so long." All those endless nights wandering the shore, waiting for the full moon, entering the shining water to search for him.

"I know. I heard you calling."

"You did?" Her boy knew. How close had she gotten to him as her limbs parted the waves, deeper and deeper? Why had she allowed everyone to convince her he was gone? How had she allowed herself to give up?

"But I couldn't find *you*, either. Sea-Mother wouldn't let me go."

Anger rose in Clem, and she clenched her fists, her fingernails digging into her palms. How dare another claim him!

Finn stepped closer, wary, like an untamed animal. A chill washed over Clem, like stepping into the ocean in winter, seaskin parting like a wound. She sucked in a sharp breath, longing to bury her nose in his hair.

But still Finn didn't reach for her. "Mama, come with me."

Clem followed him up some stairs, his footsteps silent on treads worn from ages of footfalls. The floral wallpaper faded, so multiple patterns shifted in and out of focus before her eyes.

Finn opened a door at the very top of the stairs, and she found herself in a glass tower. She had stepped out of the dimness and into the light, which shone from every window. Of course her boy would be here, in the bright, where he belonged.

Finn handed her a pile of rough-edged paper. Each piece held a sketch—the seascape, the tower, the hotel, and various boys, including the silver boy, Jack.

"You did these?" She went through them one by one, lingering on the lines and shading of each.

Finn nodded. "It's how I love the world."

Tears spilled from Clem's eyes. Once, Finn had asked her why she painted, and that was exactly what she had told him. He had said he wanted to love the world by painting too, that they'd paint it together. Later, Clem had thought they'd never have an opportunity to do that. But here he was, recreating the world he saw through his tower.

"Do you still paint?" he asked.

"I didn't for a long time. I couldn't."

"Why not?"

"That's how I lost you. I wasn't paying attention."

"Sea-Mother took me, Mama. It wasn't your fault."

"I should never have let that happen. You didn't belong to her. You only belong to me."

Again, Clem saw a lifetime of experience in her young son's eyes, an old sadness beyond losing his mother, his life. He seemed to mourn the countless sorrows of the world.

"Do you paint now? Do you still love the world?"

"I try. It's been so difficult without you in it."

Finn nodded, his eyes solemn. "I wish I could see your paintings."

"Why don't you come with me? I'll show you." She reached for his hand, longing to feel his skin against hers, but he leaned away and moved his hands under the table.

Finn looked outside, gazing at the last of the blue. "I can't leave this place."

"What do you mean?"

"Jack brought me here. I belong *here* now, not with Sea-Mother. She'll take me back if I leave here, and I don't want to go back."

"I won't let her this time. I'll stay here and take care of you. We can be a family again."

Finn smiled, the curve of his lips barely visible.

"Shall we draw together?" asked Clem. "Now? Here?"

Finn sat at the table and slid a blank sheet of paper toward her. "What should we draw?"

"Whatever you like."

He looked intently at her. "Let's draw our favorite, most precious thing."

Clem nodded and picked up a pencil. The only sound was the scribble of lead on paper, at times fast strokes, at others long whispers of a line extended. The storm brewing outside was separate from them, another world beyond the hotel tower.

They stopped drawing at the same time and slid their pages toward each other. The drawing in front of Clem was filled with lines so tender, she could feel the love emanating from the paper—her own image reflected back at her, rendered in shades of gray.

Finn leaned close to the page she had slid over to him. "It's me, Mama." When he looked up at her, his pale eyes shone. "We are each other's most precious thing."

Clem nodded, her palms flat against the paper as if they could absorb the parts of himself he had left there.

Finn flinched as the waves whispered to him through the glass tower, somehow permeating the silence, just for a moment. Sea-Mother would not let him forget her so easily.

"Mama, will you read us a story?"

"Of course I will."

Finn walked over to a shelf and pulled out a book, dusty and bedraggled. He led her back to the staircase. Downstairs, in the parlor, Finn sat on a circular rug, gesturing to Clem to sit in the middle. He continued to always keep an arm's length away from her.

She held the book in her hand as Jack led a procession of boys who joined them to form a circle. Each one held a small candle in his palm, so the center of the parlor glowed. They didn't take their eyes off Clementine, all of them struggling to remember what she was. The boys sat in silence, waiting for her to start.

"Would you like me to *tell* you a story instead?" she asked. Still, they didn't speak, looking unsure.

"How do you *tell* a story?" asked Jack.

Clem smiled. "From my imagination, inside here." She tapped the side of her head. "Although this one is mostly true."

The boys nodded in unison, and she began.

"Once, there was a family who lived in a little yellow house by the sea. The father worked hard and often spent long weeks out at sea, sucking black gold from the deepest parts of the ocean. But the mother always knew he loved her and their boy. When he was gone, mother and son would play in the waves, search for treasures on the sand, and paint and laugh together. They were very happy. The mother loved her boy so much, she sometimes forgot everyone else, including the father, who missed his family more than anything. Whenever he returned, he'd bring gifts of colored candies and shells that the boy had never seen before. And he'd cook delicious feasts so they all grew strong and healthy. He told the boy how he sailed for many miles to return to those he loved best in the world. He shared stories of his adventures fighting pirates and sea dragons.

"But one day, he returned, and they were both gone. Instead, a stranger lived in their little yellow house. The stranger told the father that the mother had run away and couldn't be found. And the boy was lost, no longer of this world. The father began his quest, searching far and wide for his beloveds. One night, though, when the moon was full, she appeared on his doorstep, like a selkie shining in the silver light.

"It took a long time for them to forgive each other and themselves. But the father did all he could to earn back her love, and they finally understood that they were meant to be together. The only thing missing was their beloved son. So the mother listened for him in the waves and never stopped loving and missing him. Until one day, a silver boy appeared and reunited her with her son in a glass tower, where he lived with all his friends. She cried with joy, and they all lived happily ever after."

Clementine looked at all the young faces encircling her. Where had they come from? What were their stories? She wondered at their sublime expressions, transfixed by her words. Except one boy, older than the others. He sat farthest away from her, his eyes hard, anger and fear disguised as mistrust. Or was it hate?

Finn rose and walked over to her, standing close. His smile radiated outward, dissolving every ounce of darkness.

Jack spoke from the edge of the circle. "Will you be *our* Mother too?"

Clementine's heart filled with love for all these lost boys. *Yes, I could do this for the rest of my days.*

Finn took a step closer and whispered into her ear. "Mama, why don't I remember him?"

"Who?"

"Father."

A rapid montage of memories flashed through her mind: Lou holding Finn close when he was a baby and singing him to sleep, just as he'd done for Clem so many times. Lou showing Finn how to mash potatoes when he was a little older, and Finn getting most of it on his hands rather than on their plates. Lou and Finn on the beach constructing elaborate structures from sand, and Lou comforting Finn when the ocean had wiped the shore clean the following morning.

Finn had tried so hard to remember him, but he could only summon absence. "When I think of him, I just remember you being sad."

"He loves you very much." Clem wanted Finn to remember. She'd make sure he did. "And I wasn't always sad. There were times when we were all very happy together." She smiled at Finn.

"I don't remember." He looked down at the floor, which wavered like his memories. "Won't you miss him if you stay here with us?"

"Perhaps he'll stay too." She hated to leave Finn, even for a moment, but she needed to tell Lou about finding their son. He was bound to stay if he knew. He was still waiting for her back at the house so they could leave before the storm hit. If he didn't want to stay, then so be it, but she wasn't going anywhere. She wouldn't abandon Finn again.

"I'll tell him I found you." She looked out the parlor windows, where light rain splattered the panes. "I must go now, but I'll be back very soon." Clem stood and again felt the older boy's intense gaze. She smiled down at Finn. "Don't worry. I won't be long." Finn's face lost a little of its glow. "I promise, *mi corazón*."

All the Lost Boys watched her leave. Jack began to follow her, but Leroy stepped in front of him before he could reach the front door. "Not now. Let her go."

"But what if she doesn't come back?"

"She will." Leroy looked at the vacant space in the middle of the circle, where Clem had told them her story and where Finn still stood. "The Father is our only obstacle." Leroy grimaced. He didn't like to think about men and their desires. "If he gets in the way, you know what to do."

Jack wasn't sure what Leroy meant. Having a Mother *and* a Father was surely even better. They could all be a family together.

"Just do what you have to do," Leroy said. "I believe in you."

Pete

Pete preferred to let fate take its course. He should probably have boarded up the windows on the house and tried to secure the trailer out back, but he never had been much of a planner. And anyway, he had *Angel* to keep him safe. A category-two storm was nothing they couldn't handle.

Of course, Carol had tried to talk him into evacuating. *For the kids' sake,* she'd said. *Personally, I don't care what you do.* He had to admit, that had stung just a bit. Luanne had called and left a message on the answering machine saying they were leaving to stay with her mother in Beaumont. She hadn't invited him to join them, knowing he wouldn't anyway.

Pete had bought a few extra supplies, just essentials—nonperishable food, water, cigarettes, whiskey, beer. He even did a little fishing in the morning, though he could smell the storm in the air, feel a tingling on his skin. Apart from that, the day had been much like all the others: fishing, cleaning and eating his catch, followed by watching TV and drinking a few beers to pass the time.

He must have fallen asleep, because he woke to the sound of the wind picking up. He figured now was the time to convene with his *Angel.* He would be safest there; she would float if the surge got too high, and he didn't fancy the idea of being landlocked during a possible flood situation. Besides, she wouldn't let him down—never had.

Angel was already aloft on the rising water that had made its way onto Pete's land. He sloshed an unsteady path and used the rope on her sides to haul himself over onto the deck. After placing his backpack of supplies into the cabin, excitement stirred. He was in for an adventure and was ready to face whatever challenges came his way; pirate blood coursed through his veins, after all.

He watched the surge move in and out, revealing flattened grass and relocating random objects. The barbecue pit had toppled on its side against a wire fence, and the pile of logs Pete stored against the house had dislodged, scattering wood about the yard like a game of pick-up sticks.

He wondered what Earle had done with his livestock. *Hope those cows can swim.* He chuckled at the image.

He knew he had made the right decision to keep his life simple. It was better to have little, expect little, not to need people or things to worry about. It was just him and *Angel* taking on the world.

Like back when he'd first gotten the boat and named her after his lost love. Now she had been a damn fine woman—one of a kind! Talk about taking on the world; she'd done that and more, a legend. 'Course, she hadn't chosen him; why would she? His wayward angel could have had whoever she wanted. Up on that stage, belting out all the pain and love she had for the world, shimmying in front of audiences who adored her as much as her fellow classmates had abhorred her. She didn't belong here, never had.

She belonged to the world. And that's what had killed her. Maybe if she had chosen him, she'd still be alive today.

Who was he kidding? The booze would have killed them both; she'd have dragged him along with her. Hell, he still wished she had, no matter the cost.

What was his life worth now? His business was going to shit. His women despised him. His kids *wanted* to love him, but Shawn had about given up and Addie would be close behind. And looking at this storm, knowing his luck, he'd lose what little he did have.

But not his *Angel.* They'd always have each other's back, no matter how bad things got.

clementine

Clem breathed in the salty brine carried by the wind that whipped at her hair, winding the curls into tight ringlets that skimmed her hips. Lou was pacing the deck when she reached the house.

"Where the hell have you been?"

Clementine recognized the expression on Lou's face—barely suppressed anger that hardened his eyes.

"We have to go, *now*. It's already looking bad out there."

"He's here." Clem didn't know how else to tell him.

"Who's here?"

"Finn. He's on the peninsula."

Lou stilled and stared at Clem, his agitation shifting to concern.

"I've seen him." Clementine clasped Lou's hands, her glassy eyes wide. Lou frowned, searching Clem's face. She knew he was looking for the signs, signs of madness. "I'm going to stay here with him."

Lou huffed out a breath of confusion and frustration,

and Clementine registered the unmistakable smell of liquor. An empty glass sat on the nearby patio table. Lou pulled his hands from her grasp and dragged his fingers through his hair. "We're not staying, Clem!"

"He's safe in his tower on High Island. With the other boys. We can stay there too."

"The other boys?" Lou spat out the words. "Look, you're upset. There are no boys. And if we don't leave now, it'll be too late."

"You can stay too. Don't you want to see your son?"

"For God's sake, Clem. Finn is dead. We can't get him back!"

Clem smiled at his foolishness. They had a second chance to be together again as a family. "Let me show you."

Lou hesitated. Then he grabbed the last of the hand luggage next to the stairs of the deck, and Clem reached for Lucille's cat carrier. She poked her fingers through the metal cage and cooed to Lucille. Lou threw the bags into the already loaded food truck, and Clem placed the cage at her feet as she sat in the passenger seat.

Water had already covered the beach, so the blanched ocean and sky were indiscernible. Waves pushed against the road, and the wind blew in gusts. Lou was forced to pull up behind a line of stalled cars halfway down highway 87. He pounded the steering wheel and cussed under his breath. Clem wondered how much he'd drunk while waiting for her. All that mattered right now was getting to High Island. The surge of water pulsed like a living creature, consuming everything in its path. Clementine buzzed with a manic energy, longing to see Finn again and share her discovery with Lou.

They'd almost reached the end of 87 where it met 124 when Lou darted out of line. "Screw this!"

He veered into the deeper water along the shoulder to cut in front of the deadlock of cars. Metal pans clanked in the rear of the food truck, and a loud clatter signaled the disarray. Lucille cried in alarm at Clem's feet.

"There. Pull over." Clem gestured to the corner where 87 met 124.

Lou kept driving.

Reaching for the door handle, Clem opened the truck door, and rain drenched the seat. She jumped out of the car, landing in water that almost reached her knees.

"Jesus!" cried Lou.

Cars started honking as the vehicle ahead of Lou moved forward. Lou angled the truck as far to the side of the road as he could before jumping out. He chased after Clem, who waded through the flooded beach.

Clem scanned the scene before her, trying to orient herself amid the floodwaters and darkening sky. Where were the woods? She should have reached them by now. Clem closed her eyes and silently called Finn to guide her, but she was met only with the roaring wind and rain.

Must be farther down. She picked up her pace again, but Lou caught up with her.

Panting, he pulled at her arm. "Where are you going?"

"Watch out for the Sea View Hotel. It can be a bit hard to see among the trees," Clem cried out. "Finn? Jack? We're here. Where are you?"

"Who the hell's Jack?" screamed Lou.

"Finn's friend. That's how I found him."

Lou tightened his grip on her arm and pulled her to a stop. "Clem, we need to go. Right now." He kept his voice measured, as if trying to reason with a madwoman. "Before it's too late."

"I told you. I'm not leaving."

Silver light shimmered between the slashes of rain pouring down on them. Clem wiped her eyes and peered into the gloom. Jack was looking at Lou. She pulled herself from Lou's grasp and reached out for the silver boy who would lead her to Finn.

"Jack, where is he?"

Jack beckoned to her, and she ran in his direction. Lou followed close behind, calling her name, which got lost in the storm. "Clem, wait. We have to go back."

When she reached Jack, she stopped and waited. Looking bewildered, Lou lost his balance and slid into the ever-rising waves.

Jack remembered the words Leroy had spoken to him. *The Father is our only obstacle.* Leroy's power rose within him. *I believe in you.* He now understood what was at stake. The Father wouldn't join them, and he wanted to take the Mother away. Jack drew closer to Lou, who struggled to stand in the moving water. He held his hand over Lou's head. Then his thin silver fingers began forcing it toward the water.

Clem panicked, confused by what she was seeing. Lou tried to rise, choking and pushing against an invisible force. Then Clem heard Finn's voice, distant and faint at first, but growing stronger. She scanned the area, eyes darting. Until suddenly, he was there, in front of her. Clem reached for him, but Finn backed away and shook his head.

"You must leave this place now. It's too dangerous." Though quiet, his voice penetrated the raging storm as if hovering above it.

Clementine felt the pain in his heart. "I don't care about any of that. I only care about being with you." Warm tears streamed down her cheeks, and she squeezed her hands into tight fists to stop from reaching for him again.

She looked back at Lou, who still struggled in the water, but she couldn't move.

Finn followed her gaze to his father. His thin face tightened with a determination he'd never felt before. He stepped toward his Mother and knelt on the ground, the water rushing around his chest. Bowing his head, he leaned toward her, close but not touching. Clementine released her fists, her hand hovering just above his hair.

Sister, I know you. You float inside her. I used to live there too—a long time ago. I forget, is it like the sea? Wavesong was once my lullaby and the briny world my cradle. Do you hear her heartbeat? Does it echo your own? Our mother doesn't know you yet—but she senses you. She knows what it is to be inhabited by another.

An electrical current moved between Clementine and Finn. It settled in her stomach and pulsated there, calming her with every beat.

"It's time for you to leave, Mama." Clem shook her head. "I wish you could stay with me forever, but it's not your time. You carry my sister inside you. You must love her the way you love me. So you can love yourself again."

Clementine bowed her head and placed her hands on her belly. A child. A daughter.

"You *can* be a Mother again."

Clem looked up at Finn. "But I *am* a mother. I'm *your* mother."

She reached for him, but he stood and went to Jack, who covered Lou like a shroud. Finn touched Jack's shoulder, and the boy froze. Bending close, he whispered into Jack's ear. His friend glowed for a moment as Finn clasped his arm, and then Finn began to absorb his silver light. Shimmering, Jack pulled away from Lou, who gulped heaving breaths of air.

Twisting out of Finn's grasp, Jack threw himself at

Clementine. She shuddered as he passed through her body, flooding her with unbearable sadness. Then he grew faint, only his tarnished outline pushing against the falling rain.

Finn stepped forward and took Clem's hand. His was icy cold, but the sadness was immediately replaced by more love than she had ever felt. As it coursed through her, she understood. She was being given a second chance, and she had to take it.

Lou struggled to stand, wavering with exhaustion and confusion. Finn took his father's hand as well, and Lou steadied himself against the rising surge. Finn led them both back to the truck, which was still parked but partly covered by the tide.

Releasing their hands, he smiled and lightly touched his mother's belly. A mingling rush of energy and light coursed through her. Then Finn turned and walked away into the veil of rain.

Clementine watched his back grow smaller. She forced herself not to run after him. Instead, she rested her hands on her belly.

september 13, 2008

ike hits bolivar peninsula at 2:00 a.m.

izzie

Izzie was tired and ready to finally head back to the apartment. She'd hung out at a coffee shop for a while to pass the time. Maybe Frankie would be asleep already or, more likely, out partying. When Izzie turned onto her street, the origami homeless guy was sitting on the sidewalk, intermittently folding sections of paper while reading the words on the page aloud: "Potent. Unforgivable. Exit. Hope . . ."

"Hi," said Izzie.

He looked up at her, a partially folded form in his hand. "You're out late. Not safe on these streets for a young girl on her own." His voice was deep, its timbre that of an old soul who had trodden many paths.

Izzie shrugged. Several completed origami cranes were lined up on the sidewalk next to him, each displaying its unique plumage. He had used whatever material he could get his hands on—glossy magazines, newspapers, discarded receipts, even a Burger King wrapper.

Izzie gestured to the cranes. "We have those where I used to live."

"Oh, yeah? Where's that, then?" His deft fingers resumed their movement, creasing the paper.

"Near the coast, Bolivar Peninsula. Do you know it?"

The old man shook his head. "I don't get down that way. Bet it's something to see."

"I guess." She never could understand what other people saw in it.

He held out the finished crane to her. Digging in her pockets, Izzie found a quarter. "This is all I have."

He shook his head. "This one's on me." He smiled, as if proud to hand her his gift.

"What's your name?" asked Izzie.

"William." He said it boldly, claiming it as his own. It was probably all he had, after all.

She held out her hand, and he hesitated. He wiped his own against his shirt and then shook hers.

"I'm Izzie."

"Nice to meet you, Izzie. Better go on home now. Not safe."

She turned toward her duplex. "See you around."

"Not safe," he repeated. "Not safe . . ." His words echoed on the concrete sidewalk, following her home.

Izzie climbed the stairs to her apartment. Walking through the front door into the living room, she stopped. A huge stack of gallon water jugs, liter bottles of soda, junk food, batteries, and other groceries took up a considerable portion of the room.

"What the hell?"

"I stocked up," Mikey said from the sofa.

"For what? The apocalypse?"

"The storm. They say it might be bad."

Izzie looked at her other roommates, who were scattered about the living room. They rolled their eyes. They'd been bored by Mikey's doomsday predictions and conspiracy theories many times—endless monologues that he favored when he was stoned. Most of the time, they just nodded and grunted, pretending to listen.

"You know they told everyone to evacuate."

"Where, here?" Izzie asked.

"No. Not yet, anyway." Mikey looked serious. "It's an official hurricane now. Hurricane Ike." He picked up a bottle of soda and a packet of powdered donuts, then headed for the hallway. "Galveston County has mandatory evacuation orders for sure. We're under voluntary evacuation here."

Izzie's heart rate sped up. Would her family leave? Her mother probably couldn't be bothered, but Uncle Rennie would make her. He wouldn't take a risk with his family.

"We're heading out again," Jules said, Dez following behind her.

"I wouldn't go back out there if I were you," Mikey shouted from the hallway. A grumble of thunder punctuated his words.

Dez and Jules just exchanged looks and laughed as they exited the front door.

Grabbing a huge bag of puffy Cheetos and a Coors Light, Frankie settled on the sofa and switched on the TV. She flicked through various channels.

Guilt descended on Izzie. She should have called her mom. Or at least Uncle Rennie.

"Whose mom is *like* that?" Frankie said from the sofa.

Izzie joined her. Frankie was watching a rerun of a *Gilmore Girls* episode. Maybe they could bond over TV, and she'd forgive her for Jess. Anyway, Izzie wanted to take her mind off her family; they'd take care of each other and be fine. Uncle Rennie would make sure of it.

Reaching for Frankie's beer, Izzie took a swig. "Why are we even watching this?" She plunged her hand into the oversize Cheetos bag, noting Frankie's preference now for the puffy ones from their early friendship.

"Shhh." Frankie grabbed hold of the bag to quiet its crinkling, not taking her eyes off the screen. She was still pissed, for sure, but it was a good sign that she'd let Iz share her Cheetos and beer.

They watched with wonder as they tried not to crunch too loudly—that storybook world of mothers and daughters who quipped playfully while sauntering through dappled streets drinking coffee and laughing ironically at everything.

Another episode played right after, and they binge-watched almost an entire season while the wind picked up outside. The panes in the old casement windows rattled like loose teeth. A flash of lightning, followed immediately by a crack of thunder, made them both jump.

Frankie turned up the volume, and Iz tried to refocus on the show.

Another flash lit up the room, followed by a click and then silence. It was pitch black except for the faint afterglow of the TV screen.

"Shit." Frankie got up and groped for the candle that always sat on the table—an image of Jesus with his arms outstretched adorning the glass holder. Stubs of incense sticks stuck out of the wax like porcupine quills. They burned them so the apartment smelled of patchouli, with slight undertones of weed.

"What the fuck?" Mikey had stumbled out of his bedroom and down the hallway. He stood before the pale glow of the candle wearing only boxers, his pale belly hanging over the waistband.

"Power's gone out," said Frankie.

"No shit, Sherlock." Mikey slumped next to them on the sofa, and they all leaned in his direction as the seat sank.

Izzie wondered how long the blackout would last. Getting up, she looked out the window. All she could make out were trees bending in the wind. The old oak outside their duplex shook its head, and leaves broke loose from its branches. The rain lashed against the window, erasing the outside world.

They all jumped again as howls from the storm entered through the open front door, which then slammed shut.

"Woohoo!" Dez and Jules staggered inside, swinging a flashlight that lit random corners of the room, which seemed to tip like a fun house.

Frankie stared in disbelief. "What the hell?"

Jules and Dez dripped water onto the floor, and Jules laughed as she shook her hair and began turning in circles so rainwater splattered in all directions.

"It's insane out there, y'all. The streets are flooding, and I swear, the wind almost scooped me away." She was laughing so hard, she could barely get the words out. "How cool would that have been?"

"Are you *high*?" asked Frankie. "You could've died out there."

"Jesus, Frankie. Lighten up!" She turned to Dez. "Wanna go back out?"

Frankie grabbed Jules by the arm. "You are not going back out there! No one is going anywhere."

A loud crack sounded outside, followed by a creak and a slow-motion thud. They all rushed to the window. The oak tree had cracked straight down the middle and split in two. It splayed across the parking lot, a car's trunk just visible beneath its heft. The roommates looked at each other wide-eyed.

"Uh, I'm going to go change," Jules said. Dez followed her sheepishly.

Izzie wished they could watch the news. If any of them had had a car, they could have listened to the radio. Though sitting in a car during a hurricane was obviously not the best idea.

Please let them be safe.

None of her roommates had a cell phone. *That's what you get for living with a bunch of dirt-broke losers,* her mom would have said.

Izzie clasped her hands and quickly drew them apart, hating herself for it. Memories of her two younger brothers begging her to play with them made her ache. And that one time her mother had made Izzie's favorite dinner, tuna casserole, to celebrate her grades for the semester she had still cared.

When her mother had still cared.

She tried to recall the last time she or her mother had said *I love you.* She couldn't remember. Izzie wiped her eyes and headed out of the room.

"Where you going?" asked Frankie.

When Iz didn't respond, Frankie knew to let her be for a bit. She was cool that way.

the lost boys

Finn willed himself not to look back at his mother. The thread that bound them grew thin again, so taut it would snap any minute. He longed to turn his head one last time, sear her image into his mind. But he knew if he did, he'd run to her, force the water to give way against him as he raced. He had to let his mother go, as she had to release him, release herself.

The surge rose higher, curling fingers reaching for Finn, stroking his skin.

Finn knew it was selfish to want his mother to stay. It wasn't her time. His sister needed to be in the world of the living. So Finn continued walking away.

The trees above him swayed and groaned against the strengthening wind. He would try to return to Sea View, search for Jack and his friends. But he had never seen Jack disappear like that before. Had he returned to Sea View? Perhaps Finn would find him there. Perhaps Sea-Mother had forgotten her Sea-Child, and Finn could stay with the Lost Boys.

The roar of the wind grew louder, disorienting. Was it the wind?

Come, my child.
    Where have you been?

Sea-Mother's roar became a whisper.

I have missed you.

Finn strained against the wind and water, searching for his glass tower rising above the treetops. The rain obscured his sight, so all he could see were vague shapes pierced by needles of glass.

Return to me, child,
    and we will be together forever.

Sound was deadened by the deluge, blinding flashes of light, and her voice.

We will be parted no more.

Finn gave in to her caress, knowing it was the only form of comfort available to him now. As the salt water entered his mouth and nose, it diffused so they again became one. His ears roared with a maternal ache now satisfied.

Sea-Mother enveloped him,
    pulled him deeper,
        down into the quiet
    where she crooned and coaxed.
Her voice now guttural gloops
    liquid clots
        bursting and bubbling,
    lulling him to stillness . . .

clementine

"What the hell just happened?" asked Lou, pale and shaking.

"We need to go, now." Clem walked to the driver's seat of the truck. "I'm driving."

"You're not in a state—"

Clem looked over at Lou's bloodshot eyes and ashen face; he had never looked so vulnerable. "I'm in a better state than you are."

Lou looked down, arms dangling by his sides.

Clem sat and gripped the steering wheel with both hands. She stared at the rain-soaked windshield that blurred the world before them, so she wasn't certain in which world she now existed. Trying to ignore Lucille's cries, Clem struggled to start the engine. Miraculously, it spluttered to life.

Lou dragged himself to the truck and sat in the passenger seat, his face slack. "I don't understand what happened back there."

Clem didn't know how to explain it. Every time she'd ever talked to him about hearing Finn in the water, Lou had looked at her with concern, sometimes even fear. She remembered when she was a little girl and told her father that her mother kissed her good night every evening before she fell asleep.

Ridiculous! His face had been hard and drained of color, his voice stern. *You're dreaming. Stop this foolishness and grow up. Your mother is dead, and nothing will bring her back to us.* He had left the room that day and avoided her as best he could ever since.

"Clem?" Lou had turned in his seat to face her, his features so close to those of her father that she recoiled. How had she not noticed before?

"Did you not see them?" she whispered.

"Who?"

She couldn't face his disbelief, couldn't afford to give him justification to doubt her sanity, to give *herself* reason to question it. "I just had to say goodbye."

Sighing, Lou raked his hands through his sodden hair.

She couldn't explain any of this, couldn't reconcile her constant need for Finn with the life she had hoped to live with Lou. And now Finn was gone for good? What was left? Her daughter, the child she and Lou had made together. The child she had to protect, from Lou's anger and distrust, from the world that could be such a terrible place.

"It's over," she said with finality. He would never accept her for who she was, for the gift she had, or the curse.

"I hope so," Lou said from behind his hands. "It's about time."

A familiar tightness gripped Clem's chest, and she tightened her hold on the steering wheel. "I mean us. This was never going to work."

Lou's stare dug into her flesh. "We got *married* yesterday."

"I'm sorry. I think it was a mistake." Her words fizzed in her mouth as she forced them out.

"Okay, so I fucked up." He kept his voice calm, but panic lurked underneath. "It was a blip. It won't happen again."

"It will."

Lou rose up and growled his fear and anguish at her. "Everyone fucks up. Look at you back there! You almost got us killed. You're losing it again, Clem."

Her hands vibrated on the steering wheel. She held on tighter to stop herself from exiting the car then and there. She imagined running into the rain and wind, but how would they survive out there in the storm alone?

Lou's voice was low. "Look. We're both in a state. We're in the middle of a hurricane, for God's sake. Let's wait to make any life-changing decisions."

Clem knew he was right, in that the priority for the moment was to get to safety. She began navigating the floodwaters, praying they'd make it through. She doubted they'd get to Lou's sister's in Houston. They'd probably need to check into a motel or something. That was her immediate goal, to keep her daughter safe.

They drove in silence, Lou staring out the passenger window, his leg jiggling. As Clem waited for the cars ahead to move forward, she stared at her whitened knuckles gripping the steering wheel. The ring on her finger glared in a flash of lightning.

Lou's eldest sister, Jean, had given it to Lou to give to Clementine, since he hadn't been able to afford to buy one yet. It was a family heirloom, and Jean had made it clear that Clem must be very careful with it.

Clementine knew Jean was wary and protective of Lou after everything that had happened. He had become a father before he was ready and had panicked at being capable of making the same mistakes his own father had. Then when Finn had died, Clem's complete rejection of Lou was unforgivable to Jean. She didn't understand.

Clem didn't need to remove the ring to recall the engraving Lou had inscribed on the inside of the band: *The tie that binds us.* It referenced a lyric from a Johnny Cash song, one Lou sang to her in the night when she woke, panicked from another nightmare about her father. She glanced over at Lou, whose head bobbed with approaching sleep.

The traffic on Interstate 10 was stalled for miles, though most people had been smart and evacuated earlier. Rain pounded the windshield, and the wipers swept back and forth ineffectually, their rhythm a heartbeat. Clem focused on the red brake lights in front of her, fighting to concentrate on pressing her foot down every few minutes as her mind took her to other places.

Absent fathers—it was something she and Lou had bonded over from the beginning.

"I never really knew him," Lou had told her when they were first getting to know each other. "He abandoned us all when we were still young, just disappeared one day. I had to help my mom raise my sisters until they were grown enough to take care of themselves."

Clem had understood then where Lou's nurturing side came from, that ingrained responsibility to take care of those he loved.

"I guess maybe I resented it at times, not being able to party with my friends, no time for girls. I had to grow up pretty quick. Perhaps that's why I tried to make up for what I missed once I was out on my own.

"But being just me and my sisters, it made us all real close, and that means a lot."

Clem had thought of her own family, or lack thereof. "I think I was almost the opposite." The loss of Clem's own mother had left her father an empty shell who had nothing left to give, especially to a daughter whom he blamed for that loss. "My father ignored me, but my *niñera* spoiled me rotten. I suppose she was trying to make up for me having a dead mother and a father who wished it was her who had been spared rather than me."

Lou had held her until all the anguish rose to the surface for the first time and poured out of her like poison lanced from an infected wound. His strength and love had absorbed the pain of not having parents who loved her.

Why does the past haunt us? Absent fathers, lost children, broken women. *How can I bring another child into this world without her father? But she's better off without him, isn't she? And me? I've done it before, first as a daughter and then as a mother.*

Clem remembered the ache when Lou was away on the rigs, the letters they'd written for months and months. And when he spent a few months in jail, she had stopped answering his letters, vowing never to see him again. It had been a struggle, but after Finn died, she hadn't cared about anything anymore. It had been easy to reject Lou then. But he had worked so hard to win her back and regain her trust.

Clem glanced at Lou sleeping next to her, the man she finally thought she deserved but who had let her down again and again. His head lolled to the movement of the car, his mouth slack. The weight of his need for her filled the space with a dull thrum, like an electric shock that immobilized her with its leaden current. She'd always thought his need meant he loved her, but now she wasn't so sure. She'd misjudged him. Dorie and Earle had been right: she should never have taken him back.

Lou awoke with a snort and sat up straight, unaware at

first of his surroundings. His hair was still damp, the ends matted and crusted with salt. He rubbed his eyes and looked at Clem, who focused only on the road ahead.

"How long was I asleep?" His voice was groggy.

"Awhile. We'll be in Houston soon."

"Want me to take over driving?"

Clem rubbed her neck. "Yeah."

Lou reached over and began rubbing her shoulders, but she shook him off. "Not while I'm driving. I need to stay alert."

He stopped but left his hand on her shoulder. "I'm sorry."

She didn't look at him, didn't want him to see the expression in her eyes, her doubt. "I was thinking maybe we should stop at a motel for the night. We don't want to be on the road when the hurricane hits."

"Pull over and let me drive. I think we can make it to Jean's before then."

rennie

The wind bellowed like a creature readying for a fight. Rennie watched from the deck as a heaving mass of water tore away six-foot dunes. A front-row house nearby swayed and leaned, foundations buckling and pulling like rotten teeth. Wooden pilings snapped, brittle as bones, and the house toppled.

Rennie stood rooted to the spot, his body tense with fear—and awe. Entire domiciles teetered and sank into the ever-widening maw. It swallowed them whole or chewed and ground as it devoured all in its path. The storm's choking breath turned into screams.

The throat of the beast spat out the remains of the house in front, which now rode the water toward Rennie. He ran into the living room just as a slow, deep groan preceded a guttural rip. The deck pulled away from the house. He had to get to the roof fast.

Squeezing his way through the attic window, he was fully exposed to the storm's wrath. Wind roared and lifted a corner of the rooftop. Rennie huddled on the remains, the wind and rain blinding him to an adversary he feared he couldn't beat.

He clung to an air vent as the rest of the roof pulled away, and he was rapidly carried into the night. Rennie scrambled to unbuckle his belt and fasten it around the vent; perhaps it would raise his chances.

Or else they'd find him dead.

Rennie floated on the roof for what felt like hours. He forced himself to block out the terror that roared like an avenging angel.

Instead, he focused on Izzie, fighting to stay alive for her. He had been there when she was born, when she sucked in her first breath. Her mother had been exhausted after a long labor, and Izzie's father had hovered in the corner of the hospital room, panic oozing from every pore. His hand had shaken as he cut the umbilical cord. He passed his daughter to Rennie almost as soon as she was placed in her father's arms.

Rennie had known he would not be sticking around for long. She was his now, his to protect and love.

The chasm below him spit up black bile that burrowed deep into his blood. A body floated face down in the water, hair tangled with seaweed and limp grasses torn from the dunes. *Izzie, is that you? Hold on tight now. Don't let go. Just keep holding on. That's right . . . that's right . . .*

He was so tired, his hands cramped, smelting ore from bone so his fingers were metallic vises. Rennie closed his eyes, his body growing limp. He mustn't sleep, but he couldn't open his eyes to the dark again. It entered him, and he gave in to it.

It tore his tattered flesh, slashed him so he was an open wound, rancid and weeping a sorrow carried by the screaming world. Teeth gnawed at bone until brittle shards eroded and everything was cartilage and flesh and gristle. Blood and piss escaped his body, warm against his thigh in the cold, dead water. He dreamed streams of clear liquid and gulped it down, spitting salt curses and retching fetid oceanbile from his lungs.

Quiet now. An opaque hollow place.

But the howling returned, filling his head with rage . . .

Iz? Iz?

Grasping for her hand . . . he forced his eyes open . . .

Gone.

She was gone. He cried out her name, over and over, but that, too, was swallowed by the insatiable beast.

All was lost.

clementine

Clem and Lou pulled up to Jean's house around ten that night, tense and exhausted from the drive.

They had attempted to find a hotel to stay in rather than risk the flooded streets. The first one they tried was fully booked, and after checking a couple more, they realized everywhere was bursting at the seams with people fleeing the storm.

Lou took over driving, insisting he could make it to Jean's. The local radio had warned of increasing intensity and recommended finding shelter as soon as possible. Clem wrapped her arms around her middle and forced herself to take deep, slow breaths.

Jean had called twice already to check on their progress. Clem wondered if she knew why they'd gotten a late start. Had Lou called her in frustration when he didn't know where Clem was? Probably. They were close and seemed to have a codependent sort of relationship, from what she could tell. When Lou was in jail, Jean had been the only one to visit him, and she'd done so every week without fail.

The back streets were worse off than the freeway. Lou had to turn around a couple of times to avoid high water, though the food truck was tall enough off the ground to handle some of the less flooded spots. Luckily, he was familiar with the area and found alternate routes, so they arrived just before the worst hit.

Turning off the truck engine, Lou grabbed their overnight bags, while Clem held the cat carrier. She followed him to the front porch, where a light shone brightly. Jean answered the door almost immediately.

"Come in, come in. Thank God you made it! You must be so tired. There's dinner I can heat up real quick in the microwave."

Lou put the bags down in the hallway and hugged his sister. Clem hovered nervously, holding Lucille's carrier close to her chest as meows emanated from within.

"Oh." Jean released Lou. "You have a cat." She backed away a little. "I'm afraid you'll have to keep it caged in your room while you're here. I'm allergic." Clem nodded. "Follow me." Jean walked toward the hallway. "Lou, why don't you go on into the kitchen and say hello to Steve. Get something to eat."

Jean led Clementine down a dim corridor to a bedroom at the far end. "Here you go," she whispered, reminding Clementine that there were three sleeping boys in the house. She opened the door to a small bedroom with two twin beds. An array of stuffed toys filled a bookcase, and a wooden railroad set was spread over much of the floor. "The two youngest are piled into Jeff's room—our eldest. Sorry about the tight squeeze."

Putting Lucille's carrier at the foot of the bed, Clem tried to quiet her.

Jean waited by the bedroom door. "I hope she won't be like that the whole time."

"I can stay here while you go back to your family," Clem said. "I'm so tired, I wouldn't mind just going to bed."

"Nonsense. You must be starving. Come on." Jean held the door for Clem, who reluctantly followed her to the kitchen.

Steve and Lou were already eating what looked like pot roast. As Clem and Jean joined them at the table, Clem realized she was indeed starving.

"Now, you make yourselves at home and stay as long as you need to." Jean looked only at Lou as she spoke.

Clem hoped that wouldn't be too long. Once the storm had passed, they could leave and head back to the peninsula and their rental by the bay.

The three of them talked about the latest predictions for the storm. Clem watched them as if from behind a window. They made no attempt to include her in the conversation—not that she minded much. She just wanted to be alone in bed and drift off to sleep, forgetting about everything for a few hours.

Jean stood to refill Lou's bowl. "Want some more, Clementine?" Her tone was so different from when she spoke to Lou, formal and clipped, as if the words were rehearsed.

Clem shook her head. "I'd really just like to head to bed, if that's okay?"

"Of course," said Jean.

Lou dug into his second bowl. "I'll be in soon."

Steve stood. "Think I'll call it a night too. Once this storm really gets going, sleep may be out of the question. Night, all."

Clem was relieved to have the bedroom to herself for a bit. Opening the door, she went straight to Lucille, who was still crying. She needed to reassure her cat that she hadn't abandoned her, so she opened the door to the carrier and gently pulled Lucille out. The cat immediately rested her head on Clem's chest as Clem hugged Lucille close.

Tiptoeing over to the bed, Clem almost dropped Lucille as she stepped on something. "Ouch! Dammit!" Bending down, she picked up a small wooden train painted with a smiley face beaming. After placing it on a nearby shelf next to a blue stuffed rabbit, she lay down on the bed, carefully holding Lucille.

"You okay, sweetheart?" Lucille purred and relaxed on Clem's chest.

The rain and wind hadn't reached their peak yet, but Clem knew it wouldn't be long now. A storm was much like childbirth: brewing quietly and then rising to a crescendo of intensity, until it finally ebbed to quiet, almost as if it had never been.

Except childbirth resulted in a new life, while she suddenly understood that this storm could end in the loss of lives. She had lost Finn a second time because of it. How many others would lose people they loved? Agnes and Earle had insisted on staying at their beloved ranch, convinced it wouldn't be dangerous. What were they tackling now? And Dorie—was she safely tucked up with Rennie and his family? She prayed they would all stay safe.

Clem focused on Lucille's rhythmic purring, and the room slowly slipped away.

She wasn't sure how long she'd been asleep, but when she woke, it seemed that Lou still hadn't come to bed. She listened for his breath but heard only the wind outside. Her throat was dry and raw, parched from the harrowing trip, and she realized she'd been so hungry, she'd forgotten to drink anything at dinner.

Leaving Lucille asleep under the bedcovers, Clem slipped on her robe. Then she crept quietly out of the room toward the kitchen, making sure not to wake the boys.

"I really thought she was doing better, but she completely lost it today." Lou spoke as if afraid of his words.

"What do you mean?" asked Jean.

Clem stopped still outside the kitchen and listened.

Lou sighed and then paused before speaking. "She hasn't mentioned Finn in a while now. But she disappeared on one of her walks today and came back in a state. She actually thought she'd found him."

"Found him?"

"I mean, people seem to forget that I lost a child too. And I don't go around talking to ghosts."

"I told you to wait and see if she—"

"It's been over four years, Jeanie."

"Have you considered maybe she's just . . . broken?"

There was a pause. Clem waited for more.

"We're all broken, somehow or other."

"Speak for yourself," Jean said defensively.

"I spent time in jail. I abandoned my kid—"

"That was an accident. You are not a bad man, Lou Walker."

"It wasn't an accident. I lost my temper and beat the shit out of a man."

"He deserved it."

"He didn't deserve being put in a coma and almost dying because of me."

"That part was an accident."

"Jean, I appreciate you always having my back, but I have a habit of losing it when I drink too much."

"So don't drink so much."

Silence filled the kitchen.

"She told me today that our marriage is a mistake." His voice was so low, Clem found herself leaning closer to the kitchen door.

"Perhaps it is," said Jean.

"Don't say that!" A chair scraped on the kitchen floor. "I can't lose her. I'll do whatever it takes to fix this."

Clem turned and walked quickly and quietly down the hallway back to their room, her heart pounding. She lay down in bed and pulled the covers over herself. Jean would hate her even more. Perhaps that was for the best, an ally to the dissolution of her and Lou's life together.

Lou entered the room. "Clem? You awake?"

She ignored his whisper; instead, she feigned sleep until he got into the other twin bed and began to snore softly almost immediately. Clem lay with her eyes open, listening to the intensity of the storm grow along with her own churning doubts and confusion, until finally she drifted off.

Pete

When Pete realized he'd made the wrong decision, he had two choices: keep drinking into oblivion or stop drinking now and use all his will to stay alive.

He had fallen asleep to the sounds of wind and rain, but it looked real bad out there now. Still, his boat would hold; *Wayward Angel* and he always stuck together, and if he chose to fight this goddamn storm, she would too.

Taking a long swig of whiskey, he hunkered down on the floor of the tiny cabin. Pete thought of his kids, especially Addie. God help her if he was her role model.

Pete took another swallow and stood unsteadily. It had been a while since he'd checked outside, but from the lurching of the boat, he knew it had gotten worse. Opening the door to the deck was like exposing a portal to another realm—a tempest of darkness and mayhem.

For the first time, he worried he might not make it. The raging sea had risen so much, he couldn't get his bearings—land and buildings were submerged underwater. Holding the whiskey bottle in one hand, he grasped the deck railing with the other to try to steady himself.

"You ain't gonna get me, you bastard!" He broke into a drunken song, which he screamed into the wind, competing with its wails and shrieks. His silver hair loosened from its bindings. His earring shone with each flash of lightning that illuminated the sky with gold-foil creases. He kept singing and staggering to keep his footing on the slick deck.

Breathless, he hugged the half-empty whiskey bottle to his chest and closed his eyes. Addie's sweet voice pleaded with him to come home. He wanted to watch her grow up, wanted to be the father she deserved.

"Goddamn you!" he screamed, hurling the bottle into the storm.

Pete made his way back to the cabin, forcing himself against the strengthening wind as the storm fought to claim another soul. He slammed the cabin door shut, muffling the madness outside.

Taking a deep breath, Pete reached for the life jacket, only to fumble with the straps and eventually give up in frustration. Instead, he lit a cigarette and waited, trusting in his *Angel* as she heaved and shuddered against the storm.

rennie

It was the stillness that prodded him back to consciousness. And the wet drops falling on his face from above.

Rennie forced his eyes open, but they wouldn't widen further than slits. After several moments, vague silhouettes emerged.

Was that land?

Scrabbling at his belt with numb fingers that fumbled and failed, Rennie eventually managed to unfasten it from the vent to which he'd secured himself. Once free, he crawled over floating tree limbs, cars, and other forms he refused to acknowledge.

Finally, he reached firm ground that rose above the water. Exhausted, he collapsed and closed his eyes once more.

Hints of daylight pulled him from a dreamless sleep. Uncurling, he groaned as every part of his body screamed.

Standing unsteadily, Rennie surveyed his surroundings. Endless piles of trash covered the ground—refrigerators, chairs and tables, wood broken and scarred . . .

He stopped looking when he caught sight of a hand protruding from a car buried under a mound of debris. It was too big to be her hand, but it belonged to a father, brother, uncle, or son.

Closing his eyes, he tried to breathe only through his mouth. He had to keep going, keep fighting through the rain and wind, the surreal terrain. His entire body ached, so he limped and loped like an injured animal. But he climbed and slipped and crawled until his hands bled and his legs cramped. Rennie's lungs heaved in the stink of death, but he focused only on the path ahead, leading to those he loved.

After a while, another sound permeated the constant drone of the rain, a rhythmic rumble. Stopping, he listened, even as exhaustion fogged his mind. A bright light pierced the dimness of the world, illuminating the horrors before him—cow carcasses, overturned trucks, beds that had once served pleasant dreams, only to become part of this nightmare.

Did I fail? Rennie wondered, staring at the light. *Am I finally dead, to be invited to join the angels?*

Pete

Pete must have passed out. When he woke, the wind had calmed to an eerie moan, each syllable a malediction against the world. Head pounding, he drank from a bottle of water. All around him, water and sky merged into one, enclosing him in a cavernous space that numbed his senses.

Am I dreaming? Or perhaps I'm dead, and this is hell. No reason, certainly, to assume he'd be let into the other place.

In the unnatural stillness and quiet, his eyes slowly adjusted, and he could make out objects floating on the surface of the water, sodden and swollen. As he peered deeper into the darkness, a flash of lightning revealed flotsam and . . . in its center . . . a sea monster, its serpentine neck stretched tall and black, ready to strike.

Pete scrambled unsteadily for the steering wheel, head pounding harder. Hands shaking, he turned the ignition key, but over and over, his *Angel* sputtered. Pete looked over his shoulder to find the serpent drawing closer, increasing in size with every second that passed.

"Come on, darlin'. Don't give up on me now!"

He turned the key again as the inky water drew him closer and closer to the monster. Terror consumed him as the beast's slick alabaster skin gleamed with every flash. Then the monster hovered, swaying slightly as it patiently awaited its prey.

Pete closed his eyes tight to the sound of scraping and cracking, as the bones of his *Angel* were broken apart.

Yet they were not devoured by the beast.

When Pete opened his eyes, the monster stood solid and still. As he watched, it morphed into the lighthouse, standing partially submerged in front of him.

His *Angel* had delivered him as he'd known she would.

Dropping anchor, Pete grabbed his supplies and pulled himself over the side of the boat. He swam toward the lighthouse, humming quietly between ragged breaths to distract himself from anything that brushed against his legs. The surge pulled and nudged, dragging him off course, so when he finally reached the rusted exterior, he was exhausted.

Only then did Pete realize he was in between levels of the tower's windows. He'd have to either climb up to reach a window above him or dive down and find an opening below. He wasn't sure he had the strength to do either.

Pete became aware of a stirring in the water and the sound of sea song—not the soothing gentleness of his days on his *Angel* but the haunting echoes of past lives calling to him.

Fuck it.

Pete dove into the water. Blinded by the muck within it, he reached frantically for the tower, forcing aside objects he was glad he couldn't see. Finally, he brushed its rough surface like a caress.

Come on, darlin'. Show me the way.

As if multiple hands had grabbed him and pulled, he

tumbled through an opening and into the innards of the tower. Returning to the surface, he gasped for breath and opened his eyes to shades and shadows that slowly dissipated into nothingness.

With the last of his strength, he climbed the steps to the top of the tower. He stood shakily, witnessing the chaotic landscape before him. He could see much of the surrounding area this high up, though most everything was covered in seawater like a black tarp.

Voices seemed to burst forth in time with the reawakening wind—cries of loneliness and despair. Pete covered his ears and closed his eyes, but nothing could block out the wretchedness forcing itself upon him.

His cries joined those beyond the lighthouse, a song of the dead. He fell to his knees as the wind wailed and the water swelled. That's when he knew the eye of the storm had passed and the worst was yet to come.

He remembered stories of the bodies found at the base of the lighthouse after the 1900 hurricane. He remembered the hundred souls who had been saved, squeezed onto the staircase that wound within the tower.

Standing, he turned to his boat, which remained anchored near the railings. "Stay safe," he whispered hoarsely. Then he went inside to share that sacred space provided to him by his *Angel.*

All night, Pete fell in and out of sleep, unsure of what was real and what was a nightmare. Screeches bellowed from outside the tower as plates of iron were ripped from the body like flayed flesh. Wind whistled through the windows and echoed throughout the brick walls, so Pete felt part of a ghostly union.

Flashes of lightning revealed shadows that moved with purpose. They crept toward him as he shivered with fear. Once, he woke to a hand caressing his cheek, gentle and cold. But these souls had saved him from the storm. He surely had nothing to fear.

Closing his eyes again, he gave in to the darkness.

clementine

Clem didn't know what time it was when she was awakened by a crash outside the bedroom window. They must have lost power, because the digital clock was out and the usual white noise of the air conditioner was missing. She had fallen asleep to murmurs from the kitchen that were mostly lost in the sounds of moaning and whistling from outside. As her eyes adjusted to the pitch black of the room, she saw Lou wasn't in the other bed.

Cries came from the hallway outside. Presumably the boys were awake.

Lou rushed into the room. "You okay?"

Clem was still groggy from interrupted sleep. "What's going on?"

"A tree fell outside, hit part of the house. I was worried you might be hurt."

Sitting up, she rubbed her eyes.

"It's bad out there. Power is out everywhere, and there's no cell phone service."

Clem heard Jean attempting to calm the boys. Getting

out of bed, Clem put on her robe, and they headed to the kitchen, where Jean was handing out snacks to appease her sons. The youngest, Henry, sat in a high chair, looking bewildered by the hubbub. Ben, the middle boy, stared at Clem with large, frightened eyes, tears still fresh on his flushed cheeks. And Jeff, who couldn't have been more than six or seven, quietly ate a cookie, concentrating on licking the icing off one half.

"I'll make some coffee." Jean lit the gas stove and put on a kettle of water to boil. "Just instant, I'm afraid."

Steve had gathered some flashlights and spread them about the room so pockets of light beamed on each face like spotlights. He sat with the boys and distracted them by making shadow puppets on the white walls.

Clem wondered at the domesticity before her amid the mess outside—a protected golden bubble of family love. Would she ever have that? She'd almost had it back when Lou and Finn were her family, a family that ate together, played, argued some, and laughed lots.

But it hadn't lasted.

Now she was being given a second chance. She knew without a doubt that she wanted to be a mother again—but a wife? That decision was far more complicated.

Jean held out a mug to Clem. "Coffee?" Her animosity hid underneath a layer of propriety. She was careful not to push too hard against Clem lest she alienate Lou.

"Thanks." Clem took the mug and savored the comforting smell.

"Bunny!" shouted Henry.

Steve had somehow made ears and a twitching nose shadow that hopped across the kitchen wall.

"No, that's a donkey," Jeff corrected.

"Kitty!" Ben cried out.

Jeff frowned at the shadow puppets. "That's not a cat—"

"There!" Ben jumped out of his chair and ran toward the kitchen door.

Clem caught sight of Lucille's tail as she ran in fright from the overly excited child. She must have forgotten to close the bedroom door, and Lucille had ventured out of the room to explore her strange, new surroundings, even more out of sorts due to the storm. Clem glanced over at Jean, who was already fuming.

"Ben, get back here this instant. I don't want you out of my sight. You hear me?" She chased after Ben as he followed in hot pursuit of Lucille.

Mortified, Clem looked at Lou.

"It's okay." Standing, he placed a hand on her shoulder before exiting the kitchen. "Back in a minute."

Lou called for Lucille, and Ben squealed with delight. Only low mumbles came from Jean, who Clem assumed was complaining about the cat being loose.

No longer playing shadow puppets with the other two boys, Steve cupped a mug in his hands. "Looks like Ike is worse than they predicted."

Jean came back in. "We don't know that for sure. There's no way to get any news right now. Hopefully, the power will come back on soon, and we can check then."

Lou followed with Ben, who was still trying to convince them to let him play with the now-contained kitty. Getting out his cell phone, Lou tried to get service, but all communication was down.

Suddenly, the room grew quiet.

"Is it over?" Jeff asked hopefully.

"'Fraid not, son. I think we're in the eye of the storm," said Steve.

Ben looked out the window. "The eye?" He looked terrified, as if afraid he would find a giant eye peering at them through the curtains.

Lou spoke up quickly. "That just means it's the quiet part of the storm, like it's resting for a bit."

"Like in time-out?"

Lou smiled. "Sort of."

"But it'll wake up again and open its eyes and be madder and madder?"

Lou shook his head. "Not exactly, but it will start back up again for a while. Don't worry, we're safe and sound here inside."

All three boys looked doubtful. The fallen tree's limbs were visible against the den window. Their leaves pounded a constant rhythm on the glass as if determined to break in.

A wave of nausea suddenly washed over Clem, and she rushed to the bathroom. Her morning sickness with Finn had been bad in the beginning.

Lou was waiting outside the bathroom door when she exited. "Not feeling well?"

Clem grimaced. "Must have been something I ate."

Lou stayed silent for what seemed like minutes. His eyes bored into hers, extracting the truth. "When were you going to tell me?"

"Tell you what?"

Lou moved toward her. "You're pregnant, right?"

Clem stuttered. "I'm not sure."

"I know what you look like pregnant, Clem. I was there last time, remember?"

Clem remained silent.

"Why do you always do this? Why do you push me away all the time? You did it with Finn, and you're doing it now. How long have you known?"

"I have my reasons." She spat the words out. "Like you being gone most of the time while I was pregnant with Finn. And after, for that matter. You being thrown in jail. You breaking your promise about staying sober—"

"Me? It's always my fault!" Lou's voice rose in the quiet of the house, and Clem became aware of others who might be listening, judging. "Don't kid yourself. You've been like this ever since I met you, and probably before, I'm guessing. Even when we were happy in the beginning, you would hole up in your room to paint or breastfeed Finn—and your endless walks. It always seemed like you preferred to be away from me than with me."

"I just need my time alone," Clem said quietly. "It doesn't mean I didn't want to be with you."

"And then the ultimate rejection—not telling me my *son* died. Running away from me and the rest of the world, from those who cared about you, who loved you."

Clem couldn't bear to be reminded of that time—all those months of wandering and searching for her boy in the waves, a purgatory of torment. But she was better now. She knew what she needed to do.

When she looked up at Lou, he had tears in his eyes. He moved closer to her. In a low voice, his words carried on breath that grazed her skin. "I refuse to give up. I won't. I love you."

Clem felt the heft of him, his contours close to hers, his scent, which she craved.

Lou continued. "And you love me too. I know it. You just haven't figured out how to do that quite yet." He leaned toward her, his eyes determined, as if willing her to agree. "But you will. I have to believe you will."

Perhaps she did love him, but that wasn't enough.

He reached for her. "What's important is that we're

bringing another life into this world. And we'll do it right this time. We'll be a family and raise our child together." He was smiling gently now, his hand on her shoulder.

Clem stepped back. "How? We don't know how to do that. I can never let what happened before happen again."

"It won't. It was an accident."

"It was my fault. I wasn't paying attention. He wouldn't have drowned if I'd been watching him like a good mother. I don't know how to be a good mother. And you don't know how to be a good father. And together . . ." She shook her head slowly and looked down, not able to say aloud that it was hopeless.

"You were a wonderful mother, Clem. And I know I've made mistakes, but I was a good father. We were young then. We've been through so much. We can do this, together."

"Look at us, though. You got in a drunken brawl with Rennie at our wedding two days ago. And the reason we're both standing here now is because of our dead son." Her voice cracked. "It's just too much."

Lou sighed. "Please don't give up on me. I promise I'll do better."

"How?"

"Whatever you want."

Clem knew that Lou's good intentions weren't enough anymore. "It's not my place to tell you how to fix this. You need to figure that out for yourself."

Clem turned and walked into the bedroom, quietly shutting the door on Lou. She needed a friend so badly and longed to call Dorie, but the lines were still down, making it impossible.

Rubbing her stomach, she willed herself to stay calm for the baby's sake.

The house seemed to grow smaller by the hour. She needed to get away from Lou and Jean and the stifling domesticity of their home. But she was stuck here. So instead, she lay down with Lucille. Accompanied by Lucille's purring, Clem hummed quietly to her daughter until they all settled into an uneasy sleep.

agnes and earle

Flames from candles placed throughout the room cast quivering shadows that licked the walls, syncopated by the rattling windows and howling wind. Rain drummed on the plywood boards. The house swayed on its skinny pilings in time with the arcing palms, a ritualistic ghost dance. Even the electrical poles listed in the strengthening gale, bowing to its power.

"Agnes, I'm going to the attic. I need to see how it looks out there." Earle wondered how long the boards would hold as the wind ripped and tore. Agnes didn't reply but held her small leather-bound Bible in her hands, her lips moving silently, eyes closed.

Pulling on the cord to the attic, Earle unfolded the rickety stairs. As he climbed, his arthritic joints complained with each step, and he had to push aside a stab of fear. A tiny ventilation window in the roof seemed too small to emit the beastly growls and shrieks that rattled Earle's bones. He followed flashes of lightning across the attic and pulled hard at the slats of the ventilation window, rainwater drenching his face and making him half blind. Wiping his eyes with his sleeve, he stretched tall to reach his head above the rooftop.

An endless ocean spread before him, churning and foul, erasing the world he knew. Cars swirled and roamed as the current pushed and pulled. A rooftop floated past, brushing against the house so it groaned and shook. A flash of lightning revealed shapes floating in the water, thin and pale as rag dolls.

Earle recalled a passage in the Bible, the flood that was God's punishment: *And all flesh died that moved upon the earth, both of fowl, and of cattle, and of beast, and of every creeping thing that creepeth upon the earth, and every man: All in whose nostrils was the breath of life, of all that was in the dry land, died.* Earle prayed to Agnes's God, begging to understand why he was destroying his beloved creation.

The water level rose higher, until it reached above the pilings of the house.

"Earle, waters comin' in." Agnes's voice was small and far away, lost in the sound of the world's end. "Where's Mabel? Mabel. Kitty, kitty?"

Earle descended the stairs, sloshing through the deluge that covered his ankles as he made his way to Agnes. By the time he'd scooped her out of the wheelchair, the water had risen almost to his knees. Wading now, he struggled to hold his wife, as frail as she was. She slipped like a fish from his grasp, and he grabbed for her again before she went under. Staggering up the stairs, he carried her shaking body and placed her carefully on their bed.

"Think it'll make it up here?" Her eyes were wide, her skin pallid and dripping.

Earle sat next to her and gently wiped her face with his handkerchief. She held her Bible out to him, and he stared at its sodden cover, suddenly afraid of what it might hold in its swollen pages.

Placing it gently on the bed, Agnes looked up at the ceiling, her eyes glazed, her voice firm. "God is our refuge and strength, a very present help in trouble." Earle watched her lips closely, hearing her words collide with the storm outside. "Therefore will not we fear, though the earth be removed, and though the mountains be carried into the midst of the sea."

Opening the drawer of the bedside table, Earle removed a pen and wrote on his forearm.

Agnes stopped her prayer. "What you doin' there?"

Earle took Agnes's arm and gently wrote her full name onto her skin. She looked down at it and then saw Earle's name written in block letters on his own arm.

"So they'll know who we are should the worst happen. Which it won't."

Earle lay down and gently pulled Agnes to him, her head resting on his shoulder, soft white hair tickling his nose. How could their God do such a thing? Or was this the devil's work? A hollow pit expanded in his chest.

Agnes picked up where she had left off. "Though the waters thereof roar and be troubled, though the mountains shake with the swelling thereof."

Mabel meowed from underneath the bed. Jumping up, she purred as she rubbed against them, as if it were a normal night, a normal storm. Earle closed his eyes and let the cadence of Agnes's voice slow his breathing. He thought of her when they first met. Her legs had been lithe and strong as she mounted her favorite horse, Levi. And when he'd first seen her ride, he'd known he would spend the rest of his life loving her. And if she loved him back, he'd make sure he deserved her.

Mabel nestled between them, still purring loudly, and Earle listened to Agnes recite in a voice that fought against the wailing wind: "The LORD of hosts is with us; the God of Jacob is our refuge." Earle willed the words to be a blessing and not a curse, willed himself to believe as she did and accept God's plan.

Earle and Agnes clasped hands. The house cried out in rage and anguish as it was ripped from its foundation. The maelstrom outside raised its voice, drowning Agnes out. Until slowly, the house tilted and rode the back of a towering wave.

the aftermath

pete

It was the silence that woke Pete. His body ached along with his head. He opened his eyes to a dismal pallor that crept in through the narrow windows of the lighthouse.

He unfolded himself from the iron stairs where he had slept, the spiral staircase twisting above and below him, refracting light. Pete stood slowly, his neck cricked from his half-sitting position. Stretching his arms and legs, he ascended the staircase, each turn bringing him closer to the platform at the top of the tower.

A simpering gray sky crouched low, as if ashamed to expose the destruction it had been part of just hours before. Spread before him was a desertscape, belied only by the lashes of water that marked the saturated sand. He barely recognized the peninsula. Surely he'd been carried by the wind and dropped into some alien place.

Everything was a surreal version of itself. No roads delineated direction, so space was abstracted. Sand covered every surface. Cars and even intact houses had landed haphazardly, like discarded children's toys. Gradually receding water left swatches of green scattered across endless expanses of ochre.

Pete tried in vain to find landmarks he recognized, to orient himself. Leaning over the railing to check the water level at the base of the lighthouse, he saw his *Angel* still anchored below. She tilted as if wounded, her bulk resting awkwardly on the grass.

Pete reentered the tower and descended the spiral, each turn accompanied by a lump in his throat, afraid of what he might find below. He could tell the surge had reached at least nine feet, and the detritus became denser the lower he got—reeds, plastic bottles, carcasses of small animals, a child's doll.

Addie. A stab of pain.

Pete longed to know if his kids were okay, but his cell phone was dead, waterlogged.

At the base of the lighthouse, he pushed at the iron door. It resisted, hinges groaning, so he leaned into it and just managed to squeeze through a narrow gap.

Angel was wedged deep in the sandy soil. Scratches, dents, and cracks marked her battle of the night before. But she had survived, as he had known she would. And thanks to *Angel* and the lighthouse, so had he.

Pete wandered, lost and disoriented, until it occurred to him he had the peninsula to himself. He could lay claim to whatever treasures it might hold. Most houses were either half gone or completely lifted from their foundations, so only the pilings remained, like vulture-picked carrion. However, up ahead, he spied a blue house that beckoned. He quickened his pace, ready for the hunt.

Avoiding gaping holes in the floor, Pete walked into the wrecked living room, where most of the furniture had washed away, leaving little trace of its inhabitants' lives. He took a moment to stare at a car that had washed into the bathroom, its bumper resting against the overturned tub. The stairs remained but led to nowhere. The entire upper floor was gone.

Pete kicked at mounds of wet sand, uncovering a sodden red tee shirt, a flaccid paisley pillow, and even a framed photograph of a family smiling awkwardly at the camera—two boys and their parents in front of a fake tropical backdrop. Pete rubbed at the glass, trying to make out how old the kids were. He knew the sort of people who had family portraits done by professional photographers at the mall.

He did not belong to one of those families. In fact, there were barely any photos of him or his family members. He'd been raised by his aunts, and they hadn't had any fancy cameras around. He could barely remember what they even looked like. Did they ever think of him?

He put the frame on the fireplace mantel, which had somehow remained intact.

Pete kept moving through the house. He checked a closet, reaching up to the highest shelf, where people tended to hide their treasures and secrets. A cardboard shoe box fell to the floor, scattering its contents into pools of water where the ground had buckled.

More photos and some letters by the looks of it. Picking one up, he tried to read it, the ink faded and smudged on the page.

> *Paul got married. Seems like a nice girl. A bit plain, but I hear . . .*

Pete dropped the page back into the water and raised himself onto his toes, straining to reach the very back of the shelf, sweeping his hand back and forth. Another box, plastic this time. Setting it down, he opened the latch.

A pistol surrounded by bullets, black and shining. Now that was more like it.

His fingers nestled around the grip, his index finger resting on the trigger. Holding it up, he aimed at the family photo on the mantel. A loud crack pierced the silence, and the frame shattered and fell to the floor, glass and wood and broken smiles.

Ears ringing, Pete whooped. He fired again and again, swinging the pistol from target to target, until the gun gave an impotent click. Grabbing handfuls of bullets, he shoved them into his pocket. There was even a holster, which he fastened around his waist and slipped the gun into, nice and snug. Then he swaggered out of the house, a satisfied grin on his face.

A kayak was his next lucky find, lodged in a shallow pool of water. No holes. The oars were even tightly packed and tied to the hollow interior. Someone had thought ahead. Pete briefly wondered if the owner had made it out.

Oh, well. One man's loss, another man's gain. Smiling, Pete pulled the boat into a nearby swath of water and got in. He rowed, each stroke bringing him closer to his bounty.

Pete's arms tired quickly. He was used to the grumble of the shrimp boat engine as he stood at the helm, but there was only silence now. Besides, it would take him some time to fix the damage his *Angel* had suffered from Ike.

Pete refocused on the task at hand. There might have been patrols watching for looters, even this early. He'd have to scout the terrain and start collecting before they let homeowners back onto the peninsula. He had maybe a week or two, so he'd have to work fast. He hummed quietly in rhythm to his rowing and the waves that sloshed against the fiberglass hull of the kayak.

Birds scratched the air, black hashtags counting the

dead below. They shrieked overhead, a cry of despair or, perhaps, a warning?

Pete stopped rowing and listened. *Were* those birds? He surveyed the landscape, mostly water and half-submerged forms he could barely make out. Movement in the distance revealed figures in the remains of a half-collapsed house surrounded by water yet to recede.

Moving a little closer, he began to make out cries for help. A small girl sat at the feet of an older boy, who stood waving his arms at Pete. He cupped his hands around his mouth. "Mister! Hey, mister!"

Shit. Better not to have heard that. Pete circled the right oar, turning the boat back toward dry land. He didn't need any kids weighing him down. No way the boat could carry them all anyway.

The cries grew fainter but more frantic as he moved farther away, each one digging deeper into his skin, and he tensed with the effort not to hear. They'd be fine. The Coast Guard would find them soon enough.

When he reached the shore, Pete pulled the kayak onto the sand next to an overturned car, half buried under sand and mud. He made sure the boat was safe before navigating the unfamiliar territory.

Pete trudged for hours across endless stretches of sand, where trenches had been gouged by the floodwaters and mounds rose from discarded lives. Pete fought disorientation as he tried to make out landmarks, but everything had shifted into a nightmare version of itself.

It didn't matter. He wasn't here to mourn. He was here to search for treasure.

With every step he took, he prayed he wouldn't come across a dead body, but he was bound to, wasn't he? He wiped his nose, unable to shake the stink of death, which burrowed deep into his bowels. He wondered how Addie and Shawn had weathered the storm. They might be without power, but hopefully that was the worst of it.

Addie's voice coursed through his head, reprimanding him for leaving the two kids at the ruined house. Her disappointment weighed heavy on him. What would happen when the sun went down? Maybe he *should* go back and pick them up—at least get them onto dry land so they had a chance to rummage for food and water.

Turning, he retraced his steps, his legs dragging as if working against him. When he reached the water, he looked in the direction of the house, straining his eyes to see if the kids were still there.

Nope, he couldn't see them. But maybe they were sheltering in what was left of the house. It resembled one of those dollhouses he'd seen in a fancy store once, its entire front opened up. Addie had put it on her list to Santa, and he'd tried to save enough money to buy it for her. Sadly, the shrimp hadn't been plentiful enough that season.

Pete dragged the boat back into the water, leaving scars on the sand. There he paused, wishing he had a cigarette. Or some whiskey.

Carol's boyfriend at the time had bought the dollhouse instead.

The birds were still shrieking when he stepped into the boat, sitting down as it wobbled on the waves. He pulled the oars through rough-hewn water, steering the boat toward the ruined house.

As he approached, the air fell silent. Was it too late? The water level had receded some. Perhaps they'd swum to shore. Though the little girl . . . she was probably younger even than his Addie, who couldn't swim yet.

Pete had always prided himself on his ability to handle

guilt. It wasn't an emotion he tended to dwell on. However, he couldn't stand the weight of guilt now heavy on his shoulders, slowing his rhythm. The water seemed denser, his muscles tiring as he dragged the oars through the waves, even just the short distance from land to the house.

When he heard the crying, it felt as if he'd discovered Addie herself, rather than one of the children he'd been searching for.

As he drew closer to the house, he could make out the older boy's face more clearly. He stared straight at Pete, sullen and unmoving. Pete pulled his boat as close to the house as he could.

"You wanna ride?"

The girl turned her tearstained face up to her brother, who still didn't move or speak.

Pete picked up the oars again. "Well, if you'd rather stay here, that's fine with me."

The boy lifted his chin. "Why'd you come back?"

Pete shifted in the tight space. "Look, you wanna ride or not?"

The boy stood, and his sister followed, still sniffling. Abruptly, she stopped.

"We can't leave without Scout. Mister, you have to help us find him."

Who the hell was Scout? Not another one—no way he could take another kid.

"My cat—he's lost, and we have to find him." She began walking away, farther into the ruins of the house.

"Get back here. Your cat's gone."

"He's not gone! He's just hiding cuz he's scared." She kept walking, stepping clumsily over various obstacles being tossed by the waves.

Pete assessed what was left of the roof, suspecting it

could collapse any minute. Suddenly, the girl cried out and stumbled to the ground. Her brother rushed over, and Pete scrambled out of the boat and into the house.

Bright red oozed from her shin, where a piece of ragged metal had gouged it. Pete picked up the wailing child and carried her toward the boat. However, in his panic, he hadn't secured it. The kayak was floating away from the house.

Goddamn it! He knew he shouldn't have bothered with these damn kids.

There was no way around it. He'd have to go in.

"Wait here." He handed the girl to her brother. "Make sure she stays put this time." Wading into the water, he swam toward the boat.

Rolag clouds covered the sun, and when he hauled himself over the side of the kayak, he realized the temperature had dropped. He shivered and grunted with every stroke of the oars as he got closer to the kids.

"Get in. You first!" He pointed to the girl. There was no extra space for her to sit, so he had to hold her on his lap as he rowed.

"You can't leave Billy!" She held out her arm as if trying to grab her brother.

"I'll get him in a bit."

"I'm not leaving him. Mama said we mustn't separate. And how will Mama find us if we leave here?" She began squirming to free herself from Pete's grasp, and the boat wobbled.

Billy cried out from the shore. "Bree, stay still. I'll be there real soon."

"Watch it, or you'll fall out and drown like everyone else!" Pete held her tightly as she began to wail, the sound rushing in his ears almost enough for him to let her go. To hell with it—the ungrateful little brat. He rowed quickly, his wet clothes clinging to his body.

Pete finally delivered the girl to dry land. "Don't you move. I'm gonna go get your brother." Pete turned back to the boat. Jesus, what was he doing?

When he reached the house again, Billy was pacing, his gaze riveted to Pete's approach. He rushed toward the boat.

Pete stood. "Wait. I need to find some dry clothes."

"There's none here. Everything's soaked. Besides, Brianna will be worried if we take too long."

"I said I need a change of clothes. It's your fault I got wet in the first place. I was doing just fine before I tried to help y'all out."

Pushing past Billy, Pete made his way over the debris covering the floor. He dug through piles of blankets and sodden clothes until he finally managed to find a waterproof jacket still hanging in a closet. Amazing what things had survived the storm and what hadn't.

He was putting on the jacket when he saw it—a foot shod in a grimy sneaker protruding from under the bed. A body was tangled between sheets and warped carpet. Shit! That must be Mom.

Pete looked back toward where Billy was waiting by the boat. Except he wasn't there. "What the fuck?" Pete scrambled over the rubble.

Billy was rowing away.

Pete could just make out Billy's words. "We won't both fit in here. I gotta get Brianna."

Pete's entire body shook with cold and rage. He had learned his lesson all right. *That's what you get when you try to help people.* Everyone he met had only ever been out for themselves. He stared after Billy, cursing him and his sister.

Only then did he notice the rope unraveling. Billy had

tied the boat to a pylon outside the house so Pete could pull it back. Pete stared at the rope silently and shook his head.

Well, I'll be damned.

When Billy reached the shore, his sister ran to him, splashing through the water and clinging to his legs as he attempted to exit the boat. He led her to the sand and knelt, holding her hands and speaking earnestly. Pete wondered what he was saying.

As Pete watched, Billy tore off the bottom of his already-ripped tee shirt and wrapped it around his sister's leg. Then he stood and looked back at Pete, nodding once and raising his hand. Pete began pulling on the rope to retrieve his boat as he watched the two children walk away from him into the distance.

As the afternoon wore on, Pete didn't find anything much worth keeping and had lost some of his enthusiasm as he dug through piles of stinking trash.

He did keep an ear out—not for the whir of helicopter blades that would warn of the Coast Guard's search for survivors or looters but rather for the sound of a girl crying or the warning shouts of an older brother. Would the kids know to be careful of wild animals out here? He thought he'd spied a coyote slinking around a trash pile earlier—they'd been sighted on the peninsula before. The little one would probably try to make friends with it to replace her lost cat.

Dead cat. Dead mom.

Shit.

Pete decided to stock up on some food. And maybe a little whisky to keep him going. The liquor mart appeared to have suffered extensive damage, but there were bound to be provisions there.

Whistling as he wheeled a shopping cart down the aisles of the liquor mart, Pete wanted to grab every bottle he saw. But he was a whiskey man.

Four bottles should do it.

And cigarettes. He needed cigarettes.

Most everything was soaked from the surge, but he found a carton of cigarettes up on a high shelf. He also threw in some bottled water and snacks.

Satisfied that that would do for now, Pete began filling his backpack.

Damn! It wouldn't all fit.

Deciding to keep two bottles of water, he left two of the whiskies. *Better safe than sorry.*

izzie

Izzie slept restlessly, sweating in the humid September heat as the window unit was dead. She hadn't dared open the window to the howling wind and strange creaks and groans of buildings and trees succumbing to the storm.

By the time she woke, the world had returned to silence. She couldn't tell what time it was, though the sun had risen.

Getting up, she found her roommates sitting around the living room, munching on chips and popcorn. Jules strummed the guitar. Mikey paced, presumably because he didn't have his computer monitors to ground him. Dez played cards with Frankie.

They looked like they might have been up all night.

Izzie sat on the couch and curled into herself, chewing her nails to the quick and scraping off all the black polish Frankie had helped her with for the show. Had it really only been two nights ago? It felt like an eternity.

Mikey sat down next to her, hunching over and fidgeting—pulling up a pocket of skin on the back of his hand, tapping his thumb and forefinger together in rhythm. Izzie looked at him out of the corner of her eye. She could feel his unease like an itch.

"I have to show you something." He spoke under his breath so only she could hear.

Izzie turned, and his anxiety burrowed into her skin. As he stood and headed down the hallway, she followed, her palms growing sticky. They entered his room, a space filled with secrets, the unknowable.

"Close the door." He sat in front of a computer screen that was blinking green code.

Izzie shut the door. "I thought we didn't have power."

"Yeah, well, this thing runs off a different power grid."

Okay, seriously, what the hell does Mikey do?

He tapped the keyboard, and the screen lit up, displaying an image of a large pale house standing in the middle of a sandscape, haunted and alone.

"It's the first image taken of the peninsula since Ike hit. It'll be in tomorrow's paper."

"How did you . . . ?" Slowly, the truth of what Izzie was seeing sank in. "Why is it by itself? Where are the rest?"

"Gone."

"How can they all be gone?"

Mikey tapped the keyboard again, and the screen went black. Izzie couldn't breathe.

"There are people at the George R. Brown Convention Center. Evacuees. You might try there."

Evacuees? An image flashed in Izzie's mind—bedraggled people in gray and brown carrying sacks over their laden shoulders and infants wrapped in rags. Evacuees came from other places, faraway places. Not here in Texas.

But the alternative was too awful to contemplate.

Izzie turned and headed to the living room.

"Where are you going?" Frankie asked as Izzie laced up her Chucks. "You can't go out in this. The roads are blocked by fallen trees and power lines. It's dangerous."

Looking at Frankie, Izzie squinched her eyes. "When did you become such a mom?"

Frankie shrugged. "Fine. Do what you want."

Izzie headed for the front door and slammed it shut behind her. Frankie and Mikey were talking on the other side as she made her way downstairs.

"Wait!" Frankie slipped on some flip-flops from a pile lying by the door and chased her friend down the stairwell. "I'm coming with you."

The fallen oak looked even more enormous at ground level. It had almost squashed the car below it flat, or what they could see of it. Izzie looked up and down the street, trying to figure out the safest route to go on foot. Frankie walked toward her, a skateboard under her arm.

"You're not going to get far on that."

"You always say that." Frankie surveyed the scene before them. Tree limbs and debris of all kinds were strewn across almost the entire surface of the street and beyond. "And I guess you're right this time." She took her skateboard back inside the apartment hallway and smiled when she found Izzie still waiting outside.

"You don't have to come, you know."

"I know."

As they started walking, Izzie dodged a board barbed with rusty nails. From then on, she was careful not to step on anything that could cause prolonged damage. She knew the kinds of dangers that could be lurking in the water that still covered much of the street. Past flooding on Bolivar had displaced snakes, rats, even gators, who roamed residual floodwaters, angry and afraid—the worst combination.

"It's like a goddamn war zone out here," Frankie said, her tone a little too upbeat for Izzie's liking. "Where are we going, anyway?"

"George R. Brown." Izzie kept her head down, focusing on where she placed her feet while managing to maintain a brisk pace. "Watch where you step, especially in those." She gestured to Frankie's flip-flops. "Why'd you wear them, for god's sake?"

Frankie ignored her. "Why George R. Brown? You know that's pretty far, right?"

"I said you didn't need to come."

Izzie wondered where William was. Hopefully he'd gotten to a shelter. She glanced at Frankie by her side and was grateful her friend hadn't given up on her.

"About the other day." Frankie paused, and Izzie kept moving, eyes to the ground. "Sorry for getting so bent out of shape about Jess."

Izzie realized she hadn't thought about Jess since the storm hit. "No biggie. I'm sorry too. I didn't know about y'all. Honest."

"Yeah, well, apparently Jess didn't know about us either." Frankie swerved around a fallen tree limb. "I guess it was wishful thinking on my part. That we were together."

"I'm still sorry." Izzie lifted her eyes from the ground to her friend. "I don't want to mess up what we have. You're pretty much the only friend I have at this point."

Frankie showed her gap in a wry smile. "Beggars can't be choosers, I guess. And you haven't messed up what we have. Jess, on the other hand, is a bitch, and I'll never forgive her."

Frowning, Izzie bit her lip.

Frankie nudged Izzie and ran her hand over her bristly blue hair. "Hell, just give me time, okay. If she's gonna be

the back door. "Kid, wake up." Pete felt her forehead—damp and hot.

Brianna stirred and half opened her eyes. "We didn't find Scout. Or Mama," she mumbled.

Pete looked back at her brother. "Did y'all eat or drink anything since I last saw you?"

The boy shook his head. Pete took off his backpack and handed it to him. "There's some stuff in there." As Billy dug through the bag, Pete carefully lifted Brianna from the car and sat her on the ground. "I need to take a look at that leg." The boy must have changed the rag, as it was no longer soaked with blood.

Brianna pushed away Pete's hand. "It hurts."

"You want a cookie?" Pete asked.

She nodded, and Pete turned to Billy, who handed one over. Pete noticed he had found the gun, along with the second bottle of whiskey, in the backpack. He was looking at Pete the way most people did—with a mixture of pity and disapproval.

As Brianna ate the cookie, Pete gently removed the makeshift bandage. The wound wasn't bleeding, but it was seeping a yellow pus. He wondered if she'd had a tetanus shot recently. This could be bad.

Pete gestured to Billy. "Hand me that bottle." Billy hesitated. "I need to disinfect the wound." Pete handed Brianna another cookie. "Here you go. Now this may sting a little, but I can tell you're a brave little trooper, right?" Brianna nodded.

Pete poured the precious liquid over the cut, even as Brianna squirmed and wailed. He wanted so badly to take a swig, but he'd need the rest to apply later if it wasn't already too late. "We need to get to the pharmacy, find some antibiotics."

Billy nodded and followed Pete, who carried Brianna in his arms.

Pete was surprised at their luck. The pharmacy at The Big Store was fully stocked—no looters to empty it out yet. He picked up some antibiotics, bandages, alcohol wipes, and ibuprofen. Maybe these kids were a good-luck charm and worth keeping around for a bit after all.

"Hey, mister?" Pete looked over his shoulder at the boy, who was filling a beach bag with food and water. "Me and Brianna are going to head over to the church for a bit, maybe camp out there tonight."

"We can stay here. It's got everything we need."

"Brianna wants to pray for our mom and for Scout."

Pete tried very hard not to scoff. He hadn't set foot in a church since he was a little kid, when his aunts made him go. He wasn't much of a believer—never had any reason to think God was watching out for him. He continued filling his backpack with supplies.

The boy and his sister headed for the door, then looked back. "You not coming?"

"Nah, I'll hole up here for a while."

The boy looked at the six-pack Pete had grabbed. "I think you should come with us."

Ignoring him, Pete tucked the beer under his arm. Brianna came over and took Pete's hand. Looking down at her, his throat constricted. When she smiled up at him, he allowed her to lead him to the store exit.

Pete and Billy took turns carrying Brianna. They were all exhausted by the time they reached the wide steps up to the closed double door of the Baptist church. Pete hoped they were locked, but when he pushed at one, it opened, and the stillness engulfed him.

Why did churches always seem abandoned when they

were empty? Although they were worse when filled with hypocritical parishioners all dressed up in their finery. He'd hated listening to the drone of the sermons and would often fall asleep, only to be woken with a sharp prod from one of his aunts.

But he had enjoyed the singing and would raise his voice with the best of them. The preacher had even invited him to join the church choir, but he declined—way too much churchin' for him.

Billy led his sister to a pew near the back where he knelt down. Brianna started to kneel beside him but cried out in pain.

"You sit there, Bree," said Billy. "God won't mind."

Hopefully those antibiotics start working soon, thought Pete.

Brianna pressed her small hands together and squeezed her eyes shut. "Please help Mama find us. I miss her. Oh, and Scout too. Amen."

Pete noticed that Billy squirmed in his seat a little, glancing at his sister with what looked like worry in his eyes. Pete watched the two of them praying, puzzled by the ferocity of their belief.

A low rumble sounded from a corridor near the back of the church. An engine of some sort? Perhaps a generator. It stopped, and silence took over again. Pete made his way down the center aisle, listening intently. Again, louder this time, short bursts of guttural growls, punctuated by heavy inhales of breath.

Every muscle in Pete's body tensed. Removing the gun from his backpack, he continued down a narrow hallway. The sound came from behind a door that led to another part of the building, storage maybe. Leaning in close, he smelled something familiar, though he couldn't quite place it.

He inhaled deeply, and it finally hit him—a zoo. The odor coming from behind the door was animal musk, excrement, a creature caged into submission.

Still, there was silence, but a heaviness of silence that came from intense listening, from both sides of the door. Pete put his hand on the doorknob.

"What was that?"

Pete started. Brianna stood next to him.

"You go on back to your brother now."

Brianna looked at the door. "Aren't you going to open it?"

"Go find Billy."

"But I want to see—"

Suddenly, the door crashed to the ground, pinning Pete beneath it. A roar reverberated through every fiber of his being, paralyzing him with fear. Then Pete remembered Brianna. Her small hand was in his. Whatever force had been behind that door had knocked it right off its hinges, and he and Brianna were both underneath it.

Pushing the door off, he rolled toward Brianna. Her eyes were shut tight, and she lay pale and rigid, her hand squeezing his so tightly, it almost hurt. Pete struggled to his knees, wiping his eyes. His hand came away streaked with blood.

"You okay?" He leaned over the girl and patted her face, smoothing her hair. "Brianna?"

She didn't answer, but she did open her eyes, which were filled with terror. Then that low rumble came again, this time from inside the sanctuary.

Billy!

Pete stumbled to his feet and ran toward the sound.

An enormous lioness stood in the center aisle, still and low to the ground. Her ears lay back, her golden eyes focused on Billy. The animal was afraid and probably hungry, maybe even injured. And that was a deadly combination.

Pete kept his voice low and steady. "Don't move."

The lioness stopped growling, though her throat still vibrated, her flanks expanding and contracting. She turned her head toward Pete. Muscle and hot breath were so close, he could smell the beast's intent to kill. Her pupils dilated as she assessed her options—stringy old meat or soft young flesh.

Pete became acutely aware of her animal scent, her pain, her hunger, her need. The lioness followed only her instincts. And those instincts enabled her to act fast. Time slowed, the standoff elongating. The moment was measured in heartbeats slowed to a pounding rhythm.

Pete's own instinct had always been self-preservation. Understanding they would be mauled swiftly and definitively, he followed the only instinct left to him. He would not allow that to happen.

A deafening roar snapped him back into real time. In a split second, the lioness was running at Billy. Pete raised the pistol, cold and heavy in his fingers, enfolding the grip with both hands to steady his aim. The distance between the lioness and Billy was decreasing rapidly.

He would not screw up this time.

Taking a deep breath, Pete pulled the trigger as he exhaled. A pop of gunfire echoed in the stale air, breaking it in two. Over and over, Pete fired as the animal lunged.

Falling to the ground, Billy crouched into a tight ball, his hands over his head. Knocked sideways by the force of multiple bullets, the lioness rolled into a pew next to Billy. She lay on her side, her body rising and falling. Her hot, labored breath filled the room, along with the metallic scent of blood. A myriad of wounds marked her golden hide.

Brianna huddled against Pete, both arms wrapped around his legs, her body vibrating with fear. Putting the gun back into its holster, he pulled Brianna off him and bent down so he could inspect her for wounds. He examined her hands, legs, face, and head, holding his breath until he was convinced the lioness had done her no harm.

Billy rose from the floor and skirted past the beast, keeping as wide a berth as possible. He stood before them, quiet and still, awaiting Pete's diagnosis of his sister. Pete nodded at Billy, who pulled Brianna to him, holding her gently as if she might still break. Pete drew close to them, not wanting to interrupt but concerned that Billy may have suffered injuries as well. When the kids pulled apart, Pete looked closely at Billy.

"You all right, kid?"

Billy nodded, still holding Brianna's hand.

"Is it dead?" asked Brianna.

Pete looked over at the lioness once more, but the silence of the room told him all he needed to know. The animal must have been injured or old to have died without more of a fight.

He nodded. "Yep, I reckon so."

"Where did it come from?" asked Billy.

"Probably Bob's. He kept a few wild cats at his place as pets."

"She was someone's *pet*?" Brianna's eyes were wide and tearful. "He's going to be really sad. And mad at you for shooting it."

"Well, it was either her or us. I didn't have much of a choice." Brianna didn't look a hundred percent convinced. Familiar anger began to rise up, and Pete clenched his hands. Turning away from the kids, he headed to the church entrance. There was no telling whether Bob would be back.

And if he did return, Pete preferred not to have to explain himself. He knew how attached Bob was to his cats.

"We should probably get out of here. Figure we'll head to The Big Store and hunker down there for the night."

The kids trailed behind him as the heavy double door slammed shut. There was no power on the peninsula and the moon and stars were veiled by clouds, so it was difficult to see.

A howl in the distance made Pete's hair stand on end. Yep, coyotes. They'd obviously been smart enough to escape the storm somehow, but they were bound to be hungry. He'd survived a hurricane and a lioness. He wasn't about to be dinner for some coyotes.

izzie

Izzie and Frankie ate quickly, Frankie because she was starving and Izzie because she wanted to resume their search.

The sandwich settled like a lump in Izzie's gut.

Still, she had to admit, the sea of cots and people appeared slightly less daunting on a full stomach. But after an hour or so of searching, Iz and Frankie found a spot on the grimy floor to take a break.

Frankie sat cross-legged across from Iz. "You okay?"

Iz shrugged.

"We'll find them. Don't worry."

Izzie had begun to wonder if they were even there. If they weren't, then what?

Biting into an apple, she chewed as she looked around the auditorium for any faces she might recognize. She had just swallowed her first bite when she heard a voice she knew better than any other.

"Get back over here now! I told you not to run around like that."

Izzie snapped her head around, just as one of her brothers raced past. "Chase?" she whispered. Then, shaking off her shock, she raised her voice. "Chase!"

Pausing, her brother looked at her quizzically. "Yeah?"

Only then did she remember her crazy faux-hawk. Together with the lack of her usual disguise due to rushing out of the house that morning—it made sense her brother might not recognize her.

"Iz?" Reaching out, he touched her shoulder as if to make sure she was real. Izzie fought back tears. "Mama's really mad at you."

"I can imagine," Izzie mumbled.

"She says you shouldn't have run away."

Izzie steeled herself as she caught sight of her mother up ahead. She looked older, tired.

"Chase, I told you—"

Her mother's face stilled. Izzie couldn't make out what her expression meant. Was she about to get yelled at in front of all these strangers, or—

"Oh, thank God!" Shelley ran toward Izzie, stumbling over a bunched-up sleeping bag. She grabbed her daughter and held on tightly. Her shoulders shook. "Thank God, he found you. Thank God . . ." Shelley held Izzie out before her and stroked her hair. "What have you done to yourself?" Tears streamed down her face, and she laughed and cried all at once.

Izzie's heart cracked open. "I'm sorry, Mom."

Shelley laughed again, her blue eyes so clear as they stared into Izzie's. Izzie had never felt so loved.

Johnny sidled up and joined them, clinging to Izzie's legs. Chase stood slightly apart, a big but confused grin on his face. Izzie motioned him over, and they all huddled together, rocking and laughing.

Another voice sounded close beside them. "You're here!" Dorie was carrying two steaming cups. Iz watched her face shift from shock to relief within seconds, like a cloudy day turned bright. Dorie glanced behind Izzie, still smiling. "Where's Rennie?"

Izzie looked around as well, expecting to see her uncle making his way over with treats for everyone to celebrate the reunion.

Dorie stopped smiling. "He's not with you?"

Shelley let go of Izzie, and the group hug dissolved.

Izzie's stomach tightened. "I thought he was with y'all."

Shelley put her hand over her face, which was suddenly devoid of color.

"Mom." Izzie's voice was high and quiet, not quite her own. "Where is he?"

Shelley reached for Izzie's hand, her fingers dry and cold. "Honey, he didn't come with us."

"Why not?"

She paused, as if assessing her next words very carefully. "He was worried you were still on the peninsula, so he stayed to look for you." Instead of the usual recrimination, her mother's eyes held only fear and sadness.

"He's okay, though, right? Where is he now?"

Her mother shook her head and looked down.

Izzie's head spun. "But he made it off safely, right?" She looked from her mother to Dorie, whose hands shook so much, coffee was spilling over the sides of the two foam cups she still held aloft. Shelley only squeezed Izzie's hand harder.

He had to be okay. *It's all my fault!* Tears sprung to Izzie's eyes, and her breathing sped up. She couldn't think straight. "We have to find him. Can't you call him?"

Shelley released Izzie's hand, her entire body slack. "Cell service is out everywhere, hon."

Izzie turned and headed for the entrance hall.

"Where are you going?" Shelley ran behind her daughter. "Come back!" She managed to block the door before Izzie could leave. "Please! I can't risk losing you again. We'll find him together. We'll figure it out."

pete

Brianna had been spooked by the lioness encounter and the coyotes howling outside, so when they reached The Big Store, Pete tried to reassure her by erecting a barrier across the broken glass doors. He and Billy used shopping carts and whatever boards they could find to fill the space.

"What if they're good at climbing?" Brianna asked when they were done.

Finding a can of pest repellent, Pete sprayed it liberally over the entrance. "That'll keep 'em away." He winked at Billy.

Brianna seemed content enough with that, but Pete decided to up the ante. "How would you like to sleep in a tent? That way, they won't even know you're here."

Brianna's eyes widened. "I love camping! But inside, right?"

"Right."

Pete led them to the camping section, where he remembered seeing a small pop-up tent. The store's slogan ran through his head: *The Big Store—where you can find just about everything under the sun!*

After they'd set up the tent, Billy put a few oversized beach towels inside, and Pete handed Brianna the last chocolate chip cookie. "Sleep tight, and don't let the bedbugs bite," he said with a wink.

She frowned at him. "Bedbugs?"

Pete could have kicked himself. He tried laughing it off. "Just joking." Brianna peered into the tent worriedly. "I sprayed that too. You're good."

Reassured, she crawled through the tent flap. "Leave the flashlight on," she cried out from inside her cocoon.

Pete was astounded by how much trust she seemed to have in him. When he checked on her a few minutes later, she was fast asleep.

Sitting nearby, Billy tied knots in a rope he'd found. Pete gestured to his busy hands. "Looks like you know what you're doing there."

"I guess. Mom made me go to Boy Scouts."

Brianna murmured in her sleep, as if responding to the mention of their mother. The beam from the flashlight on the floor between them shone on Billy's hands. Everywhere else was shadows and pockets of nightglow.

"I saw her upstairs." Billy continued knotting the rope, head bent, fingers moving deftly.

"Huh?"

"At the house. I know Mom's in heaven now."

He whispered the last, so Pete almost missed it. Pete recalled the body under the bed, caught up in the sheets. It was a good thing he'd gone back for the kids. He hated the thought of Brianna finding her mother there.

Pete didn't know what to say to the boy. He'd lost so

much himself. Well, he never really had much to begin with in the way of family, so he wasn't acquainted with mourning a loved one or the niceties of offering condolences.

"Don't tell my sister, okay?"

"Sure. But she'll figure it out sooner or later."

"Later is better." Billy glanced at the tent. "Let's get through this first."

Pete admired the kid's stoicism but knew it hid pain. He knew a lot about covering up pain. "You okay?"

Billy's hands stilled. After a long pause, he leaned over and switched off the flashlight.

"Sorry," Pete croaked.

And he was sorry. Sorry for them losing their mother and their home. For having to face a hurricane. For having to survive in this hellhole. And for what? What was next for these kids? Whatever it was, it wouldn't be easy.

"What about your dad?" Pete asked.

"Mom raised us. Don't know where he is. Don't wanna know either."

"Other family?"

"My aunt Peggy. In Houston."

"Well, we'll make sure we find your aunt Peggy, then."

Shuffling, the boy turned over. "You think we'll all make it out of here?"

"'Course."

Silence fell. Pete was beginning to wonder if Billy had fallen asleep when the boy spoke next.

"Pete?" Billy's voice sounded so small in the cavernous space.

"Yep?"

"Thanks. For helping us."

Pete folded his damp pillow in half as he tried to settle

in for the night. "You get some sleep now. We'll watch out for the Coast Guard tomorrow and get you to your aunt, safe and sound."

He closed his eyes and forced out images of all the other treasure out there that could have been his for the picking.

the lost boys

Fountains of the great deep broke open.

The hum of water a chorus of voices—
echoes prodded and poked.

Finn was shaken awake in his briny womb.

Objects floated above:
tree trunk,
pale limb,
beast,
concrete,
and steel.
Windows of light flashed through the water,
parting the obsidian depths.

Finn flailed against the churning.

Sea-Mother whipped and lashed,
sucked and sighed.
It was more than even her gluttony could consume.

Finn reached for an anchor

to stop the spinning,
grabbed a hand,
cold as his own.
But it gripped back,
drew him closer.
Four arms encircled his body,
an electric current of connection.
Two faces he knew, faces he loved.
They implored with their eyes, mouths too full to speak,
bound themselves to him, hands locked.
Sea-Mother wailed,
pulled with all her might
so their joined selves tossed and spun in the currents.
They kicked up toward the surface,
a six-legged creature
aiming for the creased flashes above.

And they kept rising, higher and higher into the light.

izzie

Take good care of my boys." Shel looked straight at Dorie, who nodded solemnly and waited as Chase and Johnny clung to their mother. "You boys be good and listen to Mrs. Edwards, you hear?"

Johnny buried his head deeper into the folds of Shel's sweatshirt. Chase looked up at her. "How long will you be gone, Mom?"

"I'll head back later today once we've found your uncle Rennie. Don't worry."

Shel extricated herself from her boys and joined Izzie and Frankie. Dorie gathered the boys close.

Rubbing Johnny's back, Dorie said, "I think Rosie is nervous. Maybe you can cheer her up." She dug her hand into her pocket and pulled out the skein of string she had saved from Clem's gift. Dorie hesitated a moment, holding it in her palm as if perhaps it were all she had left of Clementine's gift.

After a moment, she unwound it. "Rosie loves to play with string." She dangled it in front of Rosie's carrier, and a white-tipped paw poked out between the bars, batting at the string. Chase joined his brother, and they took turns holding the string and moving it up and down, a hesitant smile etching their troubled faces each time Rosie tried to grab it.

Izzie marveled at how easy it was to distract kids in such dire circumstances. But then Chase looked up at them as they turned to leave, a grave expression on his face, and her heart lurched.

"Frankie, you really should change those shoes," Shel said, her voice hoarse. Frankie looked down at her flip-flops and shrugged. "Let's stop by your place and get something more suitable." She glanced at Izzie's hair. "And while we're there, do you have a hat or something? Your uncle won't recognize you."

Izzie tried not to glare at her mom as the three of them made their way to the exit and out onto the parking lot, the air sullen.

"Are you sure the roads are drivable?" Shel surveyed the streets surrounding the convention center.

"Yeah," said Izzie. "We got here from our place, didn't we?"

"Wherever that might be," Shel mumbled.

As they pulled out of the large parking lot onto the street, Izzie thought the water had receded some, and it looked like the larger tree limbs had been cleared by road crews. Frankie directed Shel to the duplex, but it was slow going. Izzie was impatient. All she wanted was to find Uncle Rennie and make sure he was okay, not take this crazy detour. Her knee bounced, and her breath seemed to stick in her chest.

"Mom, Frankie doesn't need different shoes. She'll be fine in those. It's not like we're walking."

"We might get stuck and have to walk part of the

way. We need to be better prepared. Do you have bottled water?"

"But Uncle Rennie could be—"

"I know, honey. I know!"

The truck cab crackled with a well-worn tension. The combination of annoyance and fear in her mother's voice revealed their old patterns, cracked by the enormity of Rennie's absence but not broken. She knew how close her mom and uncle were, even though they often butted heads. Rennie was the only person who could joke his way out of a tense situation when it came to her mom, and that was saying something.

Izzie decided it was easier to just not talk, though Frankie kept commenting on the apocalyptic scene before them.

Groups of people walked the streets, their expressions ranging from shell-shocked to delirious with the novelty of surviving such a catastrophe. Teenagers splashed through gullies of water lining the roads, laughing and picking up branches that they brandished like swords. An older couple walked arm in arm, each carrying a bulging plastic grocery bag. Loose dogs limped and loped, pausing to sniff piles of accumulated trash. The sky heaved with clouds almost close enough to reach out and touch.

When they turned onto their street, it was blocked by a row of orange-and-white-striped road crew signs, almost dazzling against all the gray.

"Hang on." Izzie jumped out and began to move the signs.

Frankie went after her. "What are you doing? They're there for a reason."

Shel pulled the truck over and got out. "We're walking from here. Come on. Which way?"

Frankie continued up the street, her blue flip-flops slipping in the waterlogged gutters. Shel gave Izzie one of her *I told you so* looks.

What would her mom think of her roommates? At least she already knew Frankie. Izzie had wanted to keep her new life separate from her mother. There was no room for her here. It belonged to Iz, and she wasn't ready to share it yet.

As they turned a corner, a groan echoed from inside a large dumpster. Izzie tried to ignore it. God knew, her mom didn't need to be exposed to all the shady sides of her life at once.

When it sounded again, realization hit her. Hurrying over, she pulled herself up to look over the side of the dumpster. A figure lay half buried in trash, eyes closed, moaning as if in pain.

"William?" Izzie climbed onto some crates and pulled herself over the side.

Shel stopped. "Izzie! What are you doing?"

Izzie shook William gently. "Are you okay?"

"My head." William put his hand up to show her where it hurt, his eyes unfocused.

"What happened?"

"I climbed in last night when the storm hit. Nowhere else to go." His voice was weak, but it echoed within the metal casing of the dumpster.

Examining his skull, Izzie saw a gash of red separating the gray strands of his matted hair. A substantial tree branch lay close to him.

"You may have a concussion. You need to come with me. Can you walk?"

Frankie was looking at them over the edge of the dumpster. "Who's that?"

"William."

Frankie looked puzzled for a moment. "The origami guy?"

"Help me. We need to get him to a hospital." She attempted to lift William to his feet as Frankie climbed inside to join them. The dumpster was almost full, so with some effort, they were able to get William over the side, where Shel waited to help him down. Izzie saw her mom grimace as she dragged him over.

"Let's leave him in the truck until we get back," said Izzie. "In fact, Mom and I will stay with him and wait for you, Frankie." That way, at least her mom wouldn't see where she lived and who she lived with. They were all great, but her mom, she was sure, would not agree.

William put his arms around Izzie's and Shel's shoulders as they helped him toward the parked truck, while Frankie dashed off to the apartment. Once they were inside the truck, William lay in the back among the bags, and Shel opened her window and leaned toward it, breathing deeply. She kept glancing at Izzie and then back at William, obviously wanting to know why they were giving a ride to a homeless man.

"He's a friend," hissed Izzie. Shel's eyes widened. "He needs our help."

Shel shook her head, and Iz looked out toward the sound of voices. Frankie was making her way back to the truck, followed by Jess.

Could this get any worse?

Jess bent down to look in the window. "Hey. Okay if I come along?"

Izzie racked her brain for an excuse for Jess not to come. She didn't need any added worries.

"Jess's mom is a nurse at Ben Taub," said Frankie.

"Your uncle could be there. And they can take a look at him." She gestured to William.

"It's a Medicaid hospital," Jess added. "They'll treat him for free."

Frankie opened the door, and they squeezed over so all four of them could fit in the front. Jess got in first, sitting next to Izzie.

"How are these, Mrs. L?" Frankie held up a foot shod in leather combat boots, perfect attire for the war zone their city now resembled.

Shel nodded and started up the truck. "Which way?"

Izzie was acutely aware of Jess's skin against hers, damp from the humidity. When she realized she was tense, she forced herself to relax. But her body leaned closer to Jess, which made her tense up again. Jess's piney scent brought flashbacks of their bodies intertwined, Jess's hair in her hands. It made her want to turn around and kiss her right then and there.

But her mom would have had a heart attack if she did, and she was driving, so best not.

Ben Taub was teeming with cars, ambulances, wheelchairs, people yelling for help, medics with oxygen masks and stethoscopes. They abandoned the truck on a nearby side street and left William in the back while they went to find help.

Jess asked at the front desk if her mom was on duty and if they could page her. Shel then asked if a "Rennie Lee" had been admitted.

The receptionist tapped on the computer to check admissions. "We don't have anyone by that name, but not everyone admitted has been identified."

Izzie didn't even want to imagine what that meant. "He probably would have been brought in from Bolivar Peninsula." She could hear the desperation in her voice. The receptionist told her to try Memorial Hermann down the street or Houston Methodist. They had helipads and flew folks in via the Coast Guard.

Izzie turned to see a small, efficient woman rushing toward them. "Baby, I was so worried about you." She pulled Jess into a fierce hug.

"I'm fine, Mom."

Releasing her daughter, the woman turned to Frankie with a smile. "Frankie. Glad to see you're okay. And who are your friends?" She turned to Shelley. "I'm Naomi."

"Shelley. And this is my daughter, Izzie."

Izzie tried not to stare at Naomi. She looked so much like Jess might as a middle-aged woman with a bob wearing scrubs.

Naomi beamed. "Good to meet you."

Jess went on to tell her about William.

"Right. Let's sort this out, then, shall we?" Naomi turned and darted down the corridor to find a wheelchair.

Once William was settled and in line for a bed, they said their goodbyes.

"You saved me, child." William held Izzie's hands in his and looked into her eyes with unguarded gratitude.

Izzie had never saved anyone before. It felt good. "I'll visit you tomorrow once we've found my uncle Rennie, okay?"

William nodded and waved her off as she followed her mom and friends down the corridor to the exit. Memorial Hermann was a couple of blocks down. Shel quickened her pace, staring straight ahead and ignoring the mess around them. Every entrance they passed was clogged with people needing help. Frankie kept pace with Shel, and Jess fell in with Izzie, who was attempting to catch up.

"How are you holding up?"

"I just want to find my uncle."

"You will."

Anger flooded Izzie. "How can you say that?" Her voice rose higher. "Why does everyone keep saying that?" She heaved in a breath that stuck halfway. "It's all my fault." A tear escaped, and she flicked it away.

"I'm sorry. You're right. But we have to hope for the best."

Izzie stopped walking and tried to catch her breath. Turning, Jess hugged her. Izzie leaned into her, and they stood still and quiet.

When Izzie looked up, her mom was waiting, watching them. They began walking again, and when Izzie reached her mom, Shel took her hand.

"We'll find him, honey. I promise."

clementine

Clem looked out the window at Jean's expansive garden, where everything was already dying, drowned in the floodwaters. Flowers hung limp on bent stalks, deadheaded by the relentless wind. Tree branches littered the lawn, and the fence bowed to the ground in resignation. They needed to go home. She wanted to see Dorie and check on Agnes and Earle. She wanted to know whether her home and her paintings had survived the storm.

Lou opened the bedroom door. "You're awake. Coffee?" He walked over and handed her a steaming cup.

"When can we leave?" Clem felt like a child whining to her parents.

"We're not allowed back yet."

"How do you know?"

"Cell phone service and power just came back on."

Clem thought of her friends. She had to try to reach them.

Lou continued. "Apparently, they have checkpoints set up—to stop looters, I'm guessing."

"My paintings."

"I know. Things don't look so good down there. I heard it hit us pretty bad. The *Chronicle*'s front page . . ." Lou went back to the hallway. "Hey, Steve? Where's today's paper?"

Returning, he held out the paper for Clem to see. A lone house stood desolate. Another aerial shot showed flat concrete slabs like gravestones. Clem felt like her life had been erased. Again.

Lou put the paper on the bed, face down. "I'm sure some places survived. We don't know for sure."

Clem wiped her eyes. "Why can't I hold on to anything? Why does everything important to me disappear?"

Lou sat next to her on the bed. "I won't disappear." He waited for her to look at him.

"You can't say that. No one knows what can happen."

"Well, if I have any say in it, I'm not going anywhere. The vows I made on our wedding day meant something to me. Not that I didn't feel that way long before we got married."

"So why did you leave?"

"I didn't leave," he said softly. "I always came back." Lou paused. "You're the one who left, remember?"

"I'm scared."

"We're all scared."

"I don't know what to do."

"We'll figure it out. Your life has taught you to be alone, that love is temporary. You lost your mother before you even had a chance to know her. Your father sent you away as soon as he could. And Finn . . ." Lou's voice trailed off.

"The dead are the only ones who *do* stay."

Lou looked puzzled.

"I need to tell you something. Please listen and try to keep an open mind."

Lou nodded and took her hand.

"Back at High Island . . . that was real." She held both her hands over his, as if trying to protect him. "Finn really was there."

Lou frowned but didn't say anything.

"And my mother—I *have* seen her since . . ." The words stuck in Clem's throat. She had never told anyone except her father. "She comes to me sometimes, still."

Lou searched her face. "I'm not sure I understand."

"I've always been this way. But I only see those close to me."

"Are you sure you don't just wish they were here?"

Releasing Lou's hand, Clem looked at the wall. "Please believe me. I need you to."

Lou sighed and took her hand back.

Clem continued quietly, as if she might deny the words if he didn't believe her. "Remember when you fell into the water and struggled to get back up? Like you were drowning? That was Jack. He was holding you down."

"Jack?"

"Finn's friend. You were a threat to me staying. He wanted me to always be with them at Sea View."

Lou squeezed her hand. "It did feel strange." Clem saw him remember. "Whenever I tried to get up, it was like a physical force pushing me back under."

"Finn saved all of us. He knew about the baby. Knew before I did. He told me to go, to keep his sister safe."

"Sister? We're having a girl?"

Clem nodded and placed Lou's hand on her stomach. "Do you believe me?"

A tear escaped Lou's eye and fell onto their joined hands, which cushioned their baby, nestled in the womb of its mother.

Pete

Pete was up early. Letting the kids sleep, he searched the aisles of The Big Store for flares and found several packs. Praying they hadn't been damaged by the water, he took them outside. No matter how many times he flicked his lighter, though, they wouldn't light.

Damn it!

He left the flares outside in the sun, hoping they might dry out enough to light later. Meanwhile, he went back inside and grabbed some red paint and the biggest brush he could find. Next, a ladder.

"What are you doing up there?" Billy called out some time later. He stood on the sand below Pete, his hair sticking up in all directions. He had on a pair of chunky gold aviator sunglasses he must have found in the store. They gave him a gangsta look that made Pete smile; the kid was about as far from gangsta as one could get.

Pete turned back to the task at hand. "Painting the roof."

"Why?"

Billy climbed the ladder. When he reached the roof, Pete stood and showed off his handiwork. *HELP!* was written in huge red letters.

"For the Coast Guard, so they can find us."

Smiling, Billy nodded.

"Found some flares too. We might want to get hold of all of them. There are a bunch of duds, so let's keep looking." Pete slapped Billy on the back. When the boy faltered on the edge of the rooftop, Pete panicked and grabbed him, steadying him. "Sorry 'bout that."

They climbed down the ladder and entered the store. "They're on aisle ten," said Pete, heading that way. "How's Brianna this morning? Her fever down?"

Billy nodded. "Yeah. And her leg looks better. Still think she might need stitches, though."

"I'll look when she wakes up. Just keep feeding her those pills." Pete turned toward the sound of the tent zipper opening. "Speak of the devil."

Brianna crawled out and walked over to him, still limping. "What's for breakfast?"

"What would you like?"

"Fruit Loops?" she asked in a plaintive tone.

"Let's go see." Pete offered his hand to Brianna, who took it, and they headed for the cereal aisle.

Billy followed. "Mom doesn't like us eating sugar cereal. She says—" Billy stopped abruptly and looked down.

"She won't mind just this once," said Pete. "I'll tell her it was my idea."

"Maybe we just won't tell her," Brianna said.

Pete continued looking for the cereal, hoping the conversation would end soon. He'd never worried too much about the odd lie here and there, but somehow, lying to Brianna felt wrong.

"I'll get more flares." Billy turned back the other way.

All the cereal was waterlogged and inedible. "I got a better idea." Pete racked his brain trying to remember what kids liked best for breakfast that he might find in the store. Dairy and meat had undoubtedly gone bad by now, what with no refrigeration. They'd stuffed themselves with so many cookies and chips that offering those wouldn't be much of a treat.

"What about ice cream?" Brianna asked with a cheeky grin.

"I like the way your mind works. But the ice cream will all be melted by now. Hmm, let's think . . . aha! Follow me!"

Pete swept her up and set her down in a cart. They whizzed through the store, rushing up and down several aisles as Pete threw items into the basket. First pancake mix, canned milk, powdered eggs, and syrup. Brianna's eyes shone bright as he loaded up the ingredients.

"Pancakes?" she squealed. "How can we make pancakes without a stove?"

Next, the home-goods aisle to search for a pan or griddle, a bowl, a measuring cup set, and a whisk. Then charcoal. Pete screeched to a halt next to the barbecue grills.

"Billy," Pete yelled. "Come give me a hand."

They wheeled the grill and a tank of propane outside, and Pete began setting it up.

"What are you doing?" Billy stood next to them.

"Making breakfast. Wanna help?"

"I guess."

"You wanna light this thing up or whip the batter?"

Billy reached for Pete's lighter.

"All righty, then."

Pete let Brianna measure out the ingredients, her intense care and solemn expression filling him with a sense of hope he hadn't felt in as long as he could remember. "Now whip it up real good."

Brianna stirred the batter with enthusiasm.

"Have you done this before? You're pretty good."

She beamed and stirred even harder.

Cooking pancakes over a barbecue was a first for Pete. Getting the temperature right was the trickiest part. He kept lowering and raising the pan so as not to burn them. After a couple of failed attempts, Billy took over.

"Damn, boy!" said Pete. "How'd you learn to flip 'em like that."

Billy shrugged and prepared another pancake, his posture becoming a little straighter as Pete and Brianna oohed and aahed.

Brianna poured more syrup onto her stack. "Yummy. We did good," she mumbled around a mouthful of food. Surprised they tasted as good as they did, Pete shared his own enthusiasm with two thumbs-up.

Billy stilled, holding the pan aloft. "Listen." Pete heard a distant rumble. "You hear that?"

A helicopter suddenly appeared overhead, its blades kicking up a cloud of dust and sand. Billy looked up and waved his arms. Meanwhile, Brianna froze, her recent enthusiasm for the pancakes forgotten as she stared wide-eyed at the giant machine hovering over The Big Store. Moving to an open area, the helicopter descended, and a man jumped out and headed over to them.

"Y'all okay?"

Brianna nodded warily, and Billy stepped forward. "My sister hurt her leg, but Pete helped us." He looked back at Pete, who stood in the doorway, watching.

"Y'all need to come with us now. It's not safe here, and you're under mandatory evacuation orders."

Brianna moved forward. “My mama and Scout are still lost. Can you find them too?”

“There are others out searching, young lady. Right now, we need to get you to a doctor and make sure everyone is shipshape.” He smiled, and Brianna moved closer to him. “Let’s go.” He led her to the helicopter and helped her climb in. Billy followed.

“Wait! Where’s Pete?” Brianna cried. “We can’t leave without him.”

“Sir?” The Coast Guard yelled over the din of the rotating blades. He beckoned to Pete, who still stood by The Big Store’s entrance. “You can’t stay here. We’re picking up all survivors.”

Pete just watched with narrowed eyes. Then Brianna jumped out of the helicopter, wincing as she landed on her bad leg. She limped over to Pete and reached for his hand. “Time to go.”

Pete looked down at her and took her hand in his.

rennie

The air was different—cold and clean. Rennie recalled the angels pulling him up to the heavens, which roared and wailed. His body felt dense and dull. He tried to open his eyes, but his lids weighed heavily.

You're supposed to feel light and blissful in Heaven, not leaden.

That's when he remembered the whirring, like a hovering sea bird ready to retrieve its prey. Except he wasn't prey. He was a survivor.

He became aware of a stinging in his arm, like a mosquito bite. He must have been covered in them from his ordeal.

Cold fingers forced open his eye to a blinding light. A sharp beeping filled his ears. He remembered: the helicopter, a soldier lowering a harness and motioning for Rennie to put it on. Rennie had struggled to hook himself in, adrenaline and exhaustion numbing his fingers. Then he'd risen into the air, legs dangling below him, the nightmare receding. When he had looked up, needles of light glowed in the night, landing wet and cold on his face, rinsing away the filth. Then he was inside the helicopter, medics hovering over him, asking questions he struggled to answer. *What's your name? How long have you been out here? Is anyone else with you? Are you injured? This'll need stitches and antibiotics stat.* On and on, until they wrapped him in a blanket and let him drift into oblivion.

But now someone was patting his arm. "You're awake."

Rennie willed his eyes open and found a nurse offering him a plastic cup. *So not dead, then.* He nodded, and she held it up to his mouth. He sucked on the straw and savored the liquid, which began to wash away the horror of the past few hours.

"That's better." The nurse placed the cup on a metal table next to him. "What's your name, sir?" Rennie opened his mouth to speak, but the words were hoarse and his throat burned. The nurse leaned closer to him. "Say again?"

"Rennie. Rennie Lee.

"Well, Mr. Lee, you're our miracle patient. We still can't believe you made it. The Coast Guard was about to give up on finding any survivors, until you." She was beaming, as if rejoicing that miracles still happened in this world.

That's when Rennie remembered why he had stayed on the peninsula. "Was anyone else rescued?"

"Sure. A few." Her smile vanished. "Not enough."

"My niece. She's eighteen years old—"

"Shh, Mr. Lee. You need to rest."

"She has black hair. Name's Izzie, Elizabeth Lee—"

"Mr. Lee . . ." She touched his arm. "You were alone when they found you."

"Yes, but I was looking for her. I need to make sure she's okay." Rennie tried to sit up and swing his legs over the side of the bed.

"No, sirree. You need to stay right where you are." The nurse forced him gently back into bed. "I can check with Admissions and see if she's here. You sit tight until I come back. I'll bring you some food. How's that sound?"

Rennie didn't think he could eat. Everything hurt, both inside and out. He'd failed her. He'd never forgive himself.

"Wait, my cell phone?"

"You had no cell phone, sir. Just you. And only just that," the nurse mumbled as she left the room.

pete

Both kids were wide-eyed as the helicopter took off and rose into the air. Pete felt small and insignificant when he looked down at the patchwork of Ike's destruction. He wondered how many who stayed had survived the storm. The Bolivar Lighthouse was one of the few landmarks Pete could recognize. His *Angel* was reduced to a pale smudge next to it. He silently thanked them both for saving his life.

That's when he realized they were flying over what had once been Beauchamp Ranch. The house and barn were gone, as if they'd never been. Pete knew the pride Earle had taken in the place, the life he had built over decades for Agnes. Now that was a man who knew how to love right.

Lowering his head, Pete said the closest thing to a prayer he'd uttered since he was a boy.

"Look!" Brianna pointed to a line of pelicans flying parallel to the helicopter. Perhaps they had mistaken it for one of their own, lost from the rest of the squadron. The seabirds were so close, Pete could see their eyes, intent on their destination. Would their homes have been destroyed by Ike too?

Pete looked down again, trying to locate his property among the tangle of metal, brick, and wood half buried in sand. He couldn't see it and hoped it was just disorientation rather than the alternative.

They were told they were flying to the Med Center in Houston because UT Galveston was full. Even the bigger highways were covered in sand and debris, detritus of trees and buildings from the various towns they flew over. Miniature cars lay abandoned as if by a bored toddler. In all his years, Pete couldn't recall seeing such devastation.

When they arrived at Memorial Hermann Hospital, Brianna yelled over the noise of the blades as the helicopter lowered itself onto the rooftop helipad.

"Billy, we're landing!"

One of the Coast Guards helped them disembark and led them to the doors leading into the hospital. He waved goodbye and ran back to the still-rotating helicopter to head back and hopefully pick up more survivors. A medic escorted them into the busy innards of the hospital itself.

Brianna looked around at everyone sitting or walking past them. "Maybe Mama's here."

A nurse checked them in and gave them juice and some snacks. "So, you're not the father?" he asked when Pete gave his name.

"Nope, not me."

Brianna took Pete's hand. "He saved us."

The nurse was all efficiency and didn't seem particularly interested. "Wait here, and the doctor will see you soon."

An hour or so later, they were ushered into a room, where another nurse checked all three of them over. When the doctor arrived, the nurse told him that all three of them were dehydrated and needed rest, while Brianna needed stitches.

After inspecting Brianna's wound, the doctor looked up at Pete. "This could have been a lot worse. I'm guessing you're the reason it isn't."

"Me and her brother, Billy," said Pete. "We found some antibiotics."

"Well." The doctor looked back at Brianna. "You are a very fortunate young lady. And very brave. I need you to be brave one more time, okay?"

Brianna looked worried.

"You need a few stitches to fix your leg properly. Soon it'll be good as new."

Grimacing, Brianna reached for Billy and Pete.

Billy stroked her hair. "You'll be fine."

Brianna buried her head in her brother's chest as the nurse stitched her leg, and Pete hummed a sea shanty, substituting Brianna's name for the brave pirate who sailed the stormy seas. She giggled every time he sang out her name, and soon the nurse was joining in on the chorus.

The hallways of the hospital were lined with patients; seemed Memorial Hermann was also bursting at the seams. Brianna was given a cot there while intravenous fluids were administered. She begged Billy to lie next to her, so he reluctantly squeezed himself onto the narrow bed. But even in the hustle and bustle of the corridors, they both soon fell into an exhausted sleep.

Pete needed to speak to his kids, to make sure they were okay. Finding a pay phone in the lobby, he dialed Carol's number.

"Kids," Carol yelled as soon as she heard his voice. "It's your father. He's okay!"

Pete could hear Addie and Shawn in the background, the phone rattling as they fought over who held it. "Hey, Dad. You okay?" Shawn was keeping his cool as usual. "We were worried." His voice cracked, and he handed the phone to Addie.

"Daddy!" Addie's high voice made Pete want more than anything to be there next to her, hugging her tight.

"Tell your mom and brother I'm fine. I'm at the hospital in Houston, but I'm doing okay. I can't wait to see you both and tell you about my adventures." He tried so hard to sound confident and excited about his news, but his voice seemed to come out all wrong.

"I told Shawn you'd be okay. You're the best pirate there ever was. A hurricane couldn't hurt you."

Pete recalled the terror he'd experienced that night. Best never to mention that to the kids.

Addie's voice became muffled, as if she was holding her hand over the mouthpiece. "Mama, Daddy sounds kinda weird."

Carol got back on the phone. "What happened to you?" Pete didn't know where to start. "Are you really okay?" she whispered.

"Yep, I'm good. The Coast Guard picked us up and brought us here just to check us over."

"Us?" asked Carol.

"Oh, I'm with a couple kids."

"How'd that happen?" Carol sounded surprised.

"They were stranded, so I . . . helped them out some."

"Really? What'd they do, pay you?" Her dry laugh sounded on the other end of the line.

Pete ignored her. He was used to her berating him. "I'd like to see my kids, Carol. I think my house is gone. And *Angel* isn't faring too well right now. Could I maybe stay with you for a bit?" He hated asking, but it was all he could think of.

Carol paused for a while, and he could hear her lighting a cigarette and inhaling. The kids begged for the phone again. "I suppose. For one night, and you sleep on the sofa. Then you find a motel room or something."

"Okay. Thanks." Pete could hear the relief in his own voice.

"How will you get here?" Carol asked.

"Bus, I guess."

"I doubt the buses are running yet. You may have to hole up there for a bit, find a shelter somewhere."

"Right. Okay. Tell the kids I love 'em and will see them both soon."

"You know what? Addie's right. You do sound weird," Carol said, before hanging up the phone.

Pete wondered what they meant, but it was probably all the crap he'd just been through with the storm. He really wanted a smoke, but he was worried the kids would wake up and panic if he wasn't there. So he made his way to the elevator.

Luckily, they were still asleep, Brianna's arm flung over Billy's neck. Pete sat in a chair next to their cot and watched the rise and fall of their chests, thankful they were safe and sound.

clementine

Lying on the tiny twin bed, Clementine stared at Lou's silhouette on the other side of the room as Lucille purred loudly on her chest. Clem wasn't sure she could handle another night at Jean's. The tension between them filled every space. And she longed for her friends. She'd tried calling but had gotten no answer from Dorie or Agnes and Earle. Clem tried not to dwell on what that could mean. She refused to accept that her friends were not safe.

Closing her eyes, she tried to focus only on Lucille, her chest absorbing the cat's rumblings, her heartbeat slowing, the night receding.

Clem sank into sleep as if falling into the deepest of oceans. Water wrapped around her, its weight suffocating. She flailed in a panic, searching for the surface, kicking her legs, which were bound by the weight of the sea.

Clem gulped for air as she sank farther, swallowing salt water and choking on seaweed and silverfish that slithered down her throat. Stomach bloated with tiny shells that scraped and scarred. Lungs strained, grains of salt and sand displacing air.

Was she finally drowning like her beloved boy? Would she join him, as she'd wanted to for so long?

Clem heaved a liquid breath. Her chest opened, rose and fell. Limbs loosened, the pain receding. She gave in to the weight of the water.

Shapes tossed in the current—
all the faces she had ever known,
all the places she had ever lived.

There was her yellow house. There was Finn collecting armfuls of frogs in the rain. No, not rain—torrents of salt water drowning them all. A whisper, almost indistinguishable from other underwater murmurs—

Rise up, Mama. Fight her. Fight Sea-Mother, or she will take you too. Choose to live for me and for my sister.

Finn's face, so innocent and pure. His sunken cheeks full, his wise, old eyes young again. And on either side of him, Agnes and Earle, holding his hands.

A stirring surged inside Clementine, veins coursing with the new life she and Lou had made together. Her beloved boy drew closer, his shine entering her, binding with the new life growing inside her.

Expanses of green replaced her yellow house, an ancient oak tree in the center. Its canopy protected them from the suffocating water. Agnes stretched her free hand out toward Clementine.

I was blessed with a long life. You are young. You have an entire lifetime ahead of you. Take it. Agnes kicked her long legs, pulling them all upward toward the light. *Live each day fully. Love and be loved.* Agnes touched Finn's heart with their clasped hands, and Clem's own heartache eased. *He is our family now.*

Earle came closer, his face joyful. *Your future is full of light, Clementine. During those moments when it may dim, remember that it will pass. Fight for your life, Clem. It is precious, as you are.*

Another voice now, moving nearer. *It's time to let go of the dead, time to live.* Her mother kissed her cheek for the last time, then turned to Finn, the grandson she had never known. *Clementine, you must let Finn go now and fight for the child growing inside you, as I fought for you so long ago.*

Mountains rose from the deep, valleys writhing like snakes. There was her father's house, still and quiet. Shadows lurked, their movement slow as molasses. There he lay on his bed, draped in white linen. Was it really him, so shriveled and gray?

His lips moved. *You, too, know this liminal space we have both shared for too long.*

His only remaining companion by his bedside, her *niñera* dipped a cool compress into a hollow shell and dabbed the perspiration from his brow, oh so gently.

And then it was Clem's hand soothing her father's pain. Were those tears or the saltwater sea dripping from all their eyes?

Your mother waits for me on the other side. Do not repeat my mistakes. Your heart is full. He gasped. *Forgive me.*

Clementine kicked her feet harder, the water parting.

Rise up, rang a chorus of voices lost in the churning.

She released their hands, pulled her arms through the currents that threatened to claim her. Up, up she rose, a scream of triumph bursting from her throat . . .

"Clem! Wake up, Clem." She opened her eyes to Lou above her. "You're having a nightmare. You're safe." Over and over.

But it wasn't a nightmare. All the people she had ever loved the most were together now.

Pete

Pete waited in the hospital lobby with the kids for their aunt, whom the hospital had contacted when they first arrived. A weight descended over him; this would likely be where they parted ways for good. Still, maybe it wouldn't be so bad not having to worry about them anymore.

"Auntie Peggy!" Brianna ran toward a woman wearing a troubled expression, which shifted the instant she heard her niece's voice.

The aunt lifted Brianna into her arms and hugged her tightly. Pete noticed the aunt's smile shift again as she hid her face in Brianna's tiny shoulder. Billy joined them, and his aunt put Brianna down to pull him close to her.

"This is Pete," Brianna said, gesturing to where he stood waiting. "He's the one who saved us."

The aunt brushed tears from her cheeks, and her eyes shone as she looked at Pete. "Thank you."

Pete nodded. He could feel her assessing him, wondering how on earth her niece and nephew ended up with the likes of him. "Well, I guess I'll head off."

Brianna looked stricken. "Where are you going?"

"I got places to go, people to see," Pete quipped.

"What about us?"

"Your aunt's here now. She'll take care of you."

Brianna looked worried. "But who will take care of you?"

An awkward silence filled the air. Pete looked down and swallowed hard.

"I've been taking care of myself for a long time now, way before I met you. And I'll do it long after."

"Auntie Peggy, Pete can stay with us for the night, right?" Brianna gave her aunt that beseeching look Pete had gotten to know well over the past few days.

Pete looked at the aunt. "I'm good. I'll head to a shelter. I'm catchin' a ride outta here tomorrow, be couch surfing at the ex's for a bit."

"Nonsense," said Peggy. "Of course you can stay the night. It's the least I can do when you brought my sister's babies home." She pulled the kids closer. "Your ride can pick you up at my place tomorrow."

Brianna jumped up and down. "Auntie Peggy has a swimming pool. And a dog. He's called Bertie, and he's so funny."

Pete had to admit, the promise of a hot shower, a soft bed, and maybe even supper was very tempting. "Thank you kindly, ma'am."

"Call me Peggy, please."

They headed to her car and drove just a short distance to her house. When they pulled onto her street, they were met by a sea of ABC news vans and crew. Peggy pulled into the driveway. "What on earth?"

"What's going on?" asked Billy, craning his neck to see the commotion.

"Sandra." Peggy sighed. "She's a friend of mine who works at the TV station. I told her about finding y'all. She must have set this up."

A coiffed woman in a fitted suit approached the car. Pete wondered how she managed to look so put together under the circumstances.

"Hope you don't mind," Sandra said as Peggy exited the car.

Peggy spoke under her breath. "I'm not sure this is the best time."

"We're interviewing Ike survivors, and I thought it might help the kids find their mom."

Peggy paused and then nodded. Pete cringed in the back seat. *Here we go.* He glanced at Billy, who was already exiting the car.

Sandra focused on Pete as he exited the car. "Sir? Are you Pete?"

He nodded. "Sure am."

"I hear you have quite a story. Would you like to share it with our viewers?"

Brianna came to stand next to Pete. "Auntie Peggy, I want to be on TV too." Brianna looked up at Sandra. "Pete saved us!"

"So I hear." Sandra turned to Pete. "Our viewers would love to hear from a real hero."

"Oh, and he's a pirate too!"

Sandra laughed. She looked Pete up and down and nodded. "I guess maybe you are. Pirate Pete, are you ready?"

"Sure. Why not." He took out a cigarette, wishing he could have a quick nip, as well, to calm his nerves.

"Sorry, Pete. Can't smoke on camera." Sandra smiled apologetically, eyeing the pack.

Pete winked. "I promise to share when we're done."

Sandra held up a microphone with a large *13* on it. The cameraman indicated he was ready to roll.

"Tonight, we have with us a true hero—Pete Lafitte, or Pirate Pete as some know him." She smiled at Brianna. "As y'all know, Bolivar Peninsula was hit hard by Hurricane Ike in the early hours of Saturday morning." She turned to Pete. "How did you manage to survive the storm?"

"My *Angel* saved me."

"Your guardian angel?"

"Sorta. My boat—*Wayward Angel.* She delivered me to the Bolivar Lighthouse, where I hunkered down during the storm."

"That must have been a front-row seat to the horror. Can you describe what you saw for our viewers?"

Pete fumbled for words, his usual bravado faltering. "Well, the surge rose real quick, waves as tall as houses. Stuff started floating, and I saw homes being torn from their foundations. It was crazy, man. Biblical. All hell broke loose."

"Why did you decide to stay and not evacuate?"

"I've been through a lot of storms on the peninsula that weren't no big deal. Man, Gustav just came through a while ago, and we were told to evacuate. And all for nothin'. I fished that day—caught my best load in a while."

"Can you tell us how you found these kids?" The camera moved down to Brianna and over to Billy, who stood back a little.

"I saw them from a kayak I found. They were stranded by the floodwaters, and their house was pretty much destroyed, so I picked 'em up."

Brianna spoke up, and Sandra lowered the microphone to her level. "Pete fixed my leg." She showed off her bandage with pride. "And we camped out at The Big Store. And I made pancakes." Brianna was breathless with excitement.

"You were lucky to have found Pirate Pete, then."

"Yeah. Oh, and he saved us from a lion."

"Lion?" The newscaster laughed. "Are you sure it wasn't just a very big cat?"

"You got that right," said Pete. "She was a big 'un. Belonged to Bob. Must have taken shelter in the church."

"He shot it dead," said Brianna. "I was sad at first. But if he didn't, it would have eaten us."

"Shit, Bob's not going to like this." Pete looked at the camera. "Sorry, Bob."

"I apologize for the language folks. He is a pirate, after all!" Laughing awkwardly, Sandra gave Pete a warning look.

"Shit, sorry. I mean—"

"Well, there you have it, folks—angels, lighthouses, and lions. Quite an ordeal for everyone. Pete, you are indeed a hero."

Grinning, Pete stood a little straighter. His kids were gonna love this.

"Miss?" Brianna was pulling on Sandra's jacket.

"Yes, hon?"

"Can I say hi to my Mom? She's still lost."

"You know what? She may be watching this right now. Son?" Sandra stepped toward Billy. "Do you have anything you'd like to say to your mom if she's watching?"

Billy went pale and turned his back to the crowd. He headed to the front door of Peggy's house.

Sandra turned back to the camera. "Well, Mom. If you're watching this, or if anyone knows where these kids' mom is, they're safe and sound with their aunt Peggy."

"Come find us, Mom," said Brianna. "I miss you."

Anger washed over Pete. Anger about the injustice of

two sweet kids losing their mom. The world well and truly sucked.

Taking a deep breath, Pete took Brianna's hand. This interview was over. "Come on, pipsqueak. Time to go."

As the crew packed up to leave, Pete led Brianna into the house to find Peggy and Billy. They sat side by side on the couch, their expressions stricken.

Billy must have told Peggy the truth.

When Peggy looked at Brianna, fresh tears spilled from her eyes.

Brianna stood close to Pete, as if afraid of their display of emotion. "What's wrong?"

Pete, Peggy, and Billy all looked at each other, assessing whether they should tell Brianna that her mom would not be back.

Standing shakily, Billy went over to his sister. "Come sit down with us."

He led her to the couch, where she sat next to her aunt. Billy kneeled on the floor directly in front of his sister, his eyes focused on her face.

"There's something very important I have to tell you." He fidgeted with the zipper on the hoodie the hospital had given him from lost and found. "It's about Mama."

"Did they find her?"

"No." Billy stilled his hands by placing them into his lap. "Mama is with Jesus."

Brianna looked confused. "No, she isn't. How do you know that?" Anger and fear filled the small living room.

Billy paused. "I just know."

Brianna's eyes brimmed with tears. "So we can't ever see her again?"

"We'll see her one day."

"When?"

"A long time from now."

"I don't want to wait a long time. I want to see her now."

"You'll have to be patient, Bree. But we can talk to her in our prayers."

Brianna looked from Billy to Peggy, as if waiting for her aunt to contradict her brother. Then she pressed her palms together and squeezed her eyes shut. "Jesus, please give us our mama back. You can have her later, when we're bigger. But not yet. Okay? Jesus?"

Pete moved closer. "I'm very sorry about your mama."

Brianna opened her eyes and looked at him. "He's not answering. Why isn't Jesus answering? I want my mama."

Brianna burst into sobs, and Peggy and Billy cradled her in their arms. Pete stood close, witnessing their heart-break and wanting nothing more than to fix the unfixable.

reunion

Fluorescent lights threw the lobby of Memorial Hermann Hospital into high relief: stark glances, labored breath, stooped shoulders, prodded bodies, murmured prayers. Purified air fought against the putrid stench of fear and disease. Exhaustion and resignation hovered over it all.

Izzie had been standing in line for an hour, waiting, watching, making promises to herself, to her mother, to God, to fate, for her uncle's well-being. When she had first moved in with him, after convincing her mom she'd do better, it had felt like a new beginning. Everything had been brighter, lighter, and for the first time in a long while, she had been hopeful.

That very first night, Dorie had made a nice dinner for them to celebrate. Dorie had spent a lot of time at Uncle Rennie's, which had been weird at first, especially when she stayed over. But Izzie liked Dorie a lot, much better than Uncle Rennie's ex, Claire. Claire was a fake. She tried so hard all the time. But Dorie was just herself. And she had helped Izzie with school and other stuff. Izzie trusted her.

Izzie cringed as she recalled her reaction when Uncle Rennie made her move back in with her mom. She had yelled and blamed her uncle for giving up on her, for not caring. Then she'd stormed out of the house, slamming the door, without a goodbye, let alone a thank-you. He had done so much for her, had risked his life for her. She couldn't bear it if . . .

No. Not that.

Izzie focused her attention on some kids in the waiting room who were playing with brightly colored blocks, building a structure. A solid base, then another row and another. As the tower leaned and wobbled, Izzie held her breath. She only released it when the tower finally collapsed in a heap.

Just like all those homes destroyed by Ike, leaving God knows how many people homeless and lost. How would they all recover?

Izzie looked at her mom, who was sitting next to Frankie and Jess. Frankie was listening to music on her earphones, her knee bouncing. Jess leaned close to Izzie's mom and spoke quietly. Shelley took her hand and patted it gently. Izzie swore then and there to be a better daughter, a better friend.

After a few more minutes, Shelley joined Izzie in line. They waited for the last person in front of them to be helped, and then Shel stepped forward.

"Is Rennie Lee a patient here?"

The receptionist tapped the computer keyboard, the clacking a countdown to his fate. Izzie wondered if she'd ever breathe normally again.

"Fifth floor, room seven."

Izzie and Shel turned to each other, grasping each other's hands. Izzie tried to contain herself, knowing he was at least here and alive. "How is he?"

"It was touch and go for a while overnight, but he's stable."

The elevator took an eternity, but they were all smiles and eager questions. Only Izzie remained silent, watching the buttons light up as they ascended.

Shel checked in with the nurse's station on the fifth floor before leading them down a busy corridor to room seven. There was Rennie, lying in bed, eyes closed, a multitude of wires and tubes attached to his broken body. As they drew closer, Izzie took in his bandaged chest, the bruises and scratches that marked his skin.

When Rennie opened his eyes, he wasn't sure if what he was seeing was real. Was this another dream? "Izzie?" He reached out to her, and she clasped his hand.

Izzie hiccupped a sob and leaned against the hospital cot. "I'm sorry, Uncle Rennie. I'm so sorry."

Rennie squeezed her hand. "What are you sorry for?"

"For leaving and not telling anyone." She gasped a breath. "It's my fault you almost died."

"I didn't almost die." Except he did, though. Rennie was just grateful that Izzie was okay. Nothing else mattered.

Lines creased Rennie's face. "Where's Dorie?"

"She's fine," Shel said. "She's in a shelter, worried sick about you."

Rennie breathed a sigh of relief. "Thank you for taking care of her."

Shel shrugged. "We took care of each other." She looked at Izzie, and her daughter smiled through her tears.

"Do you have a working cell phone?" Rennie asked.

Shel handed him her phone, and he dialed. Everyone in the room could hear Dorie's joy on the other end of the line. "We'll get there as soon as we can!"

Shel and Iz stood close to Rennie's bed, watching him

with relief. He was alive, and his wounds would heal. Shelley put her arm around her daughter and held her close. As they waited for Dorie and the boys to arrive, everyone shared their stories of what happened during the storm. Rennie remained quiet, just listening, not wanting those he loved to know about the horrors he had faced.

"Hey, isn't that Pete?" Shel was looking at the TV screen on the wall across from Rennie's bed.

Everyone turned.

"Well, I'll be damned," Rennie said. "Turn up the volume."

The bottom of the screen read, *True Texas hero saves kids during Ike.*

"Not sure about that," said Shel.

Rennie sat up straighter in the bed. "Everyone can change, Shel."

Even the likes of Pete.

Rennie wondered at how this storm had changed so many people—some for the better, perhaps, and some certainly for the worse, he suspected. What would he find when he got out of the hospital? What would be left of his life and those he knew? He looked around the crowded room at his family. If this was all that was left, that would be good enough for him.

Suddenly, the door burst open, and all chatter stopped. Dorie rushed in, followed closely by Chase and Johnny, who pushed past her and ran into Shelley's open arms. Dorie beelined for Rennie's bed and bent over him, leaning her body into his.

"Ouch," Rennie said.

"Oh no, sorry." She backed off a little and stroked his face and hair. She couldn't stop touching him, wouldn't take her eyes off him.

"How on earth did you make it over here?" asked Izzie.

Dorie glanced at her quickly before returning her gaze to Rennie. "Where there's a will, there's a way."

Rennie smiled. He suspected they all had learned just how true that adage was over the past few days.

"Have you heard from Clementine?" he asked.

"Yes. My phone was out of juice, but she left several messages. It was such a relief to hear from her finally. She and Lou are safe in Houston with his sister."

"How is she?"

"Seems okay. She told me she has some news but wants to tell me in person. Can't imagine what it is." Dorie looked down at Rennie's hand, stroking his fingers. "I got the feeling it was good news, though."

"Hope so. She and Lou both need some good in their lives."

Rennie covered Dorie's hand with his and squeezed. Yep, this was more than good enough.

september 26, 2008

2 weeks later: look and leave

rennie

Rennie and Dorie left his brother's place in Austin early. The checkpoints on the peninsula were only open from 6:00 a.m. to 4:00 p.m., and it was about a four-hour drive.

Dorie was getting anxious about the time constraints and what they'd find once they got there. The freeways had been cleared of major debris, but the cruel marks of the storm remained. Highway 124 was a premonition of what was to come—crushed houses, fallen trees, and overturned cars. The closer they got to Highway 87, the worse it looked.

Dorie hadn't stopped talking for the past hour, and Rennie sensed she was filled with an odd frenetic energy based on hope and fear. She commented on the scenery they passed, at times optimistic but often crestfallen as they witnessed yet another horror.

"Look at those electrical poles!" She pointed to a line of poles that listed like stooped old men.

"Everything's dead." All vestiges of greenery had been replaced by desiccated vegetation in sepia hues.

"Oh, I can't look!" She covered her face as they passed a limp mess of feathers and red on the side of the road.

"Look!" She pointed at a squabble of seagulls hovering over a cluster of ragged reeds.

It was already close to noon when they finally reached the front of the line of vehicles at the checkpoint.

"IDs and proof of residency." The guard looked tired, bored even. He must not have been a resident.

They each pulled out their driver's license and an electric bill. "How's it look on 87?" Rennie asked as he handed them over.

The guard shook his head. "Haven't been there myself. Heard it's not so good, though." Returning the documents, he waved them on to keep the line moving.

Turning onto 87 was like entering another world—a dead one. What had once stood as barriers between the ocean and the road were now gone. Driving carefully, they searched the shoreline for Dorie's little yellow house.

After retracing their route a few times, they finally recognized a neighbor's fence with two blue dolphins attached to the posts. But the storm had torn half their house away, and a gaping wound revealed its innards—the ghostly domesticity of vacant bedrooms stripped of all but sodden rugs and displaced mattresses. What remained of the neighbor's property on the opposite side was a handwritten address sign nailed to a broken pylon.

Where Dorie's own house once stood was a cracked concrete foundation bearing frayed pilings. Next to it lay an exposed septic tank, half submerged like an ancient relic—an obscene concrete object not meant to be viewed above ground.

When Rennie turned to Dorie, she had her hand over her mouth, her eyes wide and dazed with disbelief.

As they emerged from the car, rot filled their nostrils. Rennie's chest constricted, and he fought against images of that awful night that the familiar stench dredged up.

They wandered aimlessly toward the house's foundation, where Dorie began searching the ground. Rennie hovered nearby, giving her space to grieve.

She bent down to pick up a plate, white with pale-blue flowers. How had this fragile object survived when her entire house had been completely wiped away as if it had never been?

Rennie could almost hear echoes of the house crying out in anguish as it was torn from its roots. He imagined it floating, fear dipping and tangling about its limbs, entering through cracks and crevices like the fetid seawater that filled the interior. His breathing sped up as images flickered in his mind: chairs and tables tottering and then rising to the ceiling in slow motion—a choreographed opera, where the roar of the water accompanied the howl of the wind, their voices soaring and falling in a shaky vibrato.

Dorie touched his arm. "Are you okay?" Rennie pulled himself back to her and nodded. Dorie spoke with a faraway look. "I wonder if my house is still intact, dropped onto the sand on Goat Island." Rennie doubted it. "Apparently, that's where a lot of the storm debris ended up."

"Now wouldn't that be something." All Rennie could think of, though, was scrambling in the dark up that mountain of sand riddled with the remains of what was lost to the storm.

"Maybe we could find it, bring it back." Dorie held the plate like a precious artifact.

Rennie stood close to her, but she moved away, continuing her search for vestiges of her life. But all she had left now were memories.

Pete

Pete didn't much care whether his house was there or not, but he'd spent the last few days keeping up with whatever news he could find on TV at Carol's place. All he cared about now was being there for his kids, who had been mighty spooked by the storm. And finding his *Angel*, of course.

Now that they were letting residents back onto the peninsula to check on their properties, he had asked Carol if he could borrow her car. That she agreed had surprised him, to say the least. He must have been doing something right.

He was surprised again when Carol called him to the phone.

She handed him the receiver. "It's for you."

"Hi, Pete. It's Peggy."

"Hi there." They hadn't spoken since he'd stayed with them. Pete had wondered if he'd hear from them again. He was surprised at how glad he was that she'd called.

"I just wanted to thank you again from the bottom of

my heart for taking care of the kids. They've had nothing but good things to say about you. They begged me to call you."

It was a lot to take in. Pete wasn't sure how to respond.

"They asked if maybe they could see you again."

Pete's throat constricted.

Peggy continued. "If you'd rather not—"

"No, no. I'm good with that arrangement. Um, I don't have a place right now, so they may have to wait a bit."

"Oh, that's okay. They'll be thrilled to know you want to see them both. Can I pass the phone to them now?"

"Sure," Pete said, both nervous and eager to speak to them.

"Hi. This is Billy."

"Hi there, Billy. How're you holding up?"

"I'm okay. You?"

"Yep. I'm doin' okay."

There was an awkward silence, and then Brianna's voice came on the line.

"Pete, I miss you." Pete's heart soared. "When can we see you? You promised we could go on your boat, remember?"

"Sure. She's not doing so well yet, but as soon as I get her fixed up, we'll take her out."

"Why do you call your boat a girl?"

Pete chuckled. "That's a story for another time. How's your new school?"

"It's okay. I have a best friend who's the best jump-rope girl in first grade. She's teaching me all her moves. I can show you when we visit. It takes lots of practice, but you'll get the hang of it."

Pete laughed, not sure he'd ever jump rope, even for Brianna.

"See you soon," said Brianna. "Love you."

Pete struggled to talk when Peggy came back on the line. "They miss you. If you're ever in the area, you're welcome to visit them here."

"I may just do that. Thank you."

"To be honest." Peggy lowered her voice. "Billy is struggling with the loss of his mother. My sister was a wonderful woman." Peggy's voice cracked, and the line went quiet.

"Must be difficult for you too," said Pete.

"I'm trying to put on a good face for the kids, but it's hard."

"I'm sure." Pete wasn't sure what else to say except that he knew he wanted to see those kids again. "Once I get settled, I'll invite them over. Give them a ride in *Angel*." He looked over at Addie and Shawn, who were playing in the yard. "Kids seem to like that."

"Angel?"

"My boat."

"That's a lovely name for a boat."

"Yeah, *Wayward Angel*. Maybe I'll tell you about her sometime."

"I look forward to it. The kids will be thrilled. Thank you again, Pete. We owe you so much."

"Not at all. I guess I'll see you later, then."

When Pete hung up, he realized he owed Billy and Brianna a lot too, though he couldn't quite put his finger on what that was. What he did know was that there was now something else he cared about besides his own kids and his *Angel*.

The peninsula looked much as it had when Pete last saw it. Some debris had been cleared, but it was still an eerie dreamscape of what it had once been.

He made his way to the lighthouse and was more than pleased to see his *Angel* waiting at its iron base like a loyal dog. She was worse for wear but salvageable with some attention and care, he was sure.

Pete brushed his hand over the stern where her name was painted—*Wayward Angel.* Unlike her namesake, *she* had survived her wayward journey.

But what to do with her in the meantime? He couldn't very well leave her anchored next to the lighthouse. He'd have to find a way to tow her to a storage facility somewhere so she'd stay safe until he could make repairs and take her out on the water again.

Grabbing a piece of ragged board off the ground, he searched Carol's car for something to write with. All he found were loose crayons on the floor under Addie's booster seat.

On the board, he scrawled *Property of* and added his name, address, and phone number in waxy orange letters. Then, in all caps, he added:

DO NOT MESS WITH THIS BOAT OR ELSE!!!

He placed the board in the window of the cabin and patted her goodbye for now.

clementine

Clem and Lou navigated the sand-covered terrain, craning their necks to see around displaced objects—part of a roof stuck between the branches of a large tree, overturned boats in the middle of the road, torn Texas flags flying as a show of resilience and grit, and perhaps strangest of all, an intact house that had survived the storm as if it had never been.

Clem wasn't sure she wanted to see if their place was still there, but she was grateful for any excuse to spend a day away from Jean. They had been getting along a little better since she and Lou had shared the news of the baby with the family, but Jean still seemed to keep Clem at arm's length, especially relative to her warmth and kindness to everyone else.

Lou was so happy about being a father again, and his enthusiasm was contagious. The boys were excited about getting a new cousin, though they obviously hadn't told them it would be a girl. How would they explain knowing that fact? At least, Lou seemed as sure as Clem about the gender, which was encouraging. Clem could feel a new trust forming between them.

The bayside of the peninsula had fared a little better than the oceanside. Their tiny house was still standing, but a few steps were missing, so the climb up was precarious.

"Let me go first and see how safe it all is." Lou stepped tentatively up the stairs to the deck. Clem stood below, holding her breath. Lou's long legs stretched over gaps where treads were missing, until he finally reached the door.

It was obvious from the watermark that the surge had entered the property. A stain marked the level it had risen to. When Lou fit the key into the lock and pushed, the door resisted, the wood swollen with residual moisture. He pushed against it with his shoulder, and the door opened to reveal the overpowering smell of damp and growing mildew. All the furniture was covered with a green-gray skin, and even the walls displayed what might have been an abstract floral-patterned wallpaper, if he hadn't known better.

"How does it look?" Clem called from outside.

"Not great. Mildew everywhere. I'm going to check the attic real quick."

Clem crossed her fingers that her paintings were undamaged. They were a history of her life, her struggles and her eventual healing. If they were destroyed, what would that say about her and her journey, her new life? She listened to the house bump and creak as Lou maneuvered through it. When he exited the front door, Clem could tell the news wasn't good.

"There's a lot of water damage, must have gotten in through a hole in the roof."

Clem made her way to the stairs. "I have to see."

"Be careful. That fifth step is about to go."

Clem moved slowly, testing each plank of wood before

stepping on it. Lou held out his hand to guide her up the last couple of steps.

Resting against the hallway wall was one of Clem's earliest paintings. Staring at it, she realized this new version was even more expressive than her original. The murkiness of the lower half, where the ocean was deepest, was now mottled with mold, lending it movement it had lacked before. The color of the paint grew lighter closer to the top of the canvas, but it was layered with speckles of green and gray that resembled bubbles rising to the surface.

It was as if the ocean herself had composed lines and shading to add her voice to Clem's vision. They shared these canvases now, as they had shared Finn.

Her daughter moved as if in response to the language spoken between Clem and the ocean. Clem decided she would create new paintings, ones of hope and joy, in memory of their beautiful son and in celebration of their new daughter.

But she'd had enough of the sea for this lifetime. She needed to move on, to find another place to call home.

She thought of her childhood in the mountains of Mexico, the endless plains stretching to the peaks that surrounded them. How would her father feel about this new child? He'd never even known about Finn. She hadn't told him, hadn't even spoken to him for several years now. Would that wound need to be mended, as well, for her to move forward?

Her daughter's heel slid across her belly, her watery realm slowing her movements so Clem gasped at the wonder of it all. Her daughter was strong and sure. Would she want to know her grandfather? Would *he* want to know *her*?

She ached as she remembered her *niñera* watching the car drive away as Clem left for boarding school when she was just seven years old, the closest thing to a mother Clem had ever known sobbing into her handkerchief. Her father had stood tall and straight as he watched Clem leave, his figure growing smaller the farther she traveled.

What would he look like now? He was an old man, perhaps stooped and gray. Did he think of her?

She recalled her dream during the storm, when her father had asked for her forgiveness. Was he still alive, or had her dream been portentous?

Clementine had to try to see him, try to right the wrongs they had done to each other. Give her daughter a chance to show *him* how to love again, just as Finn and so many others had done for Clem.

may 30, 2009

8 months later

onward

Rennie pounded pegs into the ground, measuring off the footprint of the new house. Stepping out of a nearby trailer, Dorie handed him a cup of tea.

"Remember the first time I brought you a cup?"

Rennie nodded and took the mug. "Sure do. I wondered what had come over you that day." He smiled, his eyes crinkling. "You'd sit there on the deck, doing your crossword and sipping on that tea. I had to bring my own flask with me since you decided you didn't like me enough to share."

Dorie swatted at him. Then she took a sip of her own tea and linked her arm through his. "But you waited for me." Smiling up at him, she kissed him.

Rennie loved to see her smile. "Hey, I made a couple of tweaks to the plans. Want to see?"

"Sure." Dorie followed him to the shed he'd set up on her land as an office.

"Oh, I almost forgot. This came for you." He motioned toward a USPS package.

She examined the address label with her name and the office address written in sharpie.

"Who's it from?" Rennie asked.

"Hugh," she replied, surprised.

Ripping open the package, Dorie pulled out a note and a handful of photographs. Rennie leaned over to take a look. Harriet smiled back at him.

Dorie went through the photographs one by one, smiling and pausing now and then. "I wasn't sure I'd see these again. He must have made copies." She opened the note and read it aloud. "I'm so sorry for your loss. I know you loved that house. Thought you'd miss seeing our lovely girl, so these are for you to put in your new home." Her voice cracked as she read the note.

"I think I might need to meet this man," Rennie said. "He sounds like a good one."

Dorie nodded. "He is. He really is." Dorie placed the note and photos back inside the package, which she tucked into her bag. Then she leaned over the table where unrolled sheets of blueprints were laid out. "Tell me about these." She put her arm around Rennie's waist as he explained the recent changes he'd made to their house plans.

"I'm adding more windows here to bring in as much light as possible and to see the ocean from east to west—one hundred and eighty degrees of water." Rennie looked down at her, awaiting her response. "No?"

Dorie's brow creased. "What happens when another storm comes?"

"I'm going to build this house stronger than any storm, don't you worry. It'll be like Noah's ark." He looked at her with such confidence, the worry slipped from her face.

"What do you think of adding a widow's walk?" Rennie knew she had fantasized about reading up in her tower, where all she could see was the ocean when she looked up from the page.

"I hate that it's called that." She'd gotten superstitious since losing her daughter and then her house.

"A captain's walk?"

"Much better. Yes, I'd love that."

"Done. And I'm adding reclaimed-wood floors so they'll have that old patina you love."

"Perfect," Dorie said. "And the house will be yellow, right?"

"Right. Whatever you want." Rennie was so happy he could do this for her, build her a dream home to soothe some of the pain of losing her first one.

"We'd better get going."

Despite her words, Dorie put both her arms around his slim waist, laying her head on his back. They stayed that way for a little longer, relishing the peace and quiet.

The moment was brought to an end by the oven timer going off inside the trailer nearby. The cake Dorie had baked still needed to cool and then be iced; no more dawdling, or they'd be late to the ceremony.

The trailer they temporarily shared was cramped and sticky in the May heat. The window unit half-heartedly blew out cool streams of air, and Dorie sighed.

"I know," Rennie said. "It won't be long now until we're in our new house together. We can handle it for a bit longer, right?"

"Right."

Some people hadn't been so lucky. According to the news, of the estimated 2,200 homes on Bolivar before Ike hit, only about 850 remained. The survivors were mostly newer homes that had been built stronger and up to code. Many of their friends' homes had been passed down from generation to generation; a lot of them hadn't even been raised off the ground on pilings.

Regulations on the peninsula had been slack. Since many of the older families had owned their homes outright, they hadn't been forced by the bank to fully insure them. People on the peninsula were fiercely independent and lived life by their own rules. Unfortunately, since Ike was deemed a flood event rather than wind, a huge number of homes had not been completely covered.

Dorie had had full insurance on her house since she'd not had it too long before losing it to Ike and the bank had demanded full coverage on her loan when she bought it. And Rennie's had been insured because he was sensible about that sort of thing.

After a lengthy dispute between homeowners, insurance agencies, and FEMA, some money had been handed out to homeowners for wind damage, but it wasn't nearly enough. A large percentage of locals had to leave the peninsula for good, and they were heartbroken. They were practically penniless, without jobs, and homeless. A way of life they'd known for generations had been wiped out in a few short hours.

Dorie and Rennie felt awful for them and a little guilty that they had come out of it as well as they had, considering. But Rennie had promised to help a number of families in the community rebuild, to restore their lives as best he could.

While Dorie got ready, Rennie scribbled notes about their soon-to-be wonderful home on Dorie's half acre of land beside the sea. She had lost almost a quarter of her plot to erosion from the storm. And they knew it would repeat over the years. Humans had claimed what was not theirs to own, and nature would prevail in the end. Inch by inch, the land would be eroded by coastal waters, until the peninsula would be only a memory.

Until then, they would continue to call it their home, and they would fight for it tooth and nail.

Clementine stood at the front of the ferry between Galveston and Bolivar, the vast ocean before her. She marveled at how different she felt from the times she'd taken this trip before—the despair, the draw of the translucent waves calling to her.

Now, Lou stood by her side, holding their daughter in his arms. Clem watched them sway to the rhythm of the boat being carried by the waves. Lou crooned into Aggie's ear, his head bent close to her rose-petal softness. His voice vibrated through Clem as if he were whispering to her. The gentleness of his breath entered her ear canal and made its way through her, soothing her, so she breathed slower and deeper.

She'd gotten back her job at the gallery in Galveston, though it wasn't the same as before. Now, she helped supervise repairs on the building, inventory the undamaged artwork, and acquire more before they reopened later in the year. Her boss let her bring Aggie to work, and she held her in a sling so her daughter rested on her chest, their heartbeats synchronized.

She and Lou had rented a loft downtown, not far from the gallery, and Lou still operated the food truck. However, Rennie was helping them fix up a space to open a restaurant later, once business started picking up again. They had committed to a lease that was ridiculously cheap because of the damage and the lack of people willing to risk opening a commercial business so soon after Ike.

Lou, though, was fearless, his confidence something Clem still envied but now appreciated more than ever. Somehow, he just knew everything would work out this time.

And she believed him.

Still, this trip was tinted with melancholy. *Can we ever really escape it?* As the ferry pulled up to Port Bolivar, they got back into the truck and crossed the ramp onto Highway 87.

Clem missed living on the peninsula, the familiarity of it, the wild beauty. But it wasn't the same now, for so many reasons. The lighthouse stood strong and proud, a beacon to all who had lost their homes. But Beauchamp Ranch was a ghost of its former self.

Still, it was turning green in the springlike weather, and the debris had been cleared, so it was an open rural landscape with grass and wildflowers growing. The large oak tree had survived, though the swing was gone. And the house and barn were just empty spaces now. White wooden chairs were arranged beneath the extensive oak canopy—similar to the ones they'd used for the wedding when everything had been so different.

Agnes and Earle's son and daughter-in-law greeted them as they approached the oak tree, the gnarled limbs gathering them into an embrace. Aggie stirred as they entered the shade.

"Welcome. Thank you for coming." Tom shook Lou's hand and congratulated them on their daughter's birth.

Sheila patted her swaddled form. "What's her name?"

"Agnes."

Tom looked at Sheila, then back at Clem. His eyes glistened, and he smiled without speaking. Aggie twitched a dream in Clem's arms, as if hearing her true name had pulled her from sleep. She turned her head toward Tom as he told Clem and Lou how beautiful their daughter was, her gaze focused just below his face.

Lou took Clem's hand, and they went to find a seat under the oak while the next guests in line approached the grieving family. *Tom's mother is your namesake, my love. You will know her and love her as I do.*

Tom smiled and thanked each person as they offered their condolences, but Clem saw the sorrow behind his eyes and knew he was aching for Agnes and Earle as she ached for them. It was difficult to imagine life without them, without their kindness and love.

Sheila and Tom said they would rebuild on the property, in honor of their family. Agnes and Earle would have liked that. They had so wanted to pass on their legacy. Clem remembered the Bible in which their family names had been inscribed, the ink now dissolved by floodwaters. But their memory would never be erased. They would be cherished in the community forever.

Lou and Tom unloaded the food Lou and Clem had brought. As Clem watched, Dorie and Rennie pulled into the driveway. Clem had been so relieved to hear from Dorie once cell service had started working again. Clem had missed her dear friend, and seeing her like this, on this day, brought tears to her eyes.

When Dorie approached, she wiped a tear from Clem's cheeks. "I'm so sorry. I know how much you loved them."

Rennie stepped forward. "They were good people. The best people."

Clem nodded, and Dorie fussed over Aggie. "I swear she's grown since I last saw her."

"It's only been a week," Clementine said. But maybe Aggie did seem a little bigger, healthier.

Arriving early, Aggie had had to spend some time in an incubator—a plastic coffin where she'd lain with her eyes shut, her breathing so shallow, she had barely moved. When Clem would push her hands through the plastic portals, their skin had been divided by a thin layer of latex—so different from when Aggie had floated inside Clem's belly.

Even as a pea-sized cluster of molecules, Clem had been aware of Aggie. When Finn had spoken to her daughter, Clem had realized she'd sensed her presence even before then. Later, Aggie's body would brush against her mother's organs, their fluids a rushing amniotic river. And then Aggie had kicked again and again against Clem's belly, so eager to enter the bright.

Aggie just couldn't bear to wait any longer.

Dorie led them to the tables that had been set up for food. There were already several platters, and Clem knew there would be much too much food after everyone showed up with contributions. The community wanted to do Agnes proud, and Clem was disappointed that stacks of paper plates and plastic utensils took the place of Agnes's beautiful collection of china and silver.

Still, Dorie had brought white linen tablecloths, which draped the temporary folding tables, and vases of flowers competed with the platters of food. It looked pretty and festive in a way that honored Clem's found family.

Izzie was suddenly self-conscious about bringing Jess, not just because she was her girlfriend but because she looked like no one else on the peninsula. Everyone stared at them with either puzzlement or shock.

She couldn't wait to introduce Jess to her cousin, Carl. He had put together a concert to raise funds for Bolivar's recovery, and he was headlining. Even though he played country, it was cool, outlaw-style country. His style was even shifting further toward blues. She suspected Jess would enjoy his set. The Stingaree Music Festival was the talk of the town—other than today's memorial, of course.

Izzie joined the line forming beside the oak tree. She had never noticed before how green everything was. The leaves were saturated with color, their will to thrive against all odds amplifying their usual verdancy. She breathed in, and the salt sea calmed her.

When Izzie reached Tom and Sheila, she shook both their hands and told them how sorry she was for their loss. Agnes and Earle had always seemed sweet, especially for old people.

Her mom was watching her and nodded, smiling. She seemed pretty okay about Jess, considering. Izzie surveyed the grounds, looking for Carl. It was so empty without the house and barn. By some miracle she didn't understand, her mom's house had survived the storm. It had suffered some damage, but Uncle Rennie had fixed that soon enough. He had built the house, after all, so it sort of made sense.

Her brothers played tag with some other kids, and her mom talked to Uncle Rennie, smiling and relaxed. Things had definitely shifted. Her mom didn't harass her the way she used to and didn't expect her to watch her younger brothers all the time.

Although, for some weird reason, Izzie didn't mind doing that so much anymore.

It was like they all understood how close they'd come to losing each other, so now they didn't sweat the small stuff.

Izzie's mom was even proud of her for enrolling in nursing school. When her mom had asked what made her decide to be a nurse, Izzie explained how she had come to realize that she wanted to help people who were suffering, like all those in the hospital when she visited her uncle.

And William. Izzie had checked on William every day at Ben Taub Hospital. She always brought healthy food when she visited, like fruit and . . . well, burgers. He loved burgers.

Reaching for Jess's hand, Izzie checked the time on the cell phone Uncle Rennie had bought her as soon as he got out of the hospital. Two more hours before the music festival. She couldn't wait.

"Daddy, can I hold the flowers?" asked Addie.

Pete handed her the cellophane-wrapped bouquet. He'd never bought flowers before and had had no idea which ones to pick, so the girls had chosen them from The Big Store. While they were there, Bree had insisted on giving Addie a tour of the place, explaining how they'd survived during the storm. Addie was notably impressed and even a little jealous, from what Pete could tell. Even Shawn had listened in.

"Hon, believe me," Pete had told Addie, "you didn't miss anything. Trust me on this one."

Billy had already told Shawn about their adventures, and Pete marveled at their resilience. He was relieved they didn't seem to have suffered PTSD stepping into The Big Store again.

He knew they were still getting over losing their mother, as he still sometimes caught them being still and silent. At least they had Peggy, who treated them as her own. Peggy had told him they were seeing a youth grief counselor, which helped a lot.

They'll be okay, Pete thought as Addie handed him the flowers so she could join the other kids at the ranch in running around the now-vacant pasture playing tag.

His own recovery involved dealing with nightmares, reliving the night of the storm. AA meetings helped; he had found a community that supported each other, not just in staying sober but in handling everyday life. Although everyday life seemed much more manageable now that he'd seen how bad things could get up close.

He watched Addie and Bree chase each other, laughing as they dodged the tagger. They really were his good luck charms. He had never considered himself a lucky man before now, but the tide had turned.

Several people approached Pete with a slap on the back or a handshake. "Saw you on the TV." His old neighbor Vern gestured to the field where the kids were playing tag. "Those the kids you saved?"

"Yep."

"Good one, Pete. Good one." He shook Pete's hand, and Pete stood a little taller.

He paid his respects to Agnes and Earle's kids. Pete still felt guilty about getting Lou drunk at the wedding. He'd encouraged him, knowing he was trying to stay sober. But Lou had been his drinking buddy for so long, it had been hard to see him any other way.

Except now.

Pete had watched Lou deal with his demons after losing Finn. He knew how much Lou had suffered and how hard it had been for him to move forward. They had run into each other often at AA meetings and were forming a new sort of connection now.

Yeah, people seemed different somehow.

Lou walked up to him. "Hey, Pete."

"How are you, man?" *Fatherhood suits him.*

"I'm good. Did you get that FEMA trailer yet?"

"Still waitin'. Got me one of them fancy tents though. The Big Store fellas gave it to me, free of charge."

"I should hope so, all the publicity you got for them."

"Yeah. Put it up on my property, but I spend most of my time on the boat. Now I'm retired, it's different—all play and no work." He chuckled.

"So you just cruise around in *Angel* all day?"

"Yeah. And I spend time with the kids . . . try to help folks who lost more than I did. Speaking of, I hear Rennie's helping out with the rebuilds. You think he might need a hand with that?"

"Sure." Lou patted Pete on the back. "I'm sure he'll take all the help he can get."

Others from the community started showing up with plates of food and flowers, and the grounds soon teemed with people coming to pay their respects. It resembled the countless parties Agnes and Earle had hosted over the years.

Except they weren't here this time.

Clem supposed it was okay to feel happy today, though. Agnes and Earle had lived good, long lives. She hoped the same for herself and Lou, and for everyone she loved.

The crowd gathered beneath the oak tree as Tom stood before them all to speak.

"I'd like to welcome y'all to this celebration of life for my mother and father, Agnes Mary and Earle Lee Beauchamp. They were pillars of this community and lived here longer than most of us present. This place was a part of them, and they will always remain a part of this place."

Amen, murmured the crowd.

Aggie stirred in Clem's arms. Her hands rested against her rosy cheeks, reminding Clem of Agnes when she was in contemplation.

"They told me they could never live anywhere else in this big world of ours, and I know their gratitude to this land and what it provided them is immeasurable. As y'all know, my parents were both devout and served our Lord as best they could, so I know they are in his arms where they belong. Therefore, let us not be sad that they're gone but rejoice in the long and beautiful life they lived."

Praise be.

"My father worked hard for everything he and my mother had—they both did—and I won't allow that legacy to be lost along with them. My father made his home with blood, sweat, and tears, and I vow to keep this land in our family and rebuild here so we, and future generations of Beauchamps, can enjoy the bounties God has blessed us with. Time marches onward and things change. One day, this place may not exist. One day, this entire peninsula may be reclaimed by the sea. But not this day."

No, sir!

"Never have I encountered a more resilient community than the one here on Bolivar Peninsula. The independence of spirit, the determination to keep going no matter the odds, and the unconditional love every single person here has for this magical place is astounding to me."

Many in the crowd nodded and clasped their hands together. Aggie let out a squeal as Clem strove to suppress her own emotion.

"Now, my mother, as y'all know, read her Bible every day and recited it often. So I will speak from a verse in Ecclesiastes that seems especially apt today:

"'There is a time for everything, and a season for every activity under the heavens: a time to be born and a time to die.'

"These words resonate for all of us who have recently experienced the destruction of land, property, precious belongings, and yes, even loved ones.

"There is 'a time to plant and a time to uproot,' as we have been uprooted from this place. We have been torn down, we have wept, and we have mourned.

"But now the time has come to build, to plant new seeds. The time has passed to weep; now is the time to laugh and dance together as we celebrate the extraordinary legacy of my parents today."

Sheila passed Tom an urn as the crowd murmured its assent. "We are grateful for this miracle. As some of you know, my parents' earthly remains were recovered and returned to us. This urn contains their combined ashes, as was their wish."

Tom removed the lid and sprinkled the ashes among the roots of the old oak tree. "In Jesus's name, amen."

The wind picked up, and a cloud of dust rose into the air. Clem pulled Aggie's blanket over her, brushing at her gossamer hair where it settled. She followed her daughter's gaze, this time directed where the white ranch house once stood. The place Clem had called home for those unbearable months after losing Finn. And before that, when Finn had loved to chase the chickens and was coddled by Agnes.

A shaft of sunlight shone over the empty lot. From it, a pool of brightness slipped apart and hovered just above the ground. When the light shifted, she saw them—Agnes and Earle smiling, Finn standing between them, holding their hands.

Aggie shifted in Clem's arms. *You see them, too, my love.*

Agnes stood tall and straight, and Mabel brushed against her long legs, circling each of them in turn. Aggie squealed again as Agnes, Earle, and Finn looked straight at them with kindness and love in their eyes.

Time to say goodbye, Aggie.

Warmth spread through Clem and into her daughter. As they watched, their beloveds waved and turned and walked into the light.

acknowledgments

Thank you to all my early readers, who provided much-needed support and insight to make this book the best it could be, especially Elise Piotrowicz, Lisa Carnochan, and Cyndy Williams.

Many thanks to my editors, Amber Meade, Roberta Templeman, and Tod Tinker, for polishing this novel and appreciating all my words—and to Charlene Templeman and Tod Tinker at Balance of Seven press for getting this book out into the world. Small, indie presses work so hard for their authors, and it's their sweat and tears that are the reason you hold this book in your hand. Thank you for believing in me and sharing my story again.

Bolivar Peninsula residents, I send love and gratitude, to both the survivors and those lost. Also, to Bolivar Point Lighthouse, which gave me inspiration for this book and offered hope and safety to so many.

Endless gratitude, as always, to my family for putting up with me while I wrote and obsessed over this book. And for helping make my dreams come true.

about the author

Georgina Key is an award-winning author whose debut novel, *Shiny Bits in Between*, received the Phoenix prize for Best New Voice of 2020 from Kops-Fetherling International Book Awards and was named a finalist for the 2022 International Book Awards in women's fiction. Her poetry has appeared in several journals and anthologies.

Born and raised in England, Georgina currently splits her time between the UK and Texas. *Syllables of the Briny World* is an homage to her beloved little yellow house on Bolivar Peninsula, which she lost to Hurricane Ike in 2008. She is currently finishing her third novel, which is set in the UK.

Printed in the USA
CPSIA information can be obtained
at www.ICGtesting.com
LVHW051239170424
777536LV00015B/1103

9 781947 012646